APPARENT POWER

DACIA M ARNOLD

Immortal Works LLC
1505 Glenrose Drive
Salt Lake City, Utah 84104
Tel: (385) 202-0116

Cover Art by Mackenzie Seidel
http://mackenzieseidel.weebly.com/

ISBN: 978-1-7324674-0-8 (paperback)
ISBN: 978-1-5323-7964-2 (ebook)

To My Dad: James R Gilliam. My Hero.
and
To Greg Arnold, for keeping me together.

CHAPTER ONE

The electricity flew from her fingers to the shower door handle. Valerie Russell yanked her hand back. The shock had not hurt, but the burst of light caught her off guard. She reached again, slowly. This time, nothing happened, and she stepped into the shower. The water flowing over her face was satisfying in that it woke her senses far better than her alarm. Startled out of her thoughts by her husband clearing his throat, she took a breath to tell him what had just happened when he cut her off.

"Who the hell are you?" Scott stood frozen, staring at her.

"Last time I checked, I was your wife." She wiped the layer of droplets to clear her view and waited for him to respond.

His lips parted to speak, but he remained silent, brows creased, and head tilted.

"What is it?" She stopped the shower. Studying his expression, Valerie pushed the door open and yanked a towel from the wall. The question he posed to her was odd, but his demeanor made her heart race. Something was wrong. She had seen him speechless twice in the seven years she had known him: once when their son was born and again when the boy had broken his arm. Scott had frozen in shock. Her mouth went dry, and the grip of fear tightened her chest.

Scott pivoted when she rushed by him, mouth still groping to form words. Valerie flew down the hall to her son's room and slapped the switch on the wall. The two-year-old scrunched his nose and threw an arm over his eyes. Relieved, she guided the switch to the off position and pulled the door until the opening was an inch wide. Valerie exhaled. Pausing to take a few long breaths, she fought to slow her heart and walked back to her bathroom.

"Stop being weird," Valerie said, shivering. The towel just covered her front, and the cold drops from her dark sienna hair annoyed her. She shoved him. "You scared me."

"Have you looked at yourself today?" Scott asked.

Tight-lipped, she raised a brow, daring him to joke about her body. Scott pulled the towel from her loose grip. The heavy terry cloth fell into a heap on the floor. He reached out to touch her bare skin, but she pushed his hand away.

"I love you, Scott, but we don't have time for this." Valerie kissed his cheek and laid a playful slap on the same spot.

He grabbed her wrist as she tried to walk away.

"I said we don't have time."

The reflection in the mirror caused her to choke on the last word. The figure moved with her as she stepped closer. She rubbed the remaining beads of dampness from her face and studied her reflection again. Her eyes narrowed, and she leaned in further. A swarm of butterflies released in her stomach. The hair stood up on her arms. Her mouth dry and uncomfortable. The thirty-five-year-old working mom stared at the image of her twenty-year-old self. All signs of age erased.

She turned back to Scott, eyeing him as if he might have something to do with what was happening. Trembling, she faced the mirror again, expecting to see the stress-worn image of the woman she saw while brushing her teeth just moments before. Tracing her hands down her body, she compared the figure in the mirror to herself. Her skin was taut and smooth. Breasts lifted and firm. Her stretch marks from pregnancy were faded. The pocket of flesh created by her C-section scar was undetectable, replaced by flat, long muscle. She raked her hands through her damp hair. The thick tresses were like dark silk through her fingers and flowed over her shoulders. Her search for gray was unproductive.

"You look amazing," Scott whispered behind her, wrapping his arms around her slender frame.

"This isn't real, Scott. Am I sick? What is this? The static. . ." She shook trying to articulate. "There was this huge static when I grabbed the shower door. I swear, like a whole twelve-inch bolt of lightning." Ignoring his gentle caress on her bare skin, she squinted into the mirror, wrinkled her nose, and pursed her lips together before resting her face. Her skin remained supple, her features soft.

"Now I kind of wish I had called off work today." Scott bent down to kiss her neck.

"Get off of me! Hon, something is wrong. This—" she turned to face him and waved her hands over her body, "—just does not happen. Fairy godmothers don't pop in and give you your twenty-year-old boobs back. And abs? I have never had abs. Pizza belongs here," she said, poking a finger into her abdomen.

"Well, how do you feel? Do you feel sick or strange?" He laughed. "Did you hit a Gypsy woman with your car recently? Should I be wary of pie?"

"Really?" Valerie rolled her eyes. "I can't go to work like this." She whipped back around to the mirror.

"Well, you need to decide because it's already five and I have to go. But that," he motioned at her body, mimicking her, "is mine when I get back."

"What am I supposed to do?" Her stomach flipped, knowing he had to leave. She wanted someone outside of her head to tell her what to do. She wanted him to stay and help her sort this out. Even if he could stay, Scott was far too distracted to be of any help.

"You can call off if you want, but you'd have to come up with a damn good reason. The staffing office was already desperate, or they wouldn't have asked you to cover a shift an hour and a half away." Scott sighed, "Think of it like this: no one there knows you any different. You'll be fine. Then you're off for a week and can figure things out." Scott kissed her head and grabbed a handful of her backside, pulling her closer to him.

"Okay. I know," Valerie said grabbing the thick straps of his overalls and pulling herself up to stand on his steel toes. "Be safe. When do you think you'll be home?"

"We're taking a train to Wyoming. I'll bring one back tomorrow around the same time. We're hauling coal. The trip is pretty routine as long as none of my engines lose power. But if you don't stop this, I'm never leaving." He kissed her mouth slow and soft. "I'll call you when I get to the hotel." He left Valerie standing naked in their bathroom, fighting the angry swarm in her belly.

Valerie continued the debate of whether or not to go to work. She would be the only nurse on shift at a stand-alone emergency room. She laughed to herself, pacing, and thinking of the least bizarre way to explain why she could not go to work. No amount of rationalization would calm the tremors in her hands and her growing queasiness. She forced herself to rush through her morning routine in hopes the more normal she acted, the more normal she would feel.

She cinched her navy-blue scrub pants as far as the drawstring would allow. Her waist had shrunk more than just a few inches, and the uniform looked like another person could fit in them with her. Frustrated, she flung the closet door open. Taking care not to trip over the shoes on the floor, she tiptoed to the back corner shelf where a pile of her old, pre-pregnancy scrubs sat. Though they also required cinching, they fit better and looked less like a circus tent over her now slender figure.

A loud chime came from a panel on the wall, making Valerie cry out. One hand white-knuckled the counter while the other clutched her chest. The nanny had let herself in, and the front door had triggered the chime. Valerie closed her eyes and inhaled for a measured three seconds before releasing. Knowing she would eventually have to face someone, her nanny, Gia, would at least be more objective than her husband had been.

Before meeting Gia on the main floor, Valerie peeked in on Caleb one more time. The shift was her third twelve-hour day in a row, and she missed him. It was difficult for her to fight the urge to hug and kiss her sleeping son, but she knew waking him would be a mistake. If he were to wake up, he would be in the worst mood for Gia. With Scott driving freight trains out of town and back, she often navigated parenting with only the help of her nanny. Knowing she would soon have an entire week home with her son helped her to walk away and let him sleep.

"Good morning," Valerie chimed, overcompensating for her internal struggle.

Gia sat her heavy school bag down next to the front door and removed her shoes but stayed by the door. Valerie kept on her path from the stairs to the kitchen, terrified Gia would notice her appearance, or worse, not notice at all.

In the kitchen, Valerie poured a cup of coffee. Breathing deeply, she hoped it would ease her tension, but found little solace in the steaming cup. She looked down at the dark beverage. Heart pounding, hands shaking, she took another breath. Her anxiety got the best of her.

"Am I crazy," Valerie asked, "or do I look significantly different to you?"

"No. Did you color your hair?" Gia shifted her weight, rubbed her forearms and elbows, and took a short glance in Valerie's direction.

"Are you serious? I lost like twenty pounds overnight, and you ask me if I colored my hair? Look at this," Valerie said, raising her voice. She pulled the drawstring free of a slip knot and stretched the waistband three inches away from her torso.

"Oh, well, now you point it out, they do look loose," Gia answered, chewing her lip and refusing to validate Valerie's concern.

"I'm losing my mind. I am having a mental break down at thirty-five." Valerie pulled her hands through her hair, gripping handfuls at the root. "Gia, please, just look at my face."

Gia took a step back as Valerie approached. The nanny made no expression, nor did she examine Valerie's face. She looked at her dead in the eye.

"I'm sorry," Valerie said backing off. "I am a wreck. And I'm late. I didn't mean to scare you."

She glanced at the clock on the stove and gathered her lunch, throwing random food items into her bag. "Scott took a train to Wyoming this morning. He won't be back today. I'm working at the ER down south, so I'm out of town, too. The number is on the fridge if you need it. I won't be home until maybe nine tonight if there is no traffic. Caleb can stay up and wait for me if he wants."

“South? Like the Springs? The drive is almost two hours away, more in traffic.”

“If you can't stay late, I can call off. The facility might have to close, and I will probably get written up, but with the day I am having so far, I have no problem staying home.”

Gia continued to chew her lip. After a few seconds, she smiled and clapped her hands together. The sound made Valerie jump. The changed expression on the nanny's face also startled her.

“No, it's fine.” Gia's voice was cheerful but exaggerated. “I will take care of everything here. No need to rush home. Take your time. Caleb and I will be fine.” She pulled her thick curly hair back and tied it with a band. It made a big light brown pom-pom on the back of her head.

The coffee in Valerie's mug rippled but did not quite splash from the tremors in her hands. She opened her mouth to protest but was cut off.

"You can go. It's fine," Gia encouraged, but even with her attempt at a natural tone, Valerie could still sense the shakiness in her voice.

Valerie hated passive aggression, secrets, or unresolved disputes. "Alright, what's going on? You are obviously not yourself. I mean, neither am I, but I've owned up to my psychosis. What's bothering you?"

“Umm, school? I have a new teacher. A new class, I mean. I'm not thinking about a guy or anything. I mean, the teacher is a guy, but it's not a boyfriend thing,” Gia scrambled for an acceptable answer but fell flat in her attempt to lie.

“I'll call you once I get settled at work if we aren't busy.” Valerie did not have time to pry any further if Gia remained adamant about her undisclosed uneasiness.

The two stood in silence for a moment, and then Caleb let out a whine from his room.

"Alright," Valerie said, "you two have a good day. Text me if you need anything at all."

Gia's shoulders dropped as she sighed with relief. Valerie curled the weight of her bag onto her shoulder and left the kitchen. When she reached for the door leading to the garage, a visible arc of electricity shot from her hand to the knob, a three-inch space, accompanied by a loud pop. Valerie shook her hand as if it had hurt, more out of habit. She let out a frustrated breath, grabbed the handle again, and was able to enter the garage without incident.

Within minutes, Valerie merged onto the highway to bypass the city of Denver. The sun had not yet given a hint of light to the sky, but the dark drive provided an isolated environment to mull over the events of the morning. When she passed the airport, two cars exited, and she was alone except for a few oncoming headlights. She replayed the conversation with Gia. The way the young woman had acted bothered her. Gia always seemed honest and straightforward. Maybe she planned on quitting . . . But Valerie needed Gia. With the unpredictability of Scott's schedule, Valerie would have to stay home with Caleb. She did not trust anyone else with him.

Or maybe Gia did notice. With increased traffic and oncoming headlights, Valerie caught glimpses of herself in the rearview mirror. Her transformation was still evident. Gia must have been lying. Valerie just could not figure out how any of this was possible. In her thirteen years of nursing, she had never heard of anything like what she was experiencing.

"You're fine. No one knows you. Just get through the day and get home. You can sort everything out then," Valerie whispered out loud to herself, repeating the speech in variations to not allow herself to turn the car around. Scott was right. After her shift, she had the week off to make better sense of the situation.

On the south end of Colorado Springs, Cheyenne Mountain loomed over the city. From the highway, she could see the dozens of antennas at the summit marking the NORAD command center, a protected government facility operating the world GPS system. To her, the towers were just part of the scenery, like the barbed wire topped chain-link fence surrounding the base. Traffic flowed with uniformed men and women going to and from their posts. Between growing up with her father in the military, her brother becoming a police officer in the Army and her marrying Scott while he still served, she felt right at home.

She had not told her family she had taken the shift near them. Her and her father, Mike Burton, had a strained but tolerable relationship. Her older brother, Kevin, was still in the military and they never had much in common. For a split second, she considered asking her father, a known conspiracy theorist, about her condition. He would demand a logical explanation and assure her nothing good would come of her transformation. She decided to leave her father out of the equation until she had a better idea of what was happening.

Still deep in thought, her classical music cut off. The gauges on her dashboard fell flat. The vehicle coasted down a hill toward a stop light just south of her destination. Valerie threw her coffee mug down to the ground and gripped the steering wheel, pumping the brakes to no avail. She employed every muscle in her upper body to maintain course without power steering. She slapped the triangular button for her hazard lights and pushed her horn, but nothing responded.

Most vehicles continued as usual, but two cars coming from the opposite direction were losing momentum up the hill. She watched one get rear-ended as she sped closer to the bottom. Her shakiness from the morning intensified. Her vision narrowed and a cold sweat broke out on her forehead. She knew what was to follow. What a hell of a time to pass out. Valerie fought against the feeling. With her last attempt at controlling the car, she pulled the emergency brake and pointed the car at a distant mile marker.

Thank God Caleb is home.

CHAPTER TWO

The vehicle shook violently. A faint whistle, like a hot tea kettle on a stove, grew louder with each passing second. Valerie opened her eyes just as a plane glided low over the street and crashed into a field she knew was just out of sight. She felt the impact in her chest. One after another, more aircrafts went down. Some she could see, and others were mere ground shaking rumbles in the distance. With every explosion, she jumped a little but remained transfixed on the destruction outside her small compartment.

Frozen, Valerie was helpless. Horrified. Her stomach ached knowing how many people could fit on a plane. She waited for the sick feeling to pass before assessing her own wellness. From the looks of things, her plan had worked. Though the airbag had deployed, she had no pain and would have guessed the accident was minor. The state of her car hood told a different story. The small mile marker appeared to have cut nearly halfway up the front end of her sedan.

She turned off her emotions to keep herself together and noticed other wrecked vehicles. Some were worse than others. Knowing those people might need medical assistance, she counted to herself. After exactly one minute without hearing or seeing another crash, Valerie pushed as hard as she could on her seat belt, but it did not budge.

Unhooking the rescue tool from her keychain, she made easy work of her restraints.

Something horrible was going on. Regardless if it was just in the immediate area or broader spread, Valerie was obligated to render aid to those who needed it. Though her car would offer a slight barrier from debris, she determined if a plane landed on top of her, there was no kind of shelter that would stop it from killing her. This measurement she did not take lightly. Her mom had been killed just outside her vehicle the year before, helping others in a snowstorm.

Once free, Valerie shouldered her bag and assessed the scene. There had not been any impacts for a few minutes. Passersby worked together to assist people who were in similar situations as herself.

"I'm a nurse. Is anyone injured?" she called out as far as her voice would carry.

"No, ma'am," a few soldiers hollered back.

"There is a small ER on the top of this hill. You can send casualties there. The next closest hospital is General."

Once her instructions were met with affirmation, she began the short walk to the facility. She came upon a mother crying and holding a baby to her chest while a little girl and a slightly older boy clung to each leg.

"Are you okay?" Valerie's heart was crushed. She could not imagine having her son with her in this mess.

"I don't know. I'm fine, and they were in their car seats, but she won't stop crying." The woman held her baby up for Valerie to see.

"Come with me. There's an emergency room at the top of this hill. She's probably just scared, Mama." Valerie took the child and cradled her against her chest. The baby quieted immediately. She looked down at the little girl who returned her gaze and cooed.

"Oh, she's super cute." Valerie smiled at the woman. "I think she's just fine. Come on."

The woman picked up the middle child and held the oldest by his hand, and they followed Valerie. She kept her emotions at bay. She made small talk about their names and where they were from because, in a military town, few are actually from there.

Valerie turned into the parking lot of the emergency room, still holding the baby who played with the zipper from the shoulder strap of Valerie's bag. The facility had once been an old movie rental store converted into a seven-bed emergency room with X-ray, lab, and CT scan capabilities. Stand-alone emergency rooms were a new concept in the area, and most of the community was skeptical of the novelty. The ER shared the parking lot with a chain drugstore, which people were running into empty-handed with just as many coming out with their hands full of random merchandise—looting, no doubt. Chaos had erupted in the strip mall across the four-lane intersection. People were screaming and running frantically.

Valerie quickly shuffled the mother and children into the emergency room waiting room, which was surprisingly empty.

"I'm Valerie. I'm covering for Shawna today," she announced to the grey-haired lady at the front desk. The woman said nothing but stared at Valerie and pushed a button to activate the door from the waiting room to the nurse's station. The night shift nurse and a tall Hispanic gentleman who popped his tongue and waved his wrist around while checking equipment were the only people she saw in the facility.

"Where's the doctor?" Valerie demanded. She did not have time for pleasant small talk. They would start receiving casualties any minute.

"I didn't know there was a student on shift today," the night shift nurse said at Valerie but to no one in particular.

In the midst of everything, Valerie completely forgot about her age regression. She no longer looked like a seasoned emergency room nurse, but a young college girl without the required experience to work for the company. Valerie knew the events of the day would catch up to her emotionally, but now was not the time to think of all the things that could have gone wrong. She had a job to do and lives to save. This fellow medical professional would, hopefully, share the same ethic.

"I normally work in Denver; I'm just filling in for Shawna." Valerie was not offended. She did not have time to be.

"Well, are you going to do this medication count or not?"

"You're not leaving," Valerie informed her counterpart. "There are planes down and car accidents. We need to start prepping to receive patients."

"Are you even old enough to work here?" the woman challenged.

Valerie could no longer mask her frustration.

"What is wrong with you?" Valerie yelled. She took a breath and coaxed her emotions back under control. She clenched her teeth. "I've been an ER nurse for thirteen years. I am thirty-five years old and fully qualified to do this job. Now, are you done interrogating me? Because I'm sure your job is not human resources. There is a mass casualty situation right outside the front doors of this place."

"I just can't handle this. Not today," the nurse said to the ceiling and let herself out the back doors where the ambulance was parked.

"You've got to be kidding me!" Valerie threw her hands in the air. A ball knotted itself in her throat, and her heart raced. She wanted to follow the woman out the door and drive home. Any other logical human in any other field of work would be doing just that. Besides, the facility was not meant to support an emergency of this magnitude. She thought about the twelve planes, the car accidents, the static that shot from her hands.

"Umm, Ms. Valerie," the older woman said with a shaky voice. "We've received an e-message from the main hospital outlining the disaster plan for our facility."

Valerie followed the woman to her desk that sat in front of a window to the waiting room.

"I'll have you back in just a second. Are you doing okay?" Valerie called out to the waiting woman.

The mother nodded and smiled.

Valerie took a seat at the desk. The receptionist walked out to the lobby to have the woman fill out some paperwork to have her children seen. The radiology technician sat with his back to Valerie at another computer, headphones on and pounding his keyboard fast and dutifully.

The office where the doctor worked remained closed. The separation aggravated Valerie to a point almost unbearable. All she could think about was opening the door. She was uncomfortable not knowing if there was even a physician in the building since she had met neither the night shift nor the day shift doctors. She stood up to knock on the door but sat back down. There was something wrong. Like when Scott first brought her transformation to her attention. With a deep breath, she willed her raging thoughts to stop. He needed to be out here, to know what exactly was happening outside the door. But there was something else making her want to tear down the door. Valerie was not usually a nervous person. In fact, there were few who were as calm as she was under pressure, but still. She had a feeling deep down that the worst had not come. Something else was not right. Even the atmosphere in the facility kept the hair on her arms standing up. No one else seemed to notice the lack of patients or the absence of the physician.

Valerie tapped her fingers on the desk in front of her, trying to still her nerves. She needed to calm down and read through her next instructions before knocking on the door. That way, she could map out the plan before demanding action.

Valerie rubbed her face with both hands and reached out to the computer in front of her to scroll down the page to see the full message. When her fingers touched the keyboard, sparks flew to the device, cracking and melting the plastic frame. The electricity surged from the keyboard to the screen, shattering the glass as well. Valerie pushed her chair back away from the machine and stood up. The tech did the same, throwing his headphones at his computer. The electricity fizzled out at the wire connected to the wall.

"What the hell did you do?" he shrieked.

"Oh dear," the receptionist said, rushing back to the desk.

The doctor's office opened, much to Valerie's relief. Destroying hospital property was not the first impression she wanted to make, but at least there was a physician in the building. The door did not open all the way at first but swung back and forth a couple of times before a tall man in a white physician coat walked out. After only a few steps he stopped, turned, and walked back into the office and shut the door.

The moment it closed again was when Valerie finally lost her cool. She needed that man, in any capacity to be in the room with her. But if no one else was going to take charge, she would.

"I am sorry I didn't catch your name," Valerie asked the receptionist.

"Oh, it's Betty. And don't you mind Roy, here." Betty motioned to the technician as if she were swatting a fly. "He just comes off rude, but he's nice. We are used to having different staff every day. We can't even keep the same rotating doctors. I have not even heard of the one that is on today."

Valerie sensed the irritation in Betty's voice when referring to the doctor who was hiding out in his office.

"Your computer exploded," Valerie said plainly, unable to explain exactly what occurred. "Has this ever happened before?" She knew without a doubt she had caused the malfunction. She felt the energy surge down her arms and release from the tips of her fingers into the machine. There had been nothing wrong with the computer before she touched the keyboard but found the idea hard to express to the strangers staring at her in alarm.

"I'd call in a ticket, but everything else kind of blew up, too, before you got here," Betty said. "Most of the lights anyway. I can start cleaning up the glass, I guess."

As if on cue, the doctor opened the door again.

Finally getting a good look at him, there was no chance the young man in the white lab coat was an experienced emergency room physician. He ignored the receptionist and the technician and stared straight at Valerie.

Like an invisible string tied between them, something inside Valerie drew her to him. He was handsome enough but possibly ten years younger than her.

"There is no way you're a doctor," the words left her mouth before she even considered her own appearance.

"I don't have time for this," he said, breaking eye contact but staying in the office doorway.

"For what? Armageddon happening outside? Jesus Christ," Valerie said, louder than she intended, but it matched the doctor's reaction.

"What's that smell?"

"The computer blew up," Valerie answered. "I'm not sure what happened. I don't usually work here." She wanted to question him, yell at him even, but there was something familiar about him.

"I wrecked my car about a half mile down the road," Valerie explained. "There were maybe three other accidents I saw on the way. There is a woman in the lobby with her kids. Their car wrecked but they all seem fine."

The doctor moved closer to her. He was tall enough to have no problem seeing past her into the lobby.

"Planes went down," he said low more to himself. "There are no other injured?" the doctor asked, standing close and looking down at her. His voice finally reflected true concern.

"None that I encountered on the way, but it's only been a few minutes."

The doctor stood close enough Valerie could feel the warmth of his body. Instead of being uncomfortable, she wanted him closer. She caught her breath and blushed, which triggered her anger. People were dying outside, and she could not fight her infatuation.

It took her a moment to realize he was no longer looking at her but out the window toward the parking lot. Turning, she saw people coming from all directions. The crowd grew to two hundred people in a matter of minutes. Only some of them had visible injuries. Valerie turned and moved past the doctor, careful not to touch him, though she wanted to.

"What are you doing?" he asked her.

Valerie picked up the phone receiver, held the plastic device to her head for a second, then slammed the handset down. She clenched her teeth and slammed three more times, knowing well her aggression would not create a dial tone.

"I was calling 911. We can't handle more than five injured people, and only one if they are critical. We are going to run out of supplies within the hour. This facility is not designed to handle major disasters.

There is glass everywhere, and I imagine the limited equipment we do have is broken as well." Valerie looked at the technician who gave an affirmative nod. She was aware a doctor would know the capabilities of the emergency room, but she still was not convinced of his credentials. She was also trying to remain objective, to keep her emotions from taking over.

"I'm sorry. You are?" he asked in a genuine tone.

"Valerie Russell. I'm the nurse on shift."

He raised an eyebrow at her and looked her over before extending his hand slowly. "I am Doctor Wilkes. August Wilkes." He held her hand a few seconds too long.

Or she held his too long; she really could not say.

He finally broke contact and continued, "From the looks of things, this isn't going to be over for a while. No doubt the phone lines and cell towers were taken out. At this point, until we do run out of supplies, we are 911. Start prepping rooms." August directed his instructions to Valerie, Roy, and poor Betty, who was trying to control her hyperventilation. "If they are all walking, they can't be that sick." He said facing the window again before delving out additional orders to the team. "Valerie, stop them outside. If they are uninjured, not in active labor, and are otherwise well, send them home. I will help triage as much as we can until something more serious comes. Exercise your best judgment as I might not be available to give recommendations. Are you comfortable with that?"

Valerie laughed at the question but remembered she looked like she just graduated nursing school. He showed little faith in her judgment, but in the moment, no one had a choice in the matter. "Triage the walking wounded and send them home if they are well enough. Got it," she answered, hoping he would dismiss her.

"Betty, help Roy. Split the patients up as they come in. Take vitals and collect their medical history. It is easy; Roy can show you how. Just get a basic idea of what's wrong with them and document it, okay?" August did not wait for her to answer. He grabbed his stethoscope, a pen, and notepad, and met Valerie before she walked out the door.

"If paramedics are on scene at the crash sites, they are going to shuttle people to the main hospitals. We are probably only going to get walking wounded." August fell silent for a few steps before letting out a small laugh. "Would it be weird to say this isn't the most bizarre thing that's happened to me today?" Valerie's heart raced as he went on. "I have felt strange all day like there was static in the air. The sensation went away when the light bulbs exploded in the building as soon as I walked in. And this morning when I woke up. . ." He trailed off again.

Valerie had not noticed until he mentioned the change, but she no longer felt shaky or anxious. She felt grounded, powerful even. Her mind was focused. They walked in step with one another out the front door of the emergency room to meet the crowd.

A mass of people gathered in the parking lot. They did not appear to have any severe injuries, just walking wounded as August had predicted. Most of them had no visible injuries; even more so, they were in excellent health.

"Please raise your hand if you are a patient," Valerie asked loud enough for the crowd to hear her. About one-third of the group raised their hands. She assumed the others were family members or bystanders assisting the wounded.

"Is anyone having chest pain or difficulty breathing?" All the hands went down. "Alright, if you are bleeding or have an open wound please step to my right, your left. Everyone else, please line up in the parking spaces on your right." The crowd parted, and the questions started. Valerie did her best to address their concerns while August examined the injured.

Most had similar experiences: they passed out, fell, hit their head. They described what Valerie had encountered in her car before she wrecked. After she had gotten the same story a third time, August called her over.

"Head inside and send Betty out here. Explain how to triage. I am going to start sending folks back for bandages. They don't all need rooms; you can patch some up in the waiting room. Send them home when you finish. No X-rays, no labs. They aren't sick. They are hurt.

Motrin, ice, et cetera."

Valerie tried not to roll her eyes at the doctor for explaining first aid to her. She took the eleven patients he identified as needing bandages and led them inside. Four she brought back to Roy to get cleaned up and the rest she sat in the waiting room while she gathered supplies to work from there.

Valerie stopped and knelt down by the woman who was still waiting with her kids. "How are you feeling?" she asked, touching each child on the head and looked them in the eyes. None of them seemed to be in any distress.

"I'm just concerned. These two said that they both fell asleep in the car. I think I might have passed out, too. None of us even remember the impact."

Something stirred within Valerie. Like butterflies, but not how she had felt earlier in the morning. She felt connected, in a way, to the family in front of her. "I understand this is all scary. Do you feel okay monitoring them at home for the time being? How far are you from where you live?"

"Not far. I mean, I feel fine, and they seem okay. Does anyone know what happened? Were we attacked?"

"I haven't heard anything definitive. I have to go now and take care of these patients. Please call us if you have any concerns, alright?"

The woman was out of the door before Valerie remembered none of the phones worked. She had a feeling deep down that they were okay, but she hated relying on those feelings when it came to medicine. Being wrong was never worth taking the chance, but there was very little she could have done differently.

"Betty, Dr. Wilkes needs you outside. If they are bleeding or have something broken, they go on the right. If they have anything minor, they wait on the other side of the parking lot. When I send one patient out, you send the next one in. You are doing a great job. You can do this." Valerie hugged the woman before sending her out the front door.

"Oh, my garsh. Oh, my garsh. I can't believe this is happening. What is going on?" Betty muttered as she scooted her feet out the front door.

Valerie collected various medical supplies into a bucket. She paused for a moment, and for the first time since the accident, she took her cell phone out of her bag. The battery was dead. The Denver Airport was a twenty-minute drive from her home. If planes were going down, they might have gone down there. She had no way of contacting Scott or Gia. Her baby was home, and she was a hundred miles away. If Scott were back, she would be less anxious.

"Valerie! We need some help back here," Roy announced, flustered. "Girl, nothing is working. All the equipment is being crazy, and I need your help."

Roy saw the phone in her hand and the emotion on her face. "We all got people. But I need help."

Valerie slid the phone into her pocket and followed him, once again turning off her personal concerns.

"The equipment works fine until you try to hook them up. So, we have to get manual vitals on all these people," Roy said, throwing his hands in the air.

"They don't need vitals right now. Expose their wounds and write on the board what their chief complaint is. We will just patch them up and send them home. No X-rays, no labs, no medications. Okay?"

Roy nodded in compliance and went to work.

Valerie returned to the lobby. Some people left as others walked in to take their place. By the time she got to each patient, their blood had dried, and their wounds had disappeared without explanation. Valerie kept her calm outward resolve, withholding her disbelief. Inside, she repeated what August had told her: This is not the most bizarre thing that has happened today. Seeing no need to document the patients, since no interventions were needed, they were dismissed.

A group waiting to be looked at chatted in the area. They took turns recapping their version of the same story:

"I was cooking breakfast for my girlfriend, and then I got light-headed. The next thing I know, I wake up on the ground covered in fried eggs. My girlfriend said I passed out for, like two seconds and the pan fell right on my head," he explained with a cold pack held up to the right side of his face. He pulled it away to show the others, but they studied him and shrugged.

"It doesn't really even hurt anymore," he said and set the ice pack down on the chair beside him.

The person listened to the story repeated by another. "I kind of felt this coming. Crazy, huh? I felt weird all morning. Now my body just feels heavy." The patients all had similar experiences with only variance in activity or location. Some people were driving and wrecked. Others were at home.

"I wonder why everyone didn't feel the electricity. I saw those planes go down in a field behind my house. No one could have survived any of those crashes, but at least they didn't go down in the neighborhoods," one man continued rambling. "An EMP, maybe? But that would have affected everything, not just random things."

Valerie tried her hardest to focus on the assessment she was giving a woman who fell in the grocery store and busted her chin open on a cart. Her thoughts were the loudest of any voice around her. Caleb. Caleb. CALEB. She wanted to run out, get in any random car, and drive home. She wanted to panic but had to focus. Any minute, the more severe trauma patients from the crashes could come pouring in.

"This was definitely an attack," one man spoke up to the others. "Russia, probably. Couldn't have been an EMP because not every car was affected. I had to drift my car to the side and use my e-brake. And I saw others freak out and do the same, but some cars kept going. My phone doesn't work either, but other people were talking on theirs. They targeted certain people. Maybe we all know something we shouldn't."

Valerie stood to politely ask the man to stop making radical speculations in the waiting room. The last thing she needed was the mass hysteria to work its way inside the ER doors.

"Valerie, come here for a sec." August walked through the waiting room and motioned her to the nurse's station out of earshot of the patients. She abandoned her confrontation and followed him as he gathered the team into a huddle.

"I have never, in over twenty years of medicine, seen people just heal themselves. Something is not right here, and all these people need to go home and stay there. We are running out of supplies fast using them on people who don't need treatment. Betty, how many people are still waiting?"

"Um, a handful of mothers with small children. They are not willing to leave until the little ones are checked out. They all seem fine to me." Betty had done an excellent job, just as Valerie knew she would.

"Excuse me? Who is in charge here?" a firm voice came from the reception desk window. A man stood in a navy-blue security type uniform with the letters CDC in white on the front.

August whispered a curse under his breath and approached the man. They spoke for a moment before August returned to the group. He rubbed the back of his neck and looked at the ground.

"Change of plans. All patients will go with the CDC for quarantine. Everyone claiming to have passed out will go for observation. Betty, please make a copy of the patient list, if you have one. I know things escalated fast. When you can throw one together, please give whatever you can gather to the gentleman over there. They have trucks in the parking lot and are already loading people up. If anyone has questions, direct them to the people in blue." August walked back to his office and shut the door.

"That must have been what the email from the main hospital said," Betty mumbled as she went to work.

Valerie heard August engage the lock on his office door. Just as earlier, she wanted to rip the door off the hinges. Something was wrong, but how typical of a doctor to protect themselves and leave everyone else to figure things out. As the only nurse on duty, she took charge and assisted Betty with compiling the list. Concerned mothers parted with children. Husbands kissed their wives before being separated. Valerie had not told anyone how she lost consciousness before her car wrecked into the mile marker. She had a feeling a trip with the CDC would postpone the reunion with her family.

The emergency room emptied of patients. The CDC collected the pedestrians waiting outside, helping them all into blue package trucks with the CDC logo.

"Did you hear him say twenty years? I think ole girl over here and him have the same baby-face condition." Roy sat behind the desk talking up a storm with Betty, trying to calm her down.

"What I find quite off," Valerie began, "is they are in security guard uniforms, and not hazmat suits like you would expect from quarantine. Something is not right."

Valerie was cut off by the television in the lobby. The monitor sprang to life loud enough to startle her from the nurse's station. The three of them rushed to see what it had to say. Two news anchors sat at the desk, a man and a woman apologizing for interrupting the regularly scheduled program.

"At exactly 12:46 p.m. Eastern Standard Time, an electrical surge passed over the surface of the Earth, what is now being referred to as 'the Event.' The CDC has put out the following statement:

"The cause of the wave of electricity is unknown but is believed to have multiple points of impact all over the globe. It is uncertain why the Event occurred or what the permanent effects will be. All airborne vessels were disabled, and we have received reports that over 4,000 planes have gone down as a result. Most motor transportation is also affected.

"The current of electricity has affected certain individuals as well. Quarantine has begun for those affected by the worldwide electrical surge. If you or someone you know has fallen, experienced a loss of consciousness, or has reported a strange sensation over their body, the CDC requests these people contact them at the 1-800 number on your screen."

The news anchors continued to talk as the three stood in silence. Inner turmoil wore visible on their faces as they each seemed to be fighting a mental battle: to stay or to go. The phone rang and surprised the group. Gia's name showed on the caller ID, and Valerie ripped the phone off the hook. Silence.

"Gia? Hello?"

Curses flew from her mouth with tears and anger. Betty put an arm on her shoulder and pulled her in to hug her.

"Shh. If you need to go, now would be the time. There is no more good any of us can do here. You have a long drive."

Valerie did not ask permission. She did not look at August's closed door or Roy or even acknowledge Betty's words. Valerie gathered her things and walked out the front door. Within five steps she remembered her car did not make it to the parking lot.

CHAPTER THREE

Valerie screamed so loud she thought her throat would bleed. She had no time to process what had happened, had no way of knowing if her husband and son were even alive, and no way to get back to them. She collapsed onto the asphalt and sat there. Mulling over multiple what-ifs. She was stuck. She finally considered going to her father for help.

"Dammit," she said, unable to think of any other way around it.

Valerie's childhood was one of extreme structure. Her father gave her and her older brother Kevin endless lessons on survival. This took away from weekends and holidays all through her adolescence. Mike taught them how to survive in many different situations. Her least favorite exercises were the four-day hikes. He showed the two how to find water, and forage if needed. He also taught them how to avoid being detected and how to apply camouflage. She honestly believed him to be a paranoid lunatic because he was so much harder on her than Kevin. It must have been a punishment for not being like her brother, a son. Mike was never mean to her, but he never showed her affection like dads on TV. He did not encourage her or ever call her princess. He just always wanted her to do better, try harder, and stop crying. Kevin would eat it up. He could not get enough of living on the land. One summer, he slept every night in the tree in their backyard, showering only when forced. Valerie was the opposite, which frustrated her father.

As an adult, she let go of most of her teenaged animosity, though Mike did little to change. She could imagine his response to her showing up on his doorstep. He would just watch her throw her tantrum without an offer of condolence and wait in silence for her to figure out a solution herself. She threw punches into her bag at the thought of having to face him. She had one last option before having to walk to her dad's house. Blood pumping, she stood up and walked back into the building.

"Roy, I need a ride. My dad lives twenty minutes from here," she yelled across the counter as she made her way through the facility to the break room, stepping around glass from light bulbs that had burst with the electrical wave. Though only a couple of hours had passed since she had fainted, the whole incident felt like a terrible distant dream. Her adrenaline was wearing off, and she had had just a few moments to piece together everything that had happened since she woke up that morning. There was a gaping disconnect between what her life was the day before and the reality of what she faced ahead. She was going to walk home, one hundred miles, whatever it took to get back to her son.

Valerie was still deep in thought when August drifted back into her mind. She snapped back to her task, fighting off the distraction he had caused during the entire ordeal. Her heart did a small flutter, and the feelings returned. She ignored them and maintained her determined standoff. Inhale, exhale.

August cleared his throat to announce his presence, but he did not catch Valerie off guard. Strange enough, she felt him enter the room.

"The roads are blocked with stalled cars. There are no clear routes. You'd be lucky to even get a vehicle out of the parking lot at this point."

"I can't just stay here and wait this out. I'll walk. My dad's house isn't far." Though the doctor was casual with her, she maintained her distance. He seemed to be genuinely concerned, but it could have been Valerie's wishful thinking. She continued to shove crackers and various other snacks into her bag. Though she was determined to get home, the idea of staying with August lingered in her mind like the sweet scent of a dessert enticing her to indulge.

He continued moving closer to her, "The president declared the entire country in a state of emergency. They have instituted martial law. It's like this everywhere."

Valerie looked up at the young doctor. She studied his face but was unsure what he was getting at.

"You don't think I am capable?" Valerie challenged. She wanted him to insult her, to piss her off. She wanted to hate him and be offended because everything in her wanted him closer.

"I don't think the CDC has anyone's best interests in mind. FEMA should have responded, not the CDC, and all federal aid takes almost twenty-four hours in any disaster. But I do think we should stick together. I want to show you something." August pulled his cell from his pocket and placed the device on the table. When he pulled his hand away, the phone sprang to life, blinking and vibrating with incoming messages. He brought his hand back to the phone, and the commotion stopped. "You try."

Valerie could not move. Her pounding heart was making her stomach sick, yet she did not shy away from his approach. She was afraid of what he was trying to tell her. More fearful of what she would see on her phone if the power came on.

"I'm going to take a stab and guess you're older than twenty," he said.

Valerie could feel him studying her reaction but did not meet his gaze. "I'm thirty-five."

"It's all right. I'm not going to turn you in."

"You're not twenty either."

"Not by a long shot."

Jaw clenched, she white-knuckled the phone in her scrub pocket for a few more moments before putting it on the table next to his. She lifted her hand away. Just like August's phone, hers sputtered and lit up. The list of messages grew until Gia's name appeared. She reached for it, but just before her hand touched the device, both phones cracked and caught fire.

"No!" she screamed into the small fiery piles on the table. She did not understand how she had caused them to explode, just like the computer. Could she have also caused the planes to go down?

"I don't know," August said to himself, less distraught about the damage she had caused. "There's like a six-inch bubble. When I get within reach of anything electronic, the power stops working. Explains why we couldn't hook up those patients to the monitors. And it isn't just you and me. The majority of those people were affected but in a different way. I don't think any vehicles we try are going work either. The cars didn't malfunction. It's the people in them. I'm just happy I wasn't on a plane today. I'm sure people like us are what brought them down."

"So, you woke up this morning looking like this?" She tried to be casual, waving a hand, deep down dreading the moment she would have to take her eyes off him.

"It's an improvement. Believe me." He smiled, and she believed him.

"I shouldn't have even come to work today. Do you think what we have is different from everyone else though?"

"Think about it. They all had injuries before coming here. If everyone were the same, the people would have started healing themselves before I was even able to see them. Tell me. How bad was your wreck?"

"I don't know. I. . ."

"Passed out? And woke up without a concussion or even a scratch?"

"You passed out, too?"

"I just think it's different for you and me. Why didn't you tell the CDC and comply with the quarantine?"

"Why didn't you? Or if you knew about me, why not give me away?"

"Because I needed to talk to you and try to figure this out." August straighten his posture.

"I still have to leave. I don't have a choice. I can't stay here. I have to go," Valerie pleaded out loud with her own heart and to him, hoping he would break her of the spell. His eyes reflected the same.

"Grab some Gatorade from the fridge. If things are as bad as they are saying, I can go with you to make sure you are safe. I just feel drawn to, I don't know, protect you? Make sure you're safe? Letting you leave alone just feels wrong." He looked away, hands deep in his pockets. He was getting at something, and Valerie could only assume what.

"Dr. Wilkes. I understand this is a traumatic and intense situation, but let me clarify something. I am a happily married woman. I have no clue what might be going on between us," Valerie motioned to the space between them, fighting against herself to narrow the separation, "but I do know it is completely inappropriate. I can manage on my own." She hoped that saying the words out loud would help to strengthen her resolve. She wanted nothing more than to jump into his arms and fall apart into a million pieces. No doubt he would let her.

Embarrassed, Valerie left without giving August the opportunity to argue her accusation. She knew if she was right, seeing his reaction might very well change her mind.

Valerie's bag was heavier than she anticipated as she flung the weight over her shoulder. The tote was impractical for her trek. She would need to get to her brother's townhouse before trying to walk to her father's. Kevin would have military gear more suitable for her trip than her two-strapped mom bag. He would also have guns, though she hoped she would not need them.

As she crested the only hill along her route, she saw the wreckage of the first plane that went down. The Colorado Springs Airport was a thirty-minute drive from where she was. Every single aircraft was brought down with the Event, leaving first responders sadly inadequate to rescue everyone. Only one firetruck was present spraying water on the flames which engulfed the nose and first half of the plane. The other end crushed like a soda can. Survivors of the wreckage were still on the scene. Others lay lifeless on orange rescue slings while the living just sat watching in shock, probably waiting for transportation to the nearest hospital. Valerie could not look any longer. The moment her eyes studied on even one child, she knew she would lose her resolve.

Her heart ached anyway. Continuing to walk went against every fiber of responsibility to treat the wounded, as if they were homeless asking for change, her pockets full and denying she had anything to offer. She was lying to those people who cried for help; saying she could not help them, but she could. She looked up one more time and sent a wave of emotion, positive energy and a breath of a prayer, "Dear God, please," under her breath. Though the words were hardly audible to herself, a boy, clear across the field, looked at her as if she had touched him, spoken to him. She broke the eye contact and continued.

Her emotional switch was stuck between her necessity to act, and her need to emotionally recognize what was happening around her. To subdue the latter, she started a mental list of things to grab from her brother's supply.

The community of townhomes was silent. From the road, she could see armed men standing at the entrance to the cul-de-sac. She would have to face them, take the risk. She surveyed the buildings. No one else was present, but for the gun-toting neighbors, she guessed them to be since they lacked any identifiable uniform. She wondered who they were guarding against. CDC? Looters? Maybe both. Empty cars blocked the throughways. Besides, trying to sneak in would be a guaranteed warning shot, if they intended to give a warning anyway.

"Do you live here?" one of the three men challenged her.

"My brother, Kevin Burton, does. I'm. . ."

"Valerie?"

"Yes."

"I'm your brother's neighbor. Madi and my wife are best friends. I've heard plenty about you, though not all of it nice."

"Yeah, well, that's Madi and anyone that isn't a fan of her Easter lasagna."

The man laughed, nodded, and waved her by.

Valerie picked up the pace until she stood at her brother's front door, thankful for the commonality with the guard. Now if she could milk this luck a little more and find a more direct way back to Denver.

A homemade pink and green tulle wreath hung crooked on the door. Valerie knocked, knowing no one would answer. She waited a few seconds, then plucked an imitation rock from the mulch bed and accessed the spare key inside.

"Madi. It's Val." She set her bag down and shut the door. A wave of relief washed over her when no one answered.

She fell onto the couch and lay there looking up at the ceiling. She relaxed her muscles, gathering herself. Without power, the building was so silent her ears rang. It was hard to focus, but she went down the list of items again: guns, ammo, medical supplies, and anything to offer her father in hopes he would be a little less judgmental of her predicament. A smart offering might soften him up to any harsh treatment from the great disappointment that was her situation.

Five minutes passed, and she felt rested enough for the haul. It did not take much searching to find Kevin's giant rucksack: a plastic framed backpack that, when full, covered the height and width of her back and stuck out almost a foot and a half. She also found a medical bag with a plethora of pockets and compartments inside. It was a solid brick of a bag when packed, but it was still smaller than the ruck. A hosed hydration system attached neatly to the smaller bag and added a convenient water source.

Valerie opened the kitchen cabinets and pulled out canned food, water filters, soap, and other random items. Her father had taught her everything she needed to know in case something like this happened. What was once Mike's paranoid preparation was now useful. With the CDC collecting people, she knew how to evade them. Without the use of a vehicle, knew how to hike long distances with heavy packs and live off the land. She hated the grueling training when she was ten, but at this moment, she was thankful.

Her next sweep through the house was to find the hidden weapons she knew her brother had squirreled away. Every year for the last three Christmases, her father gifted Kevin with a new gun hiding device. The first one took the longest to find. An inconspicuous magnet hung from one of the key hooks in the kitchen. She walked around to every air intake vent, tapping the magnet to each until the one right by the garage door released. Inside was a forty-five caliber handgun, corresponding ammunition, keys to the remaining safes, a wad of money, and a signed copy of Kevin's favorite zombie novel. She emptied the hiding place, including the book, and retrieved the remaining weapons: an AR-15 from a drop-down compartment on a bookshelf displaying more stories from the same horror writer, and a small nine-millimeter gun locked in a box disguised as a book about a witch with a lush-lipped woman wearing a locket. Valerie guessed it was Madi's.

Taking inventory, she packed what she could carry. Food, water, medical supplies, and ammo were heavy. The design of the bags would distribute the weight from her shoulders to the waistband which made the seventy-five pounds more manageable.

Without power, Valerie did not trust the food in the refrigerator to still be good. She opted for a couple of peanut butter and jelly sandwiches and packed two more to go. The walk would only take two to three hours, but she planned to carry both bags, and it had been years since she had been hiking. She guessed it was about three-thirty in the afternoon, and after eating her first meal of the day was nearly ready to step off on the second leg of her journey. But first, she needed to relieve her sister-in-law of clothing more suitable than the over-sized scrubs she had on. A black tank top and grey calf-length yoga pants would have to do.

She placed the nine-millimeter back in the first compartment she had found with a note explaining to Kevin where his stuff went. She set the magnet back on the key hook and turned to the bags she audaciously planned to carry when the front door handle jiggled. Without hesitation, Valerie pulled the forty-five from her leg holster, slammed in a full magazine, charged the weapon, and fired a bullet three inches above the door frame.

"If you don't live here, you should leave," Valerie shouted at the closed door. Inhale. Exhale. It was time to go.

CHAPTER FOUR

Judging by the distance traveled, Valerie had walked an hour. The weight she bore was awkward with the large rucksack on her back, and the smaller, yet substantial medical bag on her front. The AR-15 sat atop the larger bag, strapped down and secure.

She trekked along the railroad running parallel to the highway which was blocked by abandoned vehicles. Though the gravel was uneven, the tracks provided a straighter path. She kept a steady pace and despite the weight, Valerie felt confident she could maintain it the entire distance. A few times she spotted other people walking or riding bikes. Mothers pushed strollers and walked with children in tow carrying backpacks. Many traveled in the direction of the military base, possibly hoping to reunite with their family members on the other side of the guarded gates. Little traffic still moved, using the shoulder or the median to weave in and out between the other motionless vehicles. No one obeyed posted signs or laws. They were just people trying to get where they were going like her. Only they were not like her.

August was like her. How many others were? They could not have been the only people to wake up looking barely out of high school. And why in the world was she so damn distracted by him? Still distracted. The static, the exploding computer, the malfunctioning equipment, maybe even her attraction to August, all pointed to something electric. But how did the electricity transform her physical body? Something connected these details; she just could not figure out what or how. What was the difference between her and the people in the emergency room, or the people still able to drive cars and talk on their cell phones. What happened to cause this?

No doubt her father would have a solid theory on the matter. Though he was retired military, her father did not trust the government and would have avoided the CDC as she had. Kevin, being in the military still, would have no choice but to follow orders if he was affected, too.

A low drone of diesel engines took Valerie from her thoughts as a convoy of blue package trucks traveled north on the highway just next to her. A stalled pickup was her closest cover. She turned off the tracks and walked down the hill to the road. Ducking behind the truck, she waited for them to pass. Valerie counted twenty people in CDC uniforms moving from car to car, pushing them off to the side of the road to clear a path. She wondered how many people they had collected in the ten trucks that inched along the way heading north. Their involvement was another mystery. How had they reacted so quickly? And why were they far more concerned with the affected than the injured? The explanation of quarantine had been vague. They did not even tell parents where they were taking their children. They were only given a phone number to call for more information.

Heat rose in her face. No one could take her son out of her arms as long as she had a fighting breath. The hairs raised on her arms as the thought made her angrier. The radio in the truck she was hiding behind turned on, and a man's voice was reading the CDC 1-800 number. She nearly screamed, which only raised the volume.

"Stop!" she whispered. It obeyed.

Frozen, she waited before looking back at the northbound lane. No one appeared concerned with her direction. She took a long drink of water and carefully stood up. She would jog the rest of the way.

Valerie set the packs on the porch of her father's home. He was not expecting her, which made her more conscious of her surroundings. She did not want to be mistaken for an intruder and hoped his security cameras signaled her arrival. She knocked hard on the heavy door and waited a few seconds, listening. Nothing. She walked around to the side of the house and looked through the fence for anything to deter unwelcome guests. As she pulled the latch, the gate to the backyard opened without a problem.

Valerie collected a few pebbles and tossed them down the window wells. She knew her father would not stay on the main level of the house because he had yet to barricade the windows, leaving the first floor less secure than the basement. At the third window, her father pounded on the bulletproof glass to get her attention. Once they made eye contact, he pointed up toward the back door. She climbed the stairs to the back porch and sliding glass doors of the house and waited for him to meet her there. When he did, her father, Mike, yanked her into the house and secured the door behind her. He turned, put his hands on her shoulders and looked at her in the eye.

"What are you doing here, Val? You're not supposed to be here."

Valerie had a sudden wave of mixed emotions. Mike hugged her, squeezing the air from her lungs. The only other time she recalled her father embracing her was her wedding day.

"How did you get here?" he said, pulling her away to look at her again.

"I picked up a shift at the ER by Kevin's place. I walked. I am just stopping to rest before I walk home."

Mike gave a "Hmm," and made his way through the house to the front door. He disengaged seven locks and opened the door. At 6 p.m., the sun had already disappeared behind the mountain, yet there were no lights on—no power at all. Valerie could only make out his silhouette but noticed her father's limp. He was favoring his left leg over his prosthetic—the result of a wound retiring him from the military years ago.

"You carried these packs yourself?" Mike looked at her in disbelief.

"Is your stump bothering you?" Valerie asked, ignoring his question. She shooed Mike away from the baggage and pulled them into the house herself.

"Just today. My arthritis has always been worse on my right leg, but now I can feel every single piece of shrapnel grinding against my bone. Did you carry these?" He shut the door and reengaged the locks.

"I brought what I thought you could use."

Mike eyed his petite daughter in disbelief.

"Valerie. I am so sorry. Look at you. It was you this whole time." He held her face in his hands. "This is my fault. Where is Caleb, Val? Is he with Scott? Gia? Are they safe? I'm sorry. I can't believe I was so wrong."

"I have no idea," she said, eyeing her father suspiciously. "I can't call, my car doesn't work. Scott's on a train somewhere between Denver and Wyoming. Gia was able to call my phone at some point, so I guess Caleb is safe. I just. I need to. How am I supposed to get home? And what are you sorry for or wrong about?" Valerie broke down. Expecting her father to get uncomfortable and talk down to her for crying, she left the front foyer and sat at the kitchen table. Mike followed, took Valerie's hand, pulled her back to her feet and hugged her.

"I am so sorry. I never wanted any of this."

"What are you talking about?" Valerie pulled away from him demanding an answer.

Mike retrieved a lantern off the counter, lit the wick, and motioned for her to follow him to the basement. Valerie picked up the massive bag with the rifle still attached and followed, hoping he was going to answer her questions.

In the basement, she dropped the load in a spare bedroom. She noticed a picture of her son on the nightstand next to the bed. The photo was taken just before midnight on New Year's Eve a few months before. She flipped over the frame, removed the portrait, and folded it to fit in the small pocket of her yoga pants before going to talk with her father.

"My entire life has led up to this day," Mike said, offering her a seat at a small table. "When we were children, they told us how this might happen. Since we couldn't stop them, your mom and I spent our entire lives preparing. I hoped the gene remained dormant because of what it might mean for our family. So, we never told you. A part of me thought the government made up the story and the awakening would never come to fruition. For centuries, people passed down stories of the awakening, what they called 'The Event' on the news. The story was just science fiction after so many years. And this whole thing was just a story to me. Your mother and some others were convinced otherwise. To humor her, I figured a more hands-on approach would better equip you and Kevin if the time came."

"You know what all this is?" Valerie raised her voice to her father, unable to mask her frustration. "Why this is happening? Is this part of one of your what-if scenarios or have you known this was going to happen all along?" She wanted to scream. She felt betrayed.

"Our family is special—you, me, Kevin, and perhaps Caleb. You and your mother are especially unique. The electricity, Valerie, the energy is in you." Mike reached across the table to hold her hand. "Most people only have a little bit—enough to keep their heart beating and their metabolism going—but people like us harness power. We don't make the electricity go away; we absorb it."

Valerie was irate. Electricity meant nothing to her. She wanted to be safe in her home with her family.

"Does Scott know, too? Do they teach this in the military?"

"I don't know if he does, but chances are yes. When you reach a certain level of leadership in the ranks, they divulge a little more. They told us the population would weed itself out. They trained us on how to collect mass numbers of people. I had no idea the government was building up to this. I never put the two together."

"The CDC trained you? How do you not know the mission you're training for? Are they going to take Caleb? Tell me! Where would they take him?" Valerie stood from the table. The lights in the basement began to flicker.

Mike stood up in alarm. "Val, I don't know where they would take him if they could even find him. If he's with Gia, then he is safe, but you are not going anywhere tonight. You must rest and regroup. I am having a buddy of mine take you to Max. Kevin was supposed to go, but since he hasn't made it yet, I assume he's been detained. There will be more people like us at Max's house. He will make sure you have what you need to get home. I would never be able to make the walk."

"Who the hell is Max?" The fact Mike had already developed a plan sent Valerie over the edge. As her agitation increased, the lights that before had been only flickering were now beaming. In the brightness, Valerie could now see her father's face clearly, and it was changing. Before her eyes, Mike rapidly regressed in age just as she had. Years disappeared.

"What the hell is this? How? What is going on?" Valerie yelled in fear.

"Your ability, Valerie, but you need to calm down, or they will come here looking for you," he pleaded. "The lights will give you away."

Mike fell to the ground, gripping his war-injured leg. His jaws clenched in pain. Valerie knew there was only one way to help him. She had to get away at once. She was somehow causing the pain with her electricity. Every light in the house was burning at the highest capacity. She went to the spare bedroom where she had left her bag and shut the door. Two paintings hung on the wall. Her mother had painted both. Valerie focused on them to help calm her panic. She would have given anything to have her mother there with her, but not even her mother's memory could calm her. The room was still lit up. She could feel her energy physically shooting out to power the circuits within the house but could do little to control or even understand it. The lights pulsed with her pounding heart. The realization only made her panic more. The fixture above her burst like her phone when she saw Gia's name flash across the screen.

She pulled the rifle from the bag to remove the contents intended for her father, shaking with sobs. There were ninety-eight miles between her and her baby. Walking would take her three days without any obstacles, four if she were hung up by anything. She kept going over what her father said about the electricity. It was in her; which made little sense because it did not seem to be contained by anything at all.

Her father swung the door open, just as the light bulbs throughout the rest of the basement burst, sending glass flying behind him. A bolt of electricity shot from Valerie's hand to the wall, starting a fire in the corner of the room by the window. Mike held a finger to his lips and motioned her to the melting egress window. He pulled a release, and the window frame fell to the floor. Valerie fit hunkered down in the window well. Mike passed her the rifle. Still hidden, she could hear voices above her organizing a raid on her father's house.

"Dad! Come on! They are here," she whispered through tears. She knew what she was leaving him to. They would take him away like the rest.

"The ruck won't fit through the window, Val. You need to leave me; I won't make it. A man is waiting for you. Follow him. He will help you. Go and don't come back here. You need to evade as I taught you. Remember everything I taught you. Go! NOW!" Mike said as stern as he could without giving her away. Valerie scaled the small ladder out of the well and turned as the headlamps bounced light around the room she was just in. She clutched the rifle, pulled the charging handle back and guided the cold metal forward, but even the clicks of the bullet entering the chamber seemed loud to her. Before she could flick the safety switch, someone pushed the barrel toward the ground and grabbed her arm.

"Be quiet and follow me."

Valerie could hardly see to follow the man who gave her the command. She could tell he was wearing a variation of military uniform, but he was not her brother. She was sure she did not know him, but she trusted him for the fact he was not wearing blue, and her father had said someone would be waiting for her. They walked fifteen minutes to an underpass before the man turned around.

"Take your finger off the trigger unless you intend to use it," he said.

"I hadn't decided, yet." Valerie glared at the young blonde man and waited for an explanation. She had the rifle pointed at him but had never taken the safety off. She did not intend to shoot him but was hoping her stance would motivate him to tell her who he was and where they were going.

"You're something, you know that? They have Mike. Hope you're happy. You'd think he would have taught you some sense."

Before Valerie could throw back a witty retort, she processed what he had said.

"Oh, you think he lit up the entire house like a beacon?" he added. She must have looked confused. "Whatever you did was like a black Friday advertisement for the CDC. You're lucky I got back there when I did. But we are both screwed if you pull another stunt like that."

Valerie lowered her rifle, allowing the words to sink in.

"We have to go back. We have to get him. I shouldn't have left him."

"That's the last thing we should do." Anger and annoyance were evident in the way he spat the words at her. "I figured we'd be long gone before the CDC caught on anyone was still there. We were so careful. Your father sacrificed himself to get you out. His plan the whole time was to keep you kids safe. Away from them. You and Kevin are to be protected at all costs. So, great job, kid. Now pick up your lip. We've got a lot of ground to cover."

"The window. . ." Valerie trailed off. She was running out of fight. She replayed the scene over and over. The way her father pushed her through the window, the fact that the flashlights did not pursue her. "What just happened and who are you?"

He ignored her and walked west through neighborhoods for half an hour in silence, moving toward the mountain. Street lights helped them navigate in the dark. In time Valerie let slip a few tears for her father. He had not fought as hard as she knew he could.

The young man turned into a driveway and walked toward the backyard of a single-story home. He held the gate open for her, and she followed him inside.

Not until she sat down did she realize her luck to still have the pistol strapped to her leg. The man lit a candle and looked at her sitting on the couch.

"Don't get comfy. I'll get you another pack, and we're leaving."

"Who are you?" Valerie asked again, getting angry. The man turned and stared at her for a second.

"Jack?" a woman's voice came from the hallway. She turned on a flashlight when she got to the living room and shined the beam in Valerie's eyes before finding the man.

"Dean? What are you doing here? Who is this woman? Does your father know you're here?" She questioned him with the light shining in his eyes. "You look different. You're not using again, are you?"

"Alice, seriously? Will you stop?" the man answered, then continued to rummage through a coat closet.

"Oh, my goodness. Jack? What happened to you?" the woman questioned again with her hand over her mouth. She looked back at Valerie and scrunched her brow.

"What?" he yelled over his shoulder.

"What happened to you? Look at yourself! I thought you were Dean breaking in. Where did you go? Why do you look so young? Who is she?"

"I told you, I had to go back to Mike's. Look, I am sorry I left in such a hurry this morning, but I am fine. She—" Jack motioned to where Valerie was sitting on the couch, "—is in the wrong damn place. I've got to get her back home."

Valerie stood and greeted the woman of the house.

"Hi, I'm Valerie. I'm Mike Burton's daughter. I'm sorry if I am intruding. I can go." Sensing the tension between the two, Valerie turned to the door she had come in through. She guessed Alice was his wife and Valerie was not welcome.

"No. You sit down," Jack commanded Valerie. He gestured Alice into the next room, but Valerie stayed standing.

In their attempt at privacy, Valerie could not help but overhear the conversation.

"You cut all power to the house, leave me here in the dark, and come back to bring a strange woman into our home? You expect me just to be okay?" Alice was having a harder time at keeping her voice down.

"This isn't our home anymore. I don't have time to explain all of this right now."

“Can you at least explain to me why you look like a child?” she almost yelled.

“What are you talking about, woman?” Jack came back into the room with Alice in tow. He stopped at the mirror and grabbed the flashlight from her hand. When he did, the beam went dark. He handed the light back to her, and the ray returned. “Point it at me. Damned thing won’t work if I do it.”

“Why won’t the flashlight work, Jack? Can you please tell me what is happening around here?”

Jack stared into the mirror for a moment in silence. He tilted his head examining his reflection, doing the same facial stretches Valerie had done. He pulled a hand over his short trimmed blonde beard and laughed at himself. Then he lifted his shirt.

“You can hardly see my scar from ‘02.” He turned to Alice to show her. Valerie blushed and looked away, embarrassed to have noticed the definition of his abdomen even in the dim lighting. Alice cleared her throat giving a nod to Valerie. Jack lowered his shirt. He stared for a few more minutes trying to process his age regression. A grin spread across his face.

“Goodness, no wonder I feel amazing. Ha!”

“Well, then. How did this happen?”

“I think I did it,” Valerie spoke up, “at my dad’s house. It was an accident. I panicked while he was there and the—” she struggled to find a word to describe her ability, “—stuff spread to my dad, and I guess they both were affected. I woke up the same way this morning. I’m sorry. I’m still just as confused about all this.”

Alice huffed and disappeared into the other room and returned with a lighter. She lit another decorative candle and handed it to Valerie. “This will have to do.”

Jack vanished into the darkness of the hallway. The woman followed. Valerie sat down again on the couch. Having Alice at least acknowledge her eased her nerves but the voices in the other room continued to go back and forth. She was exhausted and had not eaten more than a few bites of food at her brother’s. She was also disoriented to time since she had given up on her watch earlier in the day. Jack reappeared with a medic bag like the one she had taken from Kevin's house. He tossed the empty carrier down on the floor along with a few loose items: a tarp, a thin blanket, and a box of 5.56-millimeter bullets for her rifle.

"What's on your leg, a .45?"

"Yes." Valerie felt out of place as he left the room again. She felt all her regrets pull tight in her chest. She patted her legs. The panic took a harder grip on her. The lights came on, though still dim. She found it harder to breathe continuing to pat around until she found the small pocket. She pulled out the photo she had taken from her father's spare room. She focused on his face. Memorized it. Inhale, exhale. She had to keep herself together if she were to hold him again.

"Is he with Gia?"

The question jarred her. How did this man know so much about her? She nodded.

"This is a good idea," Jack said pointing to the picture and looking around to ensure the episode was over. "You fight with everything you have until you make it back to your boy."

CHAPTER FIVE

"You know, Mike brags about you more than your brother," Jack sighed. "I've known your pops for a long time. We served together at a training center in Louisiana in the late nineties. He saved my butt a few times. I owe him one."

Valerie still had a hard time believing him. He looked so young, younger than her. She remembered living in Louisiana in middle school but did not recall ever meeting him. He would have looked then how he appeared to her now.

Alice's sobs coming from down the hall broke her train of thought. Jack clenched his fists and leaned his head against the wall.

"I have to come with you. You're an easy target traveling alone. We sent a messenger ahead to gather some people together. People we can trust. Since communications are down, they have no idea you're here instead of Kevin. We can hope the crew will be there and willing to join us by the time we arrive."

"Do you know what happened at my dad's house? If you and my dad are so much older, why do you look younger than me?" She was still numb, not knowing how to mentally process what had happened. She could not wrap her mind around anything her father said about the electricity or why the CDC was so involved.

"I met up with your dad earlier in the day after we realized something was wrong and the planes went down. I left for a bit to touch base with another guy to gather the group together. When I got back to your dad's place, the lights were flickering. The CDC trucks were already in the area, so I hurried and went in through the back door to warn Mike. I found him in the basement. He didn't say much other than you were there instead of Kevin and needed my help. So, I waited for you outside. The lights got so bright I couldn't look directly at the window. What I did see looked like electricity shooting from you to a hole you put in the wall. The Plexiglas melted, and the surge continued up the metal frame of the window well and into the ground." Jack rubbed the back of his neck and shook his head.

"But how was the electricity coming from me? Dad said we absorb energy."

"I absorb energy. You're something else," he answered, maintaining his thoughtful stance. "Like your dad, I just chalked all this up as a fairytale and went on with life, not thinking the awakening would ever happen."

Jack rambled on as Valerie fought to stay awake. When it was evident he was walking down memory lane without any more useful information, she surrendered to her need for rest and dozed off. Her mind and body were exhausted.

Valerie's shoulder was shaken, startling her awake. Her eyes shot open, and she was ready to sprint. Instead of the threat she anticipated, Alice stood over her with two cups of coffee. Her eyes were swollen and raw from crying.

"I'm sorry you have to see me like this. Can you imagine how unfair this is to me to not be a part of all this? To watch others regain their youth, and here I am stuck in the same aging bag of skin?" Alice handed Valerie one of the cups and sat down next to her. The older woman sniffled and wiped her eyes with a wad of tissue. "I was young and pretty once. I'd eat a baby to have my youth back. Not really, but you know what I mean. Men used to look at me, talk to me, and buy me things. Now I don't get a nod. No one bothers to hold the door anymore. Seems like society forgets about middle-aged women. I'm not a cougar; I'm like a tired old hag." Alice laughed, and Valerie could smell the whiskey from the woman's coffee on her breath.

"I left my son with a nanny this morning. I live in Denver. I can't use a car to get home or a phone to even call. I would age one-hundred years to get back to my son as soon as possible." Valerie did not mean to be insensitive to the woman. Vanity seemed like a petty consideration in the grand scheme of things.

"I mean that you get to live again. Jack might be somewhat of an asshole, but he'll get you where you need to go, but when you get there, and everything is right again, live your life. You got a second chance, don't piss it away. Alright?"

Valerie nodded. She found comfort in her reassurance of Jack's ability.

"We're not married," Alice said, motioning to Jack leaning against the wall with his own cup of coffee. "Anymore, anyway. This is, what, our third try at this?"

Jack nodded as if she had asked if he was having a good day. Like the failure was of normal conversation.

"We're not young anymore. We're both different people than before. There is nothing wrong with that. Jack is this way, with this Event, and I'm not." She patted Valerie's knee as she stood and went back down the hallway and closed a door.

Jack stood leaning against the wall, watching the exchange. Valerie sniffed her coffee to ensure there was no whiskey in her cup before taking a sip. Black and bitter. She took one more sip and set the mug down. She would give anything to be normal again. Fat, wrinkled. These things paled in comparison to being able to drive home. She could see her son within hours instead of days.

"Nap time's over. Let's go," Jack said, then took a long drink of his coffee.

The sun was not quite up, but there was enough light to see around the room, and their gear staged by the front door.

Jack held up her pack so she could slip her arms in and take the load on herself. She buckled the waistband and another band across her chest to keep the shoulder straps in place. Jack wrapped the rifle in an olive green waterproof bag and secured the weapon to the side of her pack to not draw undue attention. Opening the front door with his cup of coffee in hand, he took a deep breath and exhaled with a long sigh. He let Valerie out the door and locked the deadbolt behind them.

The pace was agreeable, to her surprise, and she could not complain. Her body complied with the weight of the pack and the speed they moved. She considered this would prove to be an easy trip.

"This reminds me of doing ruck marches back in the day, the difference being my load is lighter and my shoes more appropriate. You couldn't ask for better weather either. You might sweat a little, but the breeze keeps the heat manageable."

Despite his gruff demeanor, Valerie could tell Jack was in high spirits. His attitude was contagious and kept her motivated, making the journey feel less daunting. They started through the neighborhood walking east, away from the mountains. As the road came to an incline, their pace slowed a bit.

"Where are we going? I'm not complaining, just trying to get an idea of how far we'll be traveling."

Jack raised a hand to cut her off. He stopped and studied the road. CDC trucks moved slowly with the regular traffic of those unaffected by the Event. He continued through the neighborhood instead of down the main street.

"We are going about twenty miles north of here. There is more traffic than I thought there would be," Jack said.

"When I was walking to my dad's, I watched the CDC clear the roads to move the trucks through. They pushed them onto the shoulder to make way for traffic. Everyone else just drove on the median or the shoulder to get around the stalled cars. There are so many left abandoned still. How many people do you think they took?"

He shrugged and tossed her an energy bar. She choked down the sticky, chalky mass with water. Before long, the overpass to the highway was in view, and they could break from the road. They continued under the highway and turned left into a city park.

"We can take a break here if you need to. We've covered about five miles in an hour and a half," Jack said over his shoulder, continuing his pace. “From here, we’ll stick to the creek bed until the path ends. We aren’t going to be the only ones with the idea, but we’ll be safer than if we keep to the road. I doubt they are hunting the homeless or degenerates for quarantine, anyway.”

“We can keep going,” she said as she followed him down to a footpath running the course of the creek for as far as she could see. “Twenty miles is not far out of town. I don’t know if a GPS would be helpful or depressing at this point. Puts a perspective on things when an hour drive translates into days of walking.”

Down the creek in the opposite direction, two tents were set up, but with no signs of inhabitants. The footpath along the stream took them to another city park where they sat for their first break. The two settled at a concrete picnic table and dropped their loads to stretch. They shared salami and crackers. She studied him again in the light of day. Though he looked young, he also looked angry all the time, even as he ate. He was, however, handsome with his heavy brow and square jaw.

“Do you have any other family?” Valerie asked after five minutes of eating in silence.

“Dean, my son. Spitting image of me,” Jack spoke between bites.

“Is he a part of all of this too?” Valerie asked, making conversation and hoping to learn more about her guide.

“His mom and I were just in high school. I went away to join the army, to give them a life. When I got back from my second deployment, neither of them wanted anything to do with me. Dean grew up without a dad most of his life and decided he wanted to keep it that way. Until he got really bad into heroin. All of a sudden, he wanted to reconnect. He just had nowhere else to go. You know, I honestly thought I could fix him. I’ve led kids younger than him into gunfights that lasted days and brought them safely back home. You’d think I could raise my own kid.”

“Did he at least get help?”

“Hell no. Within twenty-four hours, that kid stole every TV in the house, two guns, and all of Alice’s jewelry I’d sent her from Korea. That was two years ago, and I have not seen or heard from him since.

I'm scared to look him up. I'd hope he'd go to jail and rehab, but I'm terrified to find out the worst, you know."

"How old are you?" She waited while he chewed his food.

"Fifty-three."

"Shut up! You're lying."

"I swear it's the truth. Here, look at my driver's license." He pulled his wallet out of his back pocket and handed her the card. The photo was indeed the man seated across from her at the age he stated. The same blue eyes were in the picture, only they were more tired with defined creases at the edges, and there were long lines on his forehead. The man in the photo also had a higher hairline.

"Mr. Jackson R. McGuire," she stated. "If you were Jackson Junior, I could believe this might be a picture of your dad. I hope you don't use this to buy your alcohol," Valerie teased.

"Okay, Ms. Valerie Marie Burton. I know I don't look," he struggled with the word, "old? That was my mug up until last night. Jesus, I even feel half my age."

"Russell," Valerie said with a mouth full of crackers.

"I'm sorry?"

"My name. Valerie Marie Russell." She waved her wedding ring in his face to help him understand. He nodded, chewing the last bite of his lunch. She looked down at his picture. She had seen him before. He stood in the back of the church at her mother's memorial service. He had appeared much older than the man across from her.

"Yeah, well, you can never stop being a Burton. I have so many stories about your dad, and Janice, too." Jack smiled. "Your mom had quite a time trying to keep us in line. You look a lot like her. Good thing, too. Your dad would make an ugly woman."

Hearing her mother's name caught her off guard. Though a year had passed since the accident, Valerie was not ready to talk about her. The guilt had yet to subside. Janice Burton's memory belonged to Valerie. Jack was a stranger who, somehow, had ghosted through her childhood. She was not special to him, and he did not have the right to tell her stories she did not already know. The immediate change in her posture conveyed he had overstepped a line.

"Please don't talk about my mother," she said, handing him back his license. Jack nodded.

Valerie threw away the trash while Jack packed up the remaining food. She felt a tinge of guilt for having cut him off and reminded herself of his loyalty to her father and their family. If he had not been such a close friend to Mike, her only other option was to make the trip alone. Jack was the more tolerable choice.

"You think my dad is okay? Where do you think they took him?" She swung the bag on her back, overestimating the weight, and knocked herself in the face with the attached rifle.

"You got that?" Jack laughed. He grabbed the top of the bag and helped her get her balance. "Mike Burton knows what he is doing. Aside from a central collection point, I could not begin to guess where they are taking them. The process is supposed to be peaceful, but we were also trained on hostile collections. Either way, there was never a jail scenario. Maybe the convention center?"

Valerie nodded and stepped off.

"To answer your question earlier, we are meeting up with everyone where Command Sergeant Major Max lives, north of town. I'm not sure if Griff—the guy I sent ahead—has gotten there yet. So, as long as Max is home and willing to take us in, we can rest tonight. He is an old friend of mine and your dad's. A bit aggressive, but he means well," Jack said with a smile like he was telling a joke Valerie did not understand. "He's retired military, also. He sold a chain of restaurants for far more money than they were worth. At least, the claim is he did. If we manage to get in the door, there will be plenty of accommodations for us."

"So, you had some guy just up and walk around town gathering people and giving messages? I have plenty of messages to send. I don't have Gia's number anyway. I blew up my phone with my mind," she laughed, listening to herself explain the story out loud. "Who memorizes phone numbers anymore? I know my husband's by heart, but I need someone to dial the number. If he could answer at all, then that would mean he wasn't affected."

"There is a chance Griff can try to call your husband. I'm sure he can call Gia too, if he hasn't already."

"Wait, what?"

"Griff and Gia are engaged."

"Engaged? She's not even dating anyone. How is she engaged? She's too young to be engaged."

"Gia is twenty-eight years old and is the head of security to the governor. She was hired by your dad to watch over you and your family. Griff got a call from her last night before everything started to let him know things were getting sticky in the capital and something was up. No one really knew what would happen, but there had been some kind of shift in the atmosphere that tipped the government off." Jack paused, awaiting her reaction.

Valerie processed everything he had said, the circumstances in which she found and hired Gia, how much they had in common, and how well they got along. Of course, her background check came back clear; it had been manipulated. She had always found the girl to be smart and mature, not realizing they were so close in age.

"Why didn't she stop me from leaving? She knew. She acted so distracted because she knew things were going to go bad. Why didn't she tell me not to go?" Valerie could not stop the tears.

"Because, the farther away you are from Denver, the better. The less you knew about what you are, the less likely they were to find you," Jack said with a heavy sigh of regret. "I'm sure she did what she thought was your best chance."

They walked in silence for a long while. When the footpath ended, they took to the railroad tracks. Jack walked straight down the middle, but Valerie had seen one too many patients hit by trains, so she skirted the wooden ties and stepped on the tracks only when she had to. After hours of walking, Valerie felt the shock of the new information subside.

"I have no perception of time. I feel like it's 5 p.m." Valerie paused for a few seconds to do the math in her head. "Why are we stopping at Max's so early in the day? At this pace, we'd get there at 3 p.m. at the latest. We'd still have four hours of daylight. We should keep going."

"If we are on mile thirty and we need to run, we won't run as fast as we would if we were only on mile fifteen. We must pace ourselves, or we'll get tired and never get there. Twenty miles a day, even to a seasoned hiker, is a decent pace for a hundred-mile hike." Jack pulled a rag from his pant pocket and wiped the cloth across his forehead. "I'm happy you asked. So far, you are holding up well. Believe it or not, I'm starting to like you."

"Why are you doing this? Helping me. Anyone else would hole up in his house until everything blew over."

"Mike is the closest thing I have to family. We have a small group we call Sasquatch International. It stands for Specially Assigned Skilled Qualified Ununiformed Armed Trappers Creating Havoc. We don't really hunt for 'Squatch. Just a bunch of old farts trying to relive the glory days. Lucky for you, we're also a network of trained and skeptical individuals. The minute the electrical current hit, I met with Mike. We knew we couldn't just sit back and be bystanders. So, I went to Griffin for help. He left to gather everyone at Max's to develop a plan. Your dad was going to meet up with us later."

"So how many people are in this Sasquatch group?"

"Only a few—me, Griff, your dad, Duke, Major, and Hyka."

"Hyka? Is that a lady's name? There is a lady in your Sasquatch group?" Valerie's smile was bigger than she intended.

"Yes, Hyka is a female. She's our woman auxiliary colonel. She's Major's daughter. She got out of the military a couple of years ago. One tough broad, though. I wouldn't pick a fight with her. She's five foot eight, maybe a buck thirty, but can outmaneuver any of us at hand-to-hand combat. She is also an expert when it comes to weapons. We'd never tell Major, but the rest of the group make bets she can outshoot her old man at the range. She's one solid woman."

They returned to the creek path when the rail turned east and came to another overpass. The CDC had cleared the road above, and there was more traffic. Valerie felt a tinge of jealousy for the regular people with their convenient means of transportation. As they got closer, they could see colored tarps hung under the bridge, offering shelter to a small group of people.

Jack and Valerie drew closer to the road and the nomadic residents of the bridge. Raised voices indicated they were approaching a conflict. Valerie recognized the blue CDC uniforms, and Jack slowed the pace. He looked to his left and right for a clear path out of their line of sight. Valerie's eyes stayed on the crowd. They had already caught the attention of one of the CDC men. Turning at this point would make them appear to be running. They would have to take their chances. Jack read her mind, and they resumed their pace.

"Just follow my lead and don't say anything."

Jack raised his voice and addressed the young man who had noticed them approaching. "Hey, troop. What's going on here?"

The kid must have been nineteen and fresh out of training. "Excuse me, sir. Have you or you, ma'am, been affected by the electric current yesterday?" His voice quivered, and he never looked Valerie in the eye, even when addressing her. He spoke as if he had rehearsed the question over and over, but still dreaded the confrontation.

"I am Sergeant First Class McGuire, and this is the daughter of Sergeant Major Burton. I'm escorting her back home to Denver. Cars are blocking her vehicle in. I assure you, neither of us was affected."

"Yes, Sergeant. I'm sorry to stop you, but we have to ask everyone, and there is a test my squad leader has. Everyone gets tested." The soldier was shaking and stuttering his words.

"Look, Private. This woman has a baby at home with a nanny threatening to leave him alone. Until we can get to my vehicle, I'm afraid delays are unacceptable." Jack spoke with such distinction. He seemed to grow three feet taller than the young soldier.

The troop nodded and allowed the two to go while his counterparts continued to deal with the upset group, oblivious to their passing.

"Pulling rank will work once. I didn't expect it to work at all, to be honest," Jack said when they were a safe distance away.

"What test do they have? Do they have a way to tell us apart? Did you see what they were doing? Are they taking everyone? Jack. What if they do have Caleb?"

"If they've developed a test, then we are running out of time. Hell, all anyone would have to do is hold anything electronic to us and if the power stops, bam, you got your guy."

Jack stopped and looked around before facing Valerie. "You can't, for a second, think they have Caleb. If you do, then you're already defeated in your mind. Right now, doubt is your worst enemy. What we are doing is not easy, but you'll convince yourself it is impossible. Keep your head, kid." He took a step back and looked around again. "I think we are far enough east to get out of the creek and head north. We'll steer clear of the main streets. The neighborhoods aren't much safer, but they offer quick cover if needed. We're almost there."

The farther they walked, the larger and more elaborate the homes became. Valerie was starting to think she overestimated herself. She felt every ounce of weight on her back from her shoulders to the balls of her feet. They came to a gated community with a sign reading Pine Bluffs Golf Club.

"Well, we're here. Max's place is just on the other side of the course." Jack slowed his pace to match Valerie's instead of taking the lead like he had most of the day.

For the last two miles, she walked hunched over, staring at the ground, weary from the long journey.

"I'm impressed. You have a lot of heart and didn't give up. You'd make a good soldier like your brother and your dad."

She knew he was trying to motivate her to push through the last stretch.

"My feet hurt," she said under her breath.

"There you go and ruin it. Went the entire day without complaining. We have half a mile left, and you just couldn't hold it in any longer." Jack threw his hands in the air.

His tone was hard and mocking, but she knew he was joking. Valerie kept her head down, watched her feet, and listened to the rhythm of her steps. A bead of sweat dripped off her nose. She pushed herself to put one foot in front of the other.

The house, like the community, was also gated. Jack pulled the massive wrought iron entrance open, and then closed it again after she had walked through behind him. The main building was a four-story home right off the golf course. Judging by the security cameras posted on the front of the house and the massive satellite dish on the roof, the home was modest compared to his budget. She understood what Jack meant earlier and doubted a restaurant chain had funded this lifestyle. Jack knocked on the door and was pushed aside by the man who answered.

"What light of God has shined upon me, that I might be surrounded by so many beautiful women?" Max wrapped his arm around Valerie's shoulder and escorted her inside, paying no attention to Jack. He looked her dead in the eyes with a smile like he wanted to lick her face. Her stomach turned. She wanted to run. Something was wrong.

"Come on in. Set your stuff down. I'll have someone take your things upstairs for you. You must be little Ms. Burton, if I knew anything. Good night, old Burton and I go way, way, way back." Max wore a red smoking jacket, with black sweat pants and house shoes. He held an unlit cigar in his teeth under a thin mustache lining his upper lip. Gray salted his black hair, more so around his temples, offering a contrast to his dark complexion.

Valerie shot an awkward look at Jack, who offered no assistance. Only then did Max break his gaze.

"Big Mac Daddy, is that you? You look like the doctor just slapped your ass and cut the cord. What kind of fountain of youth have you gotten into?"

Max was a loud man. She could not tell if he was deaf or if he had a complete disregard for everyone's comfort, though she leaned toward the latter. Unlike Jack, Max looked her father's age. His eyes wrinkled with the smile she was sure he always held. Everything from his predatory opening remarks to the way he looked at her made her want to escape. As the door closed, something felt permanent, like a prison door closing.

CHAPTER SIX

Valerie looked down the hallway past Max's foyer at the light fixtures, searching for an indication of Max's genetic standing. Though no lights were on, it was still midday and plenty of natural lighting shown through the many windows. She had at least met Jack once before, but this was the first she had ever heard of Max. She had always felt a general apprehension toward every new face she saw, but there was something about her surroundings, maybe the house itself, that felt like a threat to her. Regardless of where the danger was coming from, Valerie wanted to leave as soon as possible. Her father had trusted Jack to keep her safe, but she could not shake the feeling that some of the people he respected might have hidden agendas.

"Valerie, can I take your bag?" The thin man came out of nowhere. He was taller than the rest of the group. His short red hair appeared slept on, and he had two days of growth on his face. He looked worse off than she and Jack did after their day of walking.

"No, thank you. I can manage," she lied. She did not want to part with her gear. She needed her things close in case she found a quick escape, but the twenty miles weighed on her body. Her shoulders and feet ached.

"There is a room for you upstairs," Max interjected. "We have a lot to cover this evening, now the last of us are here. I'm sure you don't want to lug this thing around all night. You are safe. I promise."

Valerie did not hold his promises to any weight, but she had run out of energy to argue. The thin, tired man lifted the bag from her shoulders. She unbuckled the straps, shrugged off the load and peeled the sweat-matted shirt away from her torso. The cold air and relief were rejuvenating. She shivered and waited while Jack reconnected with his friends. She brushed a hand over her leg holster and the handgun. Having the weapon eased her anxiety.

Max led them through the rest of the house. The main floor was just as grand as the exterior appeared. The entire first level flowed together with elaborate flooring providing a sharp transition between each room. A full length, stocked bar ran along the wall spreading from the kitchen and into the formal dining room. Max crossed the room and picked up a crystal decanter.

"This here calls for some drinks." He lined up eight shot glasses, held the bottle higher than necessary, and poured each glass until they overflowed.

People gathered around as each shot glass was passed out. Valerie passed two shots down, one to the tired man and one to Jack before holding on to her own. She sniffed the clear liquid. Tequila.

"All right now, shut the hell up," Max yelled over the group.

Everyone fell silent.

"In our childhood, we were taught as children. But today we stand here as grown adults making grown decisions. Along with the Event came many real-life surprises. We can choose to act out of regret, spite, or malice because of how the cards played out, but retribution would be selfish and foolhardy. We are better than that. Hell, I'm better than most of you, but I love you, bastards, and have welcomed you into my home.

"Anyway, we are here because the gene is no longer dormant, and the conductors of electricity are made apparent. As the conductors draw from the energy, there is one way to ground such power. We have a grounding rod among us, what the world is calling a DiaZem. A new age is the reason we have gathered and why we are sacrificing so much for this mission. Most of us were once a part of the same organization now calling themselves the CDC. We could have been the poor blue-suited bastards out there following orders, but now we have a higher purpose. I'd much rather be drinking here with you fools than the finest in their ranks. But for the continued prosperity of all, the DiaZem must not fall into the wrong hands. So, steady your glasses and dry your tears, ladies, and gents, because this day is not a sad one. No, today we celebrate what makes us great and do what we've been born to do. To the DiaZem." Max raised his glass, and everyone followed suit.

"The DiaZem," answered the group. As Valerie lowered the glass to drink, a hand covered the liquid and pushed the glass away from Valerie's open mouth.

"You never drink to yourself," the woman said. After slamming back her own shot, she relieved Valerie of hers and treated the second tequila the same, without a wince.

The sight of the woman made Valerie freeze. She was beautiful and terrifying at the same time. With a slender but muscular silhouette, she sported many different tattoos, including a tribal eagle with wings covering her chest. She had dark hair. Bangs swept to the side, still covering her forehead. The rest of her hair was sectioned off and wrapped in tight strings extending to her waist resembling dreadlocks. She carried a once-lit cigar like Max's tucked behind her ear.

"Cheers," she said without inflection of any kind. She handed the empty glass back to Valerie and walked away.

Valerie was left with her mouth still open. She wanted to know what she meant. How did everyone seem to know who she was before she walked in the door? And why were they toasting her?

"Don't mind Hyka. She comes off a bit hostile. She likes you, or else she wouldn't have said anything at all. As for taking your drink, I'm kind of mad she beat me to your shot." Jack patted Valerie on the back and walked off to greet a couple of gentlemen across the room.

She wanted to follow him. Instead, she stood alone in the middle of the gathering while the rest of the company seemed to already know each other. She felt out of place and out of control of the situation; even the walls of Max's home overpowered her.

"Come here, young lady," Max shouted across the room.

Inhale, exhale. Valerie did not want to interact with him. His constant intensity was draining. He looked at her as if he was collecting information she was not willing to give. Acknowledging her apprehension, he and the tired man crossed the room to her.

"This here is Edward, often goes by Griff. He'll show you to your room. I can't imagine how exhausted you must be."

Griff extended his hand, and Valerie reciprocated. She had many questions.

Max looked at his watch and then addressed the group, "The time is 1500 now, dinner is at 1730, and we have a briefing at 1900. You, young lady, would find it advantageous to be at the briefing. We are going to map the process of extracting your son."

Extraction. The use of the word implied that they did not mean to just take her home. He did not say reunion. Instead of protesting, she decided to remain silent and observant. So far, no one had forced her to do anything, but they had not needed to. She had followed all their instructions because Jack had. She trusted Jack, no one else. Her attention was now on Griff and getting answers.

Valerie followed him up the stairs. Her legs ached with each step, and she could feel the dried sweat turned to salt on her skin.

"Have you spoken to her?" Valerie asked him. He knew who she was talking about.

"Yes. All she could say was she and Caleb are safe," he answered, continuing up the stairs to the second floor, then down a hallway. A sob escaped Valerie's body. The news made her want to run the hundred miles home. She sucked in air to slow her breathing enough to speak.

"Can you call her again? Are they still at my house?" Valerie caught her breath again to avoid losing her nerve in front of him.

"I don't know where they went. The CDC is monitoring her phone calls. All she said was she was taking him to a safe place, and she would leave a clue. One only you would understand. She had to be sure they couldn't find him." Griff stopped at the fourth door on the left. "She loves you and Caleb. Gia will fight with her last breath to protect him. She hated keeping the secret from you, but the less you knew, the better chance they wouldn't be able to find you. We never anticipated what to do if you were here instead of there, but she did what she thought was your best chance."

Griff looked at the corner of the ceiling behind him at a security camera and back to her. She nodded. Her suspicions were validated. Something was not right about her situation. She closed the door behind her. Solitude allowed the knot in her stomach to loosen.

The room was a generic guest room with a private bathroom. She took a seat on a beige accent chair in the corner of the room facing the bed. After removing her socks and shoes, she rubbed the soreness out of her feet. She was lucky to not have any blisters, though she could feel the beginnings of a few. A glass door to a spacious shower caught her eye in the bathroom. She pulled off the clothes she had borrowed from her sister-in-law and climbed in.

For a long while, she let the hot water run over her. She cried, thankful her son was safe, but still terrified she would never reach him. They were after him. She was not even sure who they were.

Without so much as a knock, Hyka swung the door open. In her exhaustion, Valerie had forgotten to lock either door. Startled and exposed behind a large glass shower door, she attempted to cover herself.

"Here are some clean clothes. You might have to cuff the pants, no big deal. They aren't church clothes, but at least you won't be naked." Hyka had a deep flat tone to her voice and spoke with little inflection. She sounded unimpressed, bored even. She gathered the dirty clothes on the floor. "I'll burn these for you."

Relieved to hear the click of the lock when Hyka left, Valerie finished her shower and evaluated the clothing after wrapping in a towel. No bra. No underwear. She doubted Hyka wore either garment. Then her mouth went dry. The picture of Caleb was still in the pants Hyka had taken. She was not sure if Hyka indeed intended to burn her clothes, but the concern was valid. She rushed to pull on the gray tank top and black cargo pants, not bothering to cuff them. She flung open the door and ran hard into Jack. He was more muscular than she guessed, and the impact hurt. He grabbed her arms to balance them both; then he held up the photo.

"Looking for this?"

Valerie burst into tears and snatched the photo out of his hand. The mere thought of losing his picture made her come undone. She had held herself together through the car accident, plane crashes, and even the CDC taking her dad; but the idea of losing the one thing she had left of Caleb was too much. Jack pulled her into him and held her while she shook with sobs.

"I'm sorry. I'm not normally like this. I can't be weak now, I know." She tried to get herself under control, looking at the photo of her little boy's smiling face.

"You know, I have seen grown men go through less than you and break down like babies. You have plenty of reasons to be upset right now." He walked her back into the room and sat her on the bed.

She ran her hands over the sage colored comforter trying to stifle her tears. Jack leaned against the dresser, picked up a round, glass candle holder, tossed the object in the air, and caught the orb before setting it back down.

"You don't have to be sorry. Crying isn't a weakness. Your little guy is waiting for you. Now is a good time to get all your feelings out. After tomorrow, you won't have that luxury on the road. And to be honest, nobody is going to want to hear you cry for five days."

"Nobody? Like, people are coming with us? I want to call Scott. Get Griff up here and have him call my husband. You promised me at least a phone call." Valerie's anxiety turned to anger. She knew somehow if Scott could answer the phone, everything would be fine. She needed to know her husband was safe.

"I did promise, but there is far more to this than what you and I thought. The reason why we chose to meet here is this is a secure building. Max doesn't have the gene, but he does have ties to what's going on in Denver. They are taking the conductors to the airport. Of those here, Major, Hyka, and Duke all have the gene. Griff does not, and neither does Gia. Anyway, looks like the 'Squatch team is going with you to recover Caleb." He pushed off from the dresser and crossed the room to sit in the beige chair.

"Why are you helping me, if everyone else is in the same boat? Shouldn't you all be lying low, keeping your distance from the CDC? I don't need help. I don't want help. I am going home, and that's the end of it."

"Look." Jack stood up with authority as he had to the young soldier on the road. Anger clear on his face. "This isn't a game of kickball. You don't get to pick who is on your team. If it weren't for Mike pushing you out the window, you'd already be caught. You may not like me, and I am okay with that. But whatever you think is the end of all of this, is not the end."

"What are you talking about?" she pleaded, close again to tears.

Jack lowered his shoulders and sat back down. A hint of regret on his face.

"Important people already know too much about you. A DiaZem can transfer the energy from a conductor into other objects. People like me absorb energy and over time the power builds up. Conductors have no way of expelling it, so over a short amount of time, people like me will begin to age faster than usual. You release the stored energy back into the technology around us, or the ground. Which was why Max called you a grounding rod. You released my stored energy, and now I look like the epitome of all that is man." He sat up straight and puffed his chest in an exaggerated pose. When she gave no hint of a smile, he deflated himself and continued. "The power surge at your dad's and the lightning bolt which blasted out the window was you, releasing all the energy from us."

"So, what is stopping me from being a constant lightning bolt? And why do I absorb energy too, instead of the current just passing? If I can power a house, why can't I power a car? Or a phone? This is ridiculous. I didn't ask for this. I just want my son. I want Scott. I want to be home. I want to go back to whatever life I have left. If there are people here who can drive, why don't they get Caleb? Bring him here to me? The trip would take a day."

"That was the original plan, to collect you, the kids and Gia and bring you to your dad's. This is before we knew you were already here. Griff already tried to get them. He left this morning after gathering everyone, but north of Monument a plane crashed on the highway. The pilot attempted to land, but with the traffic coming to a standstill, the landing turned into a mile-long wreckage. There is no way through in a vehicle."

She sat for a minute processing everything he had told her. After a few moments, she looked up at him.

"Jack. Thank you for today, but I need to be alone now. I'll be down for dinner. I'll play along. I will let them help me, but I do not want any part of this beyond finding Caleb."

"Alright, kid." He slapped his hands on his knees, stood up, and stretched. "My room is down the hall, the last one on the left before you go down the stairs. Let me know if you need anything, even to talk. Sorry I got a little heated. I'm proud of you." He shut the door behind him.

She laid on the bed and stared up at the ceiling. Allowing her muscles to relax, she realized how much of a toll the journey had already taken on her. She did not feel different. She did not feel like she had any power at all. There was no feeling of static in the air or a sense of storing energy from the things she encountered. She studied her hands then held them a foot apart, palms facing each other. She strained, thinking maybe electricity would shoot from one to the other like in the movies. The ceiling fan turned, and the bulbs above her flickered to a warm glow. She put her hands down and looked at the light switch in the off position. Valerie got up and flipped the small switch up and down, but the lights stayed on. She walked back to the bed and laid back down where she was before, holding her hands the same. The ceiling fan went faster. Like a fluid movement, she could feel the energy move through her to the circuits within the room. She pointed her hands out, and everything in the room sprang to life. All the lights were on, the clock radio blasted, and the TV in the room lit up with the CDC logo.

"This is unnerving, Frank," the newscaster said. "For those tuning in at home, the CDC has issued another press release outlining the dangers of those affected by the Event yesterday. Please, if you or someone you know is experiencing any of these symptoms, they need to seek medical attention or contact the CDC at the 1-800 number on your screen. Symptoms include the inability to use electronics, the ability to control electronics without touching them, or remarkable regression of age. Extreme cases can display bolts of electricity coming from an individual, or the appearance of a power overload in a home, meaning all the lights are shining brighter than they should. These people are to seek treatment immediately as they are a danger to those around them. Also, do not approach these people on your own. Call the CDC with any information you may have regarding these individuals and allow the officials to do their job.

"You know, Frank, I saw a house like they described last night in my neighborhood. The scene was terrifying. The CDC showed up in a matter of seconds and got things under control fast. I thought the entire house might explode."

Valerie pulled the energy back from the TV, and the screen went black. The CDC was using propaganda to herd the remaining conductors together. Her new acquaintances did not have a choice but to help her. The government was hunting all of them.

CHAPTER SEVEN

Valerie wanted answers. She cuffed the pants Hyka had provided, put her shoes on, and looked in the mirror to adjust her tank top, careful to maintain her modesty despite the lack of undergarments. She walked down the hall to Jack's room. The door was open, but the space was empty except for his ruck next to the bed. His room was smaller than hers and did not have a bathroom. A picture hung on the wall. Men in combat uniforms sat on a concrete barrier. She recognized many of the faces from those gathered at the toast Max had given earlier. Her father had no expression on his face, which made her smile. He never smiled for photos for as long as she could remember. Not even family ones.

"This picture was taken at the training site in Louisiana. You might have been eleven or twelve years old. Thick as thieves, we were," Jack said from the door. He gave a motion with his head to follow him down the stairs toward the sound of voices and the smell of food.

In the kitchen, a buffet-style dinner was laid out on an island table. Seven people walked around filling their plates. They joked with each other like a big, loud family. These were her father's friends with bonds stronger than blood. She looked at their faces and tried to imagine her father fighting alongside them. They must have felt a duty to help her. This offered a little more comfort and solidarity toward them, but she was still a bit apprehensive. She fell in line with Jack to fill a plate of food.

"Jack McGuire, if I didn't know you to be a dirty old man, I might give you the time of day. Nice hair, pony boy," Hyka said from across the island, a slight smirk being the only indication of her joke.

The room erupted in laughter. Only Valerie and the man standing to the right of Hyka did not join in. Instead, the man shot a disapproving look at Jack. He must have been Hyka's father. Valerie blushed and gathered her plate and utensils. Barbecue ribs, mashed potatoes, steamed vegetables, dinner rolls. When her plate was full, she found an open seat near a pitcher of water. Her body craved the nutrition, depleted by her travels, but the knot in her stomach had returned.

"Are you doing okay?" Jack asked, leaning close so she did not have to raise her voice.

"No. Did you watch the news? They are turning the collection process into a manhunt."

"Yeah, we watched that piece. Eat. Enjoy a distraction. We leave tomorrow night. You need to rest and get your strength up, and we still need more time to figure things out."

"I powered my entire room with my hands," Valerie said, too loud; she meant the comment for only Jack. She immediately regretted not keeping the incident a secret. Max looked up at her, then back at his food. She looked down at hers, a good excuse to stop talking. He had heard every word.

She filled an empty glass with water and listened to the conversations around her. The table was loud, with moods light and joyful. The men shouted remember-when stories over the course of the meal. Some included her father: the legendary Mike Burton and how he commanded his troops with an iron fist and a cold heart. They told stories of the man she remembered. Duke described a story of when he had occupied a mansion in Ramadi, Iraq, during the first elections after coalition forces liberated the country from Saddam's reign. Her father had led one hundred and fifty infantry soldiers. First Sergeant Burton made his men collect the rubble from the demolished side of the building and organize the debris into what he called a rock garden.

Even though they thought the task was ridiculous, the troops followed the order. Two weeks later, a rocket was shot into the compound, ricocheted off her father's rock garden and exploded a safe distance away, leaving the building and occupants unharmed. They never questioned the rock garden again.

Valerie could laugh at the story. She missed him. Judging from their interactions, everyone else did, too. Hearing about her father lifted her spirits. She became less skeptical of the group as a whole, and her appetite returned. She kept a careful eye on Max. He was the exception to her newfound comfort.

After they had eaten their fill and cleared the table of food, Max passed beers to those in attendance. Valerie declined the alcohol in favor of water. The transition from dinner to the meeting was marked and formal.

"Let's get down to business. I am Maximus Jonah Davis, airborne, air assault, the best damn cook this side of the Rockies, and your host." As Max took his seat, the man to his right stood.

"Edward Griffin. I go by Griff. An agent with Homeland Security."

"Jack McGuire, master gunner."

It was Valerie's turn. She was unsure of her title but followed suit the best she could.

"Valerie Russell, Sergeant Major Burton's daughter."

"And DiaZem," Max added as she sat down. His eyes followed her. No one else seemed to notice, but his gaze was invasive. She wanted to cover herself every time he looked in her direction.

"Austin Major, armorer, logistics, combatives master, tactics master, and master of anything else you can contribute to killing someone."

"Hyka Major, medic and combatives master."

"Eric Earl. I also go by Duke. Battle staff and logistics."

Valerie leaned to Jack and whispered, "There were eight shot glasses earlier when we were toasting. Where is the eighth person?"

"Mike. The eighth shot stayed on the bar. The glass was for your dad."

She was sorry she had asked. Valerie knew from attending formal military affairs with Scott that the gesture was reminiscent of a ceremony reserved for fallen comrades called "The Missing Man Table." Though this was not a formal military function, the tradition showed reverence to those unable to join them. In these circumstances, she did not know if her father was safe, or even still alive. The realization pulled at her heart and added a stronger awareness to her situation.

"Now we are all acquainted," Max started, "I'm going to give an overview of intelligence and then I'll pass the mic to the Duke of Earl to go over tomorrow's activities and suggested packing list for the mission. After him, Major will map out the route and resupply points. Right now, the party stands as Mrs. Russell, Big Daddy Jack-Mac, Griff, Major, and Hyka. Now, Duke, if you please. My beer is missing me." Max sat himself down and placed his unlit cigar back in his mouth.

Duke stood to address the group. He was not tall at all, just taller than Valerie, and stocky, but not fat. He was not as intimidating as he attempted to be with his posture. He seemed to do nothing but glare, even when he spoke to the group.

"All right, this is an extraction mission. I'm passing each of you a packing list consisting of what you'll need for at least two days and a few items necessary for the group. Those items are not negotiable. Hyka, you'll have to pack Mrs. Russell's ruck. She will be busy with Max tomorrow."

Valerie wrung her hands together at the thought of being alone with him. She looked at Jack for answers, but he did not seem alarmed by the announcement. She also hated the use of the word extraction. She considered the possibility of finding an escape from the group once they located her son.

Duke continued, "There are a couple of opportunities for resupply, but only one is guaranteed. Food will need to be rationed. Water is accessible, and each of you has a filtration device, so hydration shouldn't be an issue. Hyka is carrying the medical supplies, but iodine pills will be split amongst the group for water purification if needed."

"Question," Griff interrupted, looking over the packing list. "Why is everyone carrying a headlamp if I'm the only person who can use one?"

"Great question," Duke said, thick with sarcasm. "We are hoping when the time comes, Mrs. Russell will have figured something out."

They all turned and looked at her. She narrowed her eyes at Duke, who had done nothing but give her orders from the moment he stood up. Her frustrated focus shifted to Max, resentment evident on her face. Valerie had no idea how she was going to fill such a tall order of giving power back to everyone. The two men were giving the group a false sense of her ability. She did not put much stock in herself where her capabilities were concerned.

"The next variable is going to be if Mr. Russell comes back with us. We will have to jump that hurdle once we get on site, but keep in mind an additional member to the party is a possibility."

"If my husband is there, why would we leave? Why wouldn't I stay home with my family?" Valerie was not a soldier. There were no orders she had to follow. She was reaching a boiling point of Duke telling her what she was going to do.

"Miss Lady," Max began, "tomorrow we have a video conference scheduled with a CDC geneticist: someone with a long history in the matters of conductors and DiaZem and my main source of information, which is obviously more than you have in regards your condition. He's been in contact with a DiaZem at the Denver facility and has insisted on talking with you. Our primary goal is to keep you safe. If your safety involves relocating you and your family, so be it. So, the answer is: No, you do not have to return, and you do not have to accept our help, but I encourage you to weigh your options and the consequences if you don't." He took a casual drink of his beer.

"I am hiding from the CDC but have a conference with them tomorrow?" Valerie looked around the room, but no one seemed to see where the issue lay. No one looked concerned with the glaring conflict of interest. "If they know where I am, why don't they just come and get me?"

Max took a moment to light his cigar before answering, "I have promised Burton to keep you and your son safe. I have every intention to do so. But you are a liability, Mrs. Russell. You don't know what you are capable of. Besides, your father set up this meeting."

Breaths were held and looks were exchanged. This was news to the group. Valerie did not believe him. She was certain Max would say anything to get her to comply. There was something just under the surface of his hospitality: a hidden plan having to do with her being a DiaZem. She chewed her lip and decided not to ask any more questions during the briefing. She would pull Jack aside later.

Duke continued, "We have allotted four days there and four back. Your biggest obstacle, aside from not getting caught by the CDC, is the fluctuating elevation. We are at six thousand one hundred and thirty-five feet. Your first day of travel will be a constant uphill walk for seventeen miles. The journey is worse coming back. I'm not going to sugarcoat anything. Walking is going to suck, bad.

"I didn't have time to print timelines so write this down: Beginning tomorrow morning, from 0600 to 0730, there will be mandatory physical training. We'll be doing stretches. Hyka will need to know of any limitations or previous injuries which might cause you any issues on your trip. From 0730 to 0900 is personal hygiene and breakfast. Then from 0900 to 1500 we go over battle drills, including Mrs. Russell. Some of us need to brush up on a few skills, too. Mrs. Russell, your video conference will be in Max's study at 1400."

Valerie clenched her jaw, nodded and wrote down the time.

"At 1500, meals will be served and rations distributed. Prepackaged field rations will be the most practical. Max has spoiled us since we arrived, so a week of MREs isn't bad. From 1600 to 2100 is personal time. I encourage resting, double checking your supplies and packing list, bathing. You get the point, personal time. You step off at 2100 hours. Major, you're up."

Duke took his seat. Hyka's father walked to the head of the table with stiff arms held away from his body like they were too large to keep by his side. His hair was dark gray, cut into a high fade. He flipped a board revealing a large map, pulled a laser pointer out of his pocket and tested the device on the board with no results. Frustrated, he threw the small penlight into a trash can.

"All right." He spoke with a thick Southern accent as he walked back to the other end of the table. "As Duke said, this mission is broken up into four days there and four back. At 2100, we leave from here and head north by way of Voyager Parkway. The route will be less watched, and less utilized by the CDC. From there we go east until we reach the railroad. The tracks are clear of the Air Force Academy, makes for safer cover and a pretty direct route. We continue the uphill walk all the way to Spruce Meadows Open Space. My in-laws have an RV parked out there, which should do us some good for getting some sleep during the day. Day one is a little under twenty miles. This location is also a food and ammo cache. We shouldn't need to resupply so early in our trip, but this location is the only option we have. Also, this is the only substantial resupply on our route. A contingency plan is to send Griff to purchase supplies if needed. He's the only one who should interact with anyone outside of our squad.

"Day two is uphill still, but I'd like to push to Lone Tree, even though we'll be clocking thirty miles in one day. I want to start day three at the bottom of E-470. If we stay away from downtown Denver and the general population, we can finish up the two days on E-470 with no problems. Three extra miles versus the trouble of going through downtown are manageable.

"Hotels are out of the question. We hold the risk of being turned in or trapped with limited escape routes, so those last two nights will be spent sleeping on the road. Weather is optimal, but the temperature will drop down at night. Even so, you should not require more than a thin sleeping bag. Max can touch on the threat of the general population." Major took his seat beside his daughter.

Max rose.

"The CDC has created propaganda to strike fear into the hearts of our fellow man in a feeble attempt to continue to gather conductors and any remaining DiaZem. They estimate a quarter of the world's population, two billion people, carry the conductive gene. This group is what they are considering conductors of electricity. Ten thousand in the world hold the DiaZem gene, which is a sort of royal lineage of conductors. The CDC wants to recover as many of both as possible. If

DiaZem remain at large, the CDC cannot move on to part two of their mission. Don't even ask me what part two is. They have yet to reveal anything else to even the most senior of command. The President doesn't even know what part two of the mission is. As long as we can keep a DiaZem out of CDC hands, the longer the general population—Griff and me included—can gather information and plan.

"After much discussion, Griffin will be accompanying the mission not only because of his personal interest but because he is the only one of us without the conductor gene who is physically capable of walking the distance.

"Most people are scared. They will be afraid of conductors and turn you in as soon as they sense something is wrong. I've already seen them stand behind people in line at a store holding up their cell phones or watches. Having Griff with you is essential if you find the need to interact with anyone unaffected outside of your group. Also, he refuses to stay behind.

"So, on that note, are there any caveats? Questions? As discussed, fire watch begins in an hour. Two hours each beginning with Duke, then Jack, myself, and we will cycle back through with Duke and Jack at an hour and a half each. Mrs. Russell, is five-thirty a good wake-up time for you?"

The group dispersed, even though Valerie had not answered. She was confused as to what fire they were watching for. She displayed enough confusion to warrant clarification because Max continued.

"In case you have an episode, we'll have someone on hand to stop you. There will be someone outside your door all night watching for signs of electrical power. The second a light flickers, we will wake you. Just a precaution. The walls would stop any power surge from being revealed to the outside, and the exterior lights are on a different and protected circuit of their own. I don't want you burning my house down from the inside out."

The words stung. She started to get a sense that he did not like her and, as far as she was concerned, the feeling was mutual. All of his pleasantries were a front, and the idea of him watching her sleep intensified her feeling of contempt for the man. She wished Jack or even the scary woman would stay with her, but they had to rest as much as everyone else. She was thankful Jack volunteered to help, at least. Duke and Max were not traveling with the rest of them, so it made sense for them to get the least amount of sleep.

Valerie realized she was left alone in the dining room with Max. A swell of panic balled in her throat, like he caught her in a trap. The walls were smothering and contained her energy. Without another word, she walked away in search of Jack. His door was still open. Empty. A single chair sat across from her door. She balled her fists and quickened her pace. They had better not expect her to keep the door open all night while she slept. She walked into her room, but before she could get far enough in to reach the door handle, someone grabbed her arm, yanked her into the room and shut the door. In the darkness, all she heard was the click of the lock.

CHAPTER EIGHT

"Everyone find a seat and listen up." The thick Southern accent came from somewhere in the pitch black of the room. She heard others shuffle around her and waited for her eyes to adjust before following the instruction.

"Curse it, does anyone have a light?" Jack asked after a thud came from the back of the room. Someone produced a lighter. The flame was enough light for her to find the edge of the bed to sit.

"There's a candle on the far end of the dresser," Valerie offered, despite the rude yank into the room. Judging by where she stood, Hyka was the one to pull her in. She was as strong as she looked—and as rough, too. Griff passed the round candle to Major, who held the lighter. Once lit, he placed the orb back on the dresser in front of the mirror to better light the room. Valerie could see everyone. Hyka stood between her father and the door. Jack moved to the beige accent chair, and Griff was sitting behind her on the bed. Duke stood in the bathroom doorway with his arms crossed over his chest, the same glare on his face. She felt a little better without Max there, but the way Duke treated her like a subordinate was beyond irritating.

"Alright, Duke. You have the floor," Major announced. In the candlelight, she could see how Eric Earl's nickname suited him. His short stature was disproportionate to his muscle mass, reminding her of a mean little dictator with a complex. He did not belong there. He was not going with them—the only conductor to stay behind. Any comfort she felt before had retreated with his presence. He was the goon watching over her while she slept. She shuddered.

"So, a few more pieces of this puzzle are coming together. I think Max has been in on this thing for longer than he is letting on. What side he's playing for is the real question. Mike might have put too much trust in our old friend. I think the biggest curveball is we all suspected Kevin Burton to be the one sitting here," he said with a breath of annoyance. "Anyway, this scientist you are talking with tomorrow, he's told Max they have another DiaZem in a facility underneath the Denver airport, where they are holding the conductors."

"What?" Jack interrupted. "You mean the conspiracy theory about there being a hidden city under the airport is true? You have got to be kidding me. Is this the New World Order mumbo jumbo? It's real?"

"The whole thing goes way beyond a conspiracy, Jack. There are five thousand cities across the world being used for containment areas for conductors. We can assume one of two things could come of this segregation: they will eradicate us conductors or complete a mass genocide of the general population. Regardless, Mrs. Russell cannot be taken by the CDC. Not if we hold a moral bone in our bodies. We are dealing with the real Center for Disease Control. They have taken over all government assets, including all military branches of service, to follow through with this plan. The word is FEMA has even set up in places with high fatalities to mask the processes of collecting conductors. Shit's bad out there. Really bad."

"I'm sorry, but I still have no idea what is going on," Valerie interjected. "Why am I being hunted by the CDC? How do they already know I am a DiaZem when I just found out a couple of hours ago? What do I have to do with genocide?" She felt far too out of touch with the situation. They all spoke like she knew everything there was to know about her new status.

"We think your dad might have had ties to the CDC," Duke answered. "Likely going back before any of us knew him. He was so adamant about protecting you and your brother if this ever happened. It was news to us, but there is a possibility Mike did, in fact, arrange your meeting tomorrow. As far as your identity as a DiaZem, the episode causing Mike's capture is what tipped them, and us, off."

"So, are we leaving now?" Griff asked. He still looked tired, but anxious to move.

"No. We stick out the timeline," Hyka spoke up. "We couldn't leave even if we wanted to unless Max let us. I've done a recon on this entire house. The place is a glorified prison. He can hear everything we are saying right now. It's disgusting. I mean, not much we can do in the ways of privacy. He might as well be standing in this room right now. I can't imagine what his reasoning for surveillance was before we all got here." Hyka was direct. Despite her expression of disgust, she still carried little inflection in her voice.

"Val, you'll continue with this meeting you have tomorrow," Major said.

"Ask questions and find out as much as you can from this geneticist," Hyka added. "Even go as far as to comply with every request, even your firstborn child. Whatever you do, don't give them the impression you won't cooperate. You will make things far more difficult for all of us if they think they have to force you."

"Okay," Valerie agreed. She was good at playing with a poker face. She was satisfied to have received a few answers and was on the verge of more. Soon she could leave this prison and get back to her family.

"Griff?" Valerie called over her shoulder.

"Yes, ma'am."

"Could you try calling my husband for me?" Griff looked up at Major for approval.

Major nodded.

"I'll grab my phone once we finish here."

Valerie let a tear fall, hoping the darkness would conceal her emotion.

"What else you got, Duke?" Major was pushing at something specific Duke was reluctant to say.

"Mike and Kevin were taken to Denver. They are alive and okay. We don't have solid contact, but Max has been keeping tabs on them.

Valerie, if they need to, the CDC will use them as leverage over you. They made a pass at collecting Caleb, but they couldn't locate him. I'm hoping Gia is as bright as Griff said and left you a great clue as to where to find him."

Valerie felt the color leave her face and her chest tighten. Though Griff had told her Caleb was safe, the fact that the CDC was being so aggressive in finding him unraveled her core. They had been in her home. Her safe place. The ceiling fan spun and the lights came on in the room, blinding everyone. The bulbs began to grow brighter. Visible energy currents pulled from each person to Valerie. A large bolt shot from her hands and bounced around the room, looking for an escape, creating small fires on the walls. She panicked and could not control herself or stop what was happening. Hyka took two steps toward her, and with one left hook, ended the episode. Valerie's vision went black.

When she woke, Hyka was taking an IV out of her arm.

"I had to punch you in the face. How're you feeling?" she asked, continuing to work.

"Fine. I actually feel great, considering. What did you give me?"

"Benadryl. Jack switched rooms with you since you almost burnt yours down. Hey." Hyka got close to Valerie's face. "We'll get them back, all of them. You didn't let my dad finish. Gia is one of us. She knows what she's doing. The good news is they don't know where your kid is, which means she's doing her job. Just remember what I said last night. Play along, understand?"

Valerie nodded and was glad this woman was on her side. Valerie would have agreed to anything she said for fear of being punched again. She sat up on the bed, thankful the fireguard had come and gone. Thanks to Hyka, she had slept through Max hovering over her. The thought still made her shudder. She did not even want to know if the watch had happened at all.

"Duke went out last night and got you some clothes for the trip. Your ruck is packed, too. Get ready to meet up in the courtyard. Griff said you have about thirty minutes." Hyka finished bandaging the injection site and left Valerie to get dressed.

The clothes Duke had gotten her were comfortable and adequate.

He had also provided undergarments: a pleasant surprise. There was a small mirror on the wall over the dresser. A faded bruise covered her jaw on the right side. The faint yellow mark looked older than what it was and did not hurt. Hyka had knocked her clean out with one hit, though out of necessity and not anger. Valerie could not think of a more efficient, less violent way to have handled the situation.

She made her way down to the first floor to meet the rest of the group. The doors leading to the courtyard were open, offering a contrasting fresh breeze to the stuffy feeling of the house. She walked outside and breathed in the air. Jack, Major, Griff, Hyka, and Duke were stretching. Hyka puffed on a cigar while leaning this way and that. The men laughed about how much they drank the night before.

"When was the last time you walked a hundred miles, Major?" Griff asked.

"I could walk two hundred miles straight at this rate. Look at me." Major stood straight up and flexed his biceps and puffed his chest. Upon second glance, he appeared the same age as his daughter standing behind him. Hyka had not changed much, and neither had Griff. Duke and Jack looked like muscle-headed frat boys, having started a push-up competition in the grass. Duke had a baby face, versus the scruffy man who brow-beat her the whole time he explained the logistics of their journey the night before.

In her panic, Valerie had triggered whatever drew the energy from her companions. She touched her jaw again and felt the blood rush to her face, embarrassed about her panic attack. She stood away from the group and stretched on her own.

Major kicked Duke's arms between push-ups, and soon they were a rolling ball of arms and legs, wrestling on the lawn of the courtyard. While Jack stood by and laughed, Hyka came up behind him and torqued his arm behind his back, bringing him to his knees without much effort. They soon grappled in the grass.

Mike had taught Valerie jiujitsu when she was young, and Scott would sometimes wrestle her; otherwise, Valerie only practiced her hand-to-hand combat skills on drunken men in the emergency room.

Hyka broke free of Jack's hold and they faced each other in

fighting stances, both with smiles on their faces. Hyka made the first move and slapped Jack open-handed in the face before he wrapped his arms around her torso and threw her to the ground.

"Want to have a go?" Griff asked Valerie. "I'm pushing fifty, so you'll have to go easy on me."

"No, I'd rather not." Valerie was not one to wrestle for fun. She was also put off by the fact that he was engaged to Gia, a woman nearly half his age. "You think we could call my husband now?"

"Do you think those CDC soldiers are going to go easy on you, once they realize what you are?" Max asked, leaning against the threshold of the French doors, puffing his cigar. The sweet smell of the burning tobacco fit him. His outward appeal was all right, but like the cigar, deep down he was creating cancer. "I'll help you call him after our meeting later."

After five rounds, three of which she won, Griff gave his approval and sat to rest. The others were still grappling. Major, somehow, had picked a fight with everyone. Jack, Duke, and Hyka teamed up against him. Major maneuvered from one to the other. Valerie was in awe of the agility each displayed. Griff broke up the battle with the mention of the time. The four shook hands before returning to final stretches. Valerie felt like she had stretched every muscle in her body at least ten times before the hour was over. Her mood had changed with the display of camaraderie. With the exception of Duke, who stayed too close to Max for her comfort, the small group of conductors slowly grew more familiar. She could only hope that, over time, the 'Squatch team would consider her one of them.

Breakfast was elaborate, though she had little interest in the food. The spread was another buffet-style meal with far more food than was required. She filled her plate out of necessity and ate in silence, listening to the over-excited men gloat of past battles won. She remembered her uneasiness when she had first seen her younger self in the mirror. Unlike her, they had the luxury of understanding their transformation. The novelty had worn off for Valerie. For the older gentlemen, the regression was a second lease on life. Valerie wanted to celebrate with them, but her meeting with Max and the geneticist loomed like a shadow over her mood.

Battle drills covered a broad range of subjects she remembered her father teaching when she was young but had forgotten over the years. Everything was necessary, down to what order they would walk on their journey. They also went over land navigation skills and how to determine a rallying point if they were to get separated. She did remember a few things, like how to tell rise in elevation by looking at a terrain map and how to identify and match live landmarks to drawn ones. The mountains were always to the west, so north was easy to find. Jack was impressed with how much she already knew considering her lack of official military training. The lessons were nostalgic, and she felt guilty now for fighting her father over learning them as a child.

Duke passed out compasses to everyone but Griff, who used a digital compass. Valerie opened hers, but the dial did not move. The north end of the needle pointed to her body, no matter which way she turned. Major shook and slapped at the round metal object before throwing the compass in the trash.

Hyka, who stood about twenty feet away from Valerie, spoke up. "Got it. Digicam here creates her own magnetic field. Looks like you're on your own if we get lost. Good thing you know something about terrain features."

Valerie did not correct the woman about her title. Even though Hyka did not laugh, or show any expression for that matter, the play on DiaZem was a much-welcomed joke. They would never be friends in any other setting, but Valerie could not think of a better ally than this terrifying and beautiful woman that seemed to lack all ability to display emotion.

The last thing on the agenda before lunch was the firing range. They made their way to the basement in single file. At the bottom of the stairs, there was a table where each grabbed hearing protection and safety glasses before going through the heavy door. Valerie was the last person in line with Jack. Everyone found a lane and loaded their weapons. Hyka was the first to fire at her target across the room. The men followed suit. Jack guided Valerie to her firing station. This was not the first time she had been to a firing range. Her father had taken her many times as a child. She loaded the .45 and aimed the weapon. Inhale, exhale. She fired six rounds into her target. Once the bolt of the pistol locked to the rear, Valerie placed the safety on and set the gun down. Jack pushed the button to retrieve her silhouette. The paper had two holes: one large within the profile where five rounds had hit in the same spot and one a little high and right of the silhouette.

"What happened to this one?" Jack laughed and pointed to Valerie's stray shot.

"I always pull my first shot."

"Nerves. Don't anticipate the recoil. I'm sure Mike's told you before."

Valerie smiled, but the recoil did not make her nervous. The consequences of pulling the trigger did. She had seen the implications in the emergency room more times than she could count. No matter their offense, few people deserved to be on the business end of a gun. She had simply reacted when she fired the warning bullet into her brother's wall. Valerie knew what she was doing. The reality of having to defend herself to the death might be a choice she would have to make. The military was under the command of the CDC. The enemy. The kid Jack had talked out of testing them was out there collecting people, just taking orders. She was as nervous as he had been. The possibility of shooting someone so young out of necessity was terrifying, but something she could do if the circumstances called for lethal force.

The next target was up, and she tried to shake the anxiety from her mind. She thought of Max and the meeting they were about to have. Six rounds hit the silhouette. She had found her muse.

CHAPTER NINE

Wringing her hands, Valerie sat in front of the large cherry wood desk across from Max. Certificates and plaques hung along the walls next to photos like the one in Jack's room. She was not impressed with the display of coins, ribbons, and badges he had earned throughout his life. She knew he was a snake.

Max ignored her, typing and clicking demands into the computer. Looking far too pleased with himself. He glanced up and motioned her attention to the monitor. The computer screen displayed three parts. She and Max occupied separate sections, and a third was blank, awaiting the other member of the conference. She wanted to slap Max for the way he looked at her but maintained her poker face as promised, though her heart skipped as the screen indicated they were dialing into the conference.

The blue screen disappeared, and a handsome young man appeared in a tailored navy suit and deep red tie. His brown hair was short and connected to a trimmed beard. His smile curled at the corners of his mouth. Valerie was not intimidated by the image. She coughed to cover a laugh. If the CDC were sending young go-getters after her, she would have no problem evading the government entity.

"Ah, hey there, old friend," came the voice through the speaker. "Thank you for arranging this meeting."

If the men were old friends, she had no way of knowing how old the gentleman on the screen was. She knew they had a DiaZem at the Denver facility, so that would explain his age regression. Valerie hated how his low, smooth voice made her feel. His tone was warm and familiar, like an old blanket. She hated him more for it. Her hands in fists under the table, she focused her energy on maintaining her façade.

"You know I always keep my word," Max answered.

"Yes, you do. Now, would you be so kind as to step out and allow Ms. Burton and me some privacy?"

Max's smile faded, but he stood and crossed the room to the door. The man on the screen had more authority than Max in his own home. Valerie noted the observation, but did not know what to make of it. The man on the screen was nothing to her. She would give enough respect to get what she needed. Nothing more.

"Good afternoon, Ms. Burton. My name is Doctor Lucas Jarrett. I am a geneticist with the CDC and have been assigned to Denver as the Head of Research for the United States. I understand you have several questions, as do I, but you may go first."

"Where are my father and brother?" Valerie kept her tone pleasant despite the disdain she felt for him. She would let the use of her maiden name slide. If this was her father's arrangement, her proper name was inconsequential.

"Yes, of course. Your family is fine. Comfortable and well. Would you like to speak with them?"

"Yes, please," she answered with tight lips. He was smug and mocking in his tone. She had worked with plenty of doctors with the habit of talking down to her. Lucas was not an exception. In normal circumstances, she could stand her ground, but Valerie had to muster every ounce of will to keep her agreeable posture toward the man on the screen. She could not show fear or anger; she did not want to give herself away.

The display on the monitor changed to show a sterile white room. At a white table, seated in white chairs, were her father and brother in white clothes.

"Valerie," her dad said, sitting upright. He looked young and healthy as the doctor had promised. His shoes were not the regular ones he wore over his prosthetic foot. Kevin sat beside him. The two men looked like twins rather than father and son. Valerie's emotions swelled in her throat, which she swallowed hard to keep from bubbling to the surface.

"Hi, Dad. Kevin." She hoped her father would take the lead in the conversation because she could not speak without choking on her words. Valerie was unsure of how much Lucas already knew about her and assumed Max had kept him informed of her every move.

"We are fine. Nothing bad is going to happen to any of the conductors." He paused for a long time with a blank look.

She understood his underlying message. The general population was in danger. Valerie was too scared to ask him anything. She nodded in understanding, and he continued.

"They are having a hard time locating Caleb. Once you find him, Gia will know. . ."

The video cut back to Dr. Jarrett.

"Now, you see they are happy and healthy. But there are matters you and I need to discuss, Ms. Burton." The curled smile spread deeper across his face, making her stomach turn.

"Mrs. Russell," she responded, tightening her fists under the table, thankful the words did not come out as a scream. She took a deep breath and gave him a rehearsed smile. Yes, she would play along, but he would know that the power he assumed he had over her was minimal. Lucas could treat other people as less, but not her.

"Yes, Mrs. Russell." His smile widened. "Mr. Davis shared with me a rather disturbing video, among others. We know you have been affected by the Event, but not in the way that your friends have. The awakening of the dormant gene has also brought into effect a type of system of checks and balances. Conductors, like the members of your family and a few of the people in your company, can absorb electricity. Hence the term used to describe those with the gene."

The doctor paused and took a sip of water. "This is the mark of a higher civilization. Something we need to protect. The government has recognized this and set into motion the collection of such individuals.

We estimate two billion people in the world have this gene. But with change often comes fear, and the majority of the world's population may not want to acknowledge our superior genetics. We want to protect you from becoming a target of the general public by providing alternate living arrangements until we can eliminate any threat to the preservation of this gene. A sort of safe house."

Valerie wanted to spit in his face. The propaganda developed by his organization caused animosity; herding conductors like cattle by using their neighbors was the tactic the CDC had developed to segregate them. A strategy used by Hitler in World War II. Many people would believe their lies, but she was not one of them.

"Furthermore, you are the key to a new society."

"You mean I am a DiaZem."

"Yes, and with every passing day, we are learning more about what this means and how vital you are to the future of our society."

"You talk like society is going to change," Valerie probed like Hyka had coached her, though she was having trouble remaining neutral.

"Oh, society will change, in the most glorious way. There has already been a realignment of power all over the globe. But the key to unlocking the power is in your abilities as a DiaZem."

"What abilities are you referring to? How do you know so much about me?"

"I have studied the dormant gene for decades. Dia is a Greek word meaning between, and Zem is the Czech word for earth; so, a grounding rod of sorts. I discovered the conductor and DiaZem genes in the seventies, but since Germany was the first to pinpoint the abilities of the DiaZem, they coined the term. In short, you are like a small but essential piece of a battery. With careful training, you can convert a small amount of a conductor's stored energy into electricity. The facilities we have established are being engineered to run off the energy of conductors by way of DiaZem, like a giant electrical circuit. A clean energy power plant."

"You are mistaken." Valerie gave a genuine laugh.

Lucas was not amused.

"I blew up my cell phone. I can't power a car or even turn on a light."

"On the contrary, Ms. Burton."

The display on the screen switched again. This time Valerie watched herself in the room Max had provided the day before when she thought she was alone. Her face became hot. Max had watched her the whole time. His fireguard had been a front, an excuse to hover over her. There was no need for anyone to stand outside her door. She tried to slow her breathing. She had known her privacy was in question, but seeing proof of him violating her solitude made her blood boil. But she needed to cooperate, or she would never get to Denver. Inhale, exhale.

"A fluke. I have no idea how I powered those things or how to control my ability to do so. I'm sure you've seen more video from later in the evening. I could have burnt the entire house down."

Lucas leaned forward and pointed at her on the screen, "You, my dear, are a unique piece of a larger circuit. This society will not function without you here at the facility with another DiaZem. There is no order unless we have all the pieces to complete the circuit. Alone, you can't even begin to harness the power you hold within. You are weak and lack the proper setting to tap into your abilities. Two DiaZem are required to complete the circuit and maintain a self-sufficient society. The Central United States, as far as Kansas City, to Salt Lake City, and even Albuquerque, can be powered by two DiaZem maintaining proximity."

He sat back in his chair and adjusted his suit jacket. His smile curled even more than before. There was something he was not sharing, but she had enough information. She had played the game and remained cooperative. He would, no doubt, track her until she led him to Caleb. There was a reason they were not more aggressive in pursuing her. She looked down at her hands and twirled her wedding ring, out of habit.

"Any word from my husband, Scott?"

Lucas' smile faded into a sneer. For as well as Valerie could mask her emotions, he wore his plainly on his face.

"He was recruited and is now employed by the CDC. With his

background, he has become quite an asset to the collection and transport of conductors. He is, at this exact moment, about to cross County Road 59 heading back out to rural Kansas."

The screen changed to a black and white surveillance feed of Scott sitting in the engineering chair of a train, wearing a CDC uniform. Valerie's mouth went dry, and a gasp escaped her lips. She fought back the tears. She was thankful her husband was alive but disheartened to see him wear the same uniform of the people she was trying to avoid. Lucas had almost all the leverage he needed to bend her to his will.

Valerie rubbed her forehead, trying to find the words to move forward. She needed to remember that Caleb needed her protection, but the 'Squatch team also required her to gain the upper hand.

"How can I help you, Dr. Jarrett?" Hearing herself say the words made her physically sick. She swallowed back nausea.

"I will allow you to take your journey to find your son. I cannot guarantee you will not be collected by agents of the CDC along your way. They have explicit and unwavering orders to detain suspicious individuals, but I can tell you I will make no direct orders to collect you unless, of course, you have no intentions of coming to the facility on your own free will."

"Well then, I guess you have all your bases covered."

Valerie reached to the computer and pulled the energy from the conference. The call ended, and the screen went black. She opened the door and walked past Max who did not try to hide the fact he had been eavesdropping on their conversation. She was no longer afraid of him. He had no authority over her. He could watch her all he wanted. In a few hours, she would leave, and he would receive whatever reward Lucas promised for his role in her cooperation.

Valerie walked down the stairs to the first floor. Gear and boxes of the prepackaged food rations were being handed out. She fell in line with Hyka and accepted her rations for the trip: familiar military-style MREs. None of them tasted good. Even with the food and ammo packed, her bag still seemed lighter than what she had brought with her. Valerie would have carried all their packs if doing so meant she could leave sooner, but she still had to stick with the timeline. The minute the CDC suspected her of running, they would hunt her down. She would play nice until she found her son. Then she would fight with every ounce of her being to evade the CDC. Her father tried to convey a warning, of what the CDC planned to do. She knew she needed to stay far away from where he was.

When she returned to the first bedroom Max had designated for her, Valerie noticed the burn marks which peppered the walls. A yellow and white quilt replaced the comforter she had damaged in her fit. She laid on the bed and looked up at the fan and around the corners of the room, searching for the device Max used to watch her.

"There is a small camera mounted above the TV," Max said. He had opened the door without her even noticing. She cursed under breath as she sat up for forgetting to lock the door, again.

"Can I help you?" She tried to remain neutral, but she overcompensated and came off exactly how she felt.

"Yes, Mrs. Russell, you can. I know you don't care for me much, and understandably so. As you can tell, I'm not a conductor. My sons are. I have three talented boys with bright futures. You hadn't met them because the CDC took them to the facility with the other conductors before you arrived. You see, I might have a fancy house, smoke expensive cigars, and live very, very comfortable, but all this means nothing without my boys, as I am sure you understand."

Valerie remained tight-lipped, but her heart weakened ever so slightly to the man. The CDC had not taken her son, but if they did, she would walk with open arms wherever they wanted her to go if she could have him back.

"My fate had been undetermined until you came along. Ole Mike Burton put all this together for you and Kevin. In the planning stages, this was all hypothetical, and I just assumed I would be like one of you before people absorbed electricity and before DiaZem were the diamonds to the ring. You and your brother mean far more to your father than his own life. Now you are a precious commodity to everyone, young lady, even more than our friends realize."

Valerie's face grew hot.

"You sold me out for what? My dad said nothing bad is going to happen to the conductors. Your sons are safe, like my father and brother. Dr. Jarrett said they would be released soon. Why would you betray my father's trust like this?"

"I can see you are angry, and deep down I understand why, but humor me. Nothing happens in my house without me knowing. I replayed your discussion with Lucas many times, and there is something clear to me that you may have missed: what your father was trying to tell you. Nothing is going to happen to the conductors." He paused and waited to see if she would understand.

Valerie was so full of rage she could not think straight.

"The general population will suffer. The government will eradicate us. The New World Order has found a way to eliminate all but a fraction of the population to raise a globalized central government: harbor the conductors and destroy the rest."

Duke had mentioned genocide before, but the idea seemed unbelievable at the time. Max would be among the victims of mass genocide.

He moved across the room toward her, waiting for the realization to wash over her. "My sons will be released, but I won't be around to see them. At least, this was the case until you came along. Yes, they know where you are and where you are going. They will track you every step of the way. Once you find your son, they will take you both to the facility. They are hoping you passed the DiaZem gene on to him. In exchange for your detention, I receive a spot in the new society along with my boys. Please, don't look so surprised. You would have done the same to be with your son. We both win. You'll be happy in the New World."

"I'll be happy when I get the hell out of this house," she said, nearly spitting the words at him.

He raised his hand to touch her shoulder but did not. Instead, he smiled and nodded in defeat. She could see where he was coming from; however, if she were in his situation, she knew she would have found a better way.

Once the door clicked shut, she pulled the photo from her cargo pocket. She missed Caleb's chubby baby cheeks. His hair was so long in the picture, swept to one side out of his eyes. His back was to the camera, and he was sitting on her father's living room floor. She remembered he was pulling the carpet and pushing his fingers deep into the threads, exploring. He had only turned his head when she called his name. Valerie regretted not holding him closer, not giving him enough kisses. She wanted to hug him tight and breathe him in. He looked just like Scott. She missed them both so much. Four days felt like an eternity, without a guarantee to be reunited.

She thought about Scott wearing the CDC uniform. Shocked the one person in her life she trusted might be the one to turn her and Caleb in. She had to continue to believe he would prove to be the man she married, who loved them more than anything. She prayed he did not know the truth of the situation. Once he was aware of what he was contributing to, he would fight to protect her and Caleb from the organization he served. She could still trust him. She had to. Scott was the one who could keep her from falling apart. She just needed to find him.

CHAPTER TEN

The crisp evening air gave instant relief from the stuffy confines of Max's fortress. Valerie kept silent pace with Major as she had been instructed to earlier in the day during battle drills. Hyka stayed a moderate distance behind them with Jack at a similar distance ahead. Griff had gone far ahead with a can of spray paint. Every thirty minutes, Valerie spotted a green mark on a tree or an abandoned vehicle notifying the group of safe passage. Twice Jack forgot to stay clear of the street lights and walked so close they flickered. Major yelled curses at him both times, making Valerie laugh. But the moon was high and bright, and she could see her footing without the use of any artificial lighting. After three hours of walking, they caught up to Griff leaning against a sign for Dirty Woman Park.

"You're home, Hyka!" Jack yelled back, laughing.

Aside from a huff, her expression never changed. Hyka shoulder-checked Jack as she walked by, then dropped her bag at a picnic table. Valerie found an empty table away from the group.

"Look," Major announced, "we are stopping for twenty minutes. Eat, do your business, and we are back on the road." He and Jack stood together and unpacked their MREs. They spoke just low enough Valerie could not hear.

Griff sat down with Hyka and asked her questions about her

medical background. Without a word, Hyka stood up, collected her meal, and walked away. As she approached, Valerie moved the items on her table to make room for the scary woman to join her. She sat opposite of Valerie on the picnic table. Valerie did not dare speak first.

"Figure out how to work your magic yet?" Hyka asked, referring to the tall order everyone anticipated Valerie could deliver.

Had they not witnessed her panic attack, they would not have believed she had any abilities at all.

"No. The moon is so bright out here I'd forgotten about the headlamp. I guess now would be a good time, huh?" Valerie started to dig in her bag.

"No worries. Griff has his lamp on. You're not a monkey, you know."

Valerie was caught off guard by the statement. She knew well she was a human. Hyka blew her bangs off her forehead and rolled her eyes.

"I meant you don't have to sit here and do every trick they tell you. Yeah, you got super powers or whatever, but having magic doesn't mean you have to jump when they say jump. Keep your voodoo to yourself. You don't have to prove anything to anyone. It's not dark out here, anyway." Hyka took a bite of a mystery food from an unlabeled green plastic wrapper and proceeded to talk with a full mouth. "You did good playing cool, though. What did the geneticist have to say? Why didn't they come to pick us all up from Max's? That creep. I never trusted the guy, even before all this went down."

"Dr. Lucas Jarrett is in charge of research for the entire country. He works in Denver. The CDC must already have a DiaZem because I couldn't tell how old he was." Valerie took a bite. She mulled over how much she should share with the group. Hyka still scared her, and she had a strong gut sense Major did not like her at all. Griff represented a lie from someone she had allowed in her home and had trusted with her son. She had just met Jack. She went along with the group out of necessity.

"I got to see my dad and Kevin," Valerie said into a substance labeled Chili Mac.

Hyka looked up and stopped chewing. “They alright?”

“Yeah. Dad said they were fine and the conductors are not in danger. He also said the CDC couldn’t find Caleb, but once I do, Gia would know something. I didn’t hear the rest because that prick cut the feed.”

“What else did you find out?” Hyka continued eating what looked like a compressed piece of bread that she covered with cheese with a strong odor of jalapeno, which she squeezed from another green plastic pouch.

“They think we are genetically superior to everyone else and are pieces of a giant electrical circuit. Ridiculous. The CDC is developing some way to harness the electricity absorbed by conductors, but the facility requires two DiaZem to power the entire Midwest.” Valerie tried to play down what Lucas told her.

“Sounds like Atlantis.” Hyka studied Valerie’s face for acknowledgment.

Valerie had no idea where Hyka was going with her statement.

“The lost city of Atlantis? They were a self-sustaining, advanced technological civilization without explanation. Could be we are just descendants of them. When the gene went dormant, the city sank. Makes sense to me.” She shrugged.

“Oh,” Valerie nodded. She decided not to tell Hyka much more. She was also going to keep her conversation with Max to herself. Despite her animosity toward him, she did not want to complicate things further.

Their time was almost up, and Valerie realized she had not eaten much. She took bites of what she could identify. The mystery food did not deter Hyka, and she finished all but a couple of green pouches.

“I heard your mom died.”

Valerie stopped chewing and looked up at Hyka, who continued without reverence for her comment.

“I never knew my mom. My dad was in love with her. She left us when I was two. He still hasn’t gotten over her leaving. We stay close with her family because knowing my Native heritage is important to my dad, but sometimes I wish she had died so he could move on." Hyka gathered her things and walked away.

Valerie sat with a blank expression on her face, unable to chew. Shocked, she tried to process what Hyka meant, but Jack walked up and snapped her out of her reflection.

"How are you holding up, kid? Ready to move?"

"Could be better. You know the CDC recruited Scott? He's driving transport trains for them, helping them collect conductors. I saw him on video during my conference call. He's not a conductor. Well, he's a train conductor, but he's not like us. He doesn't have the gene." Saying the words out loud brought another realization to her mind. They would try to kill him. If she wanted this ever to end, she would need to figure out her abilities to save her husband and every other person within a five-hundred-mile radius. Grief rolled over her, and she tried to think about anything else. She did not want to risk throwing herself into another episode and giving away their location.

"Valerie, look at me," Jack said in a stern tone. "You are losing focus. Stop thinking about what-ifs and think about what you need to do now. Keep your mind busy with the task at hand. We have a few more hours until daylight. Then you can rest. You can't change what has already happened. But you can choose how to react. You can stay here and feel sorry for your luck, or you can pull yourself together and unleash mama bear on anyone who gets in your way."

Valerie smiled. Jack was right. She would sooner tear someone apart with her bare hands before playing the victim. She felt her cargo pocket and pulled out the picture of Caleb. She could feel the rage building at the thought of someone taking him, but she would get to him first.

"Form it up," Major called over the group, signaling the time had come to continue their journey. Griff started off first, and each person fell in behind him at a measured distance. Valerie walked with Major with no need to know the measurement.

"I would not be here if not for Hyka," Major said after a while. Much like his daughter, he spoke from a place in his mind ten steps further than the actual conversation. "She talked me into coming. I couldn't care less what happens to this world, but she has a bleeding heart. She said helping you would give me purpose."

Major remained silent for a few moments. Valerie found his claims of Hyka's soft spot unbelievable but dared not admit it. At any moment, he would reveal why he did not like her. Valerie remained silent.

"I've done things in this life I am not proud of, Mrs. Russell. I've hurt people. Hell, I've been responsible for the deaths of hundreds, and I've carried the guilt on my shoulders for years. If there is even the slightest chance of redemption in this. . ." He sighed. "I guess what I'm trying to say is someone must stand up and do the right thing. For once, it's going to be me."

Dawn was close to breaking on the horizon and with the moon hidden by the western mountains, small fires glowed in the distance. The plane wreckage spread over a mile of visible highway. Gridlocked vehicles had been pulled to the shoulders, abandoned. The body of the plane lay across the four lanes, blocking all directions of travel. The group crossed the highway and headed west to an RV park. Their first campsite.

Major pounded on the door of the new, thirty-foot RV which looked out of place compared to its neighbors. There were a few much smaller RVs with more permanent additions; concrete stairs, brick and mortar fire pits, and even couches sat in front of a few.

Major reached his hand into the front wheel well and did two sweeps of his hand before pulling out a magnetic box. He opened it to reveal a key. With a silent nod to Jack, everyone pulled out their handguns. Major jerked open the door and allowed Jack to go in first, then followed behind.

"Clear," Jack said first.

"Clear," Major said and walked to the door to motion everyone inside.

Hyka holstered her handgun as she walked past Valerie, up the stairs, and into the RV. Valerie followed, ready to sit down after their twenty-mile hike.

Once everyone was inside, Major stood by the driver's seat and gave orders. "The ladies will share the full bed in the back. I'll take first watch. Jack and Griff, you take the loft beds and get some rest. The time is about 0630. Griff, set your alarm for four hours. Jack, you'll cover the watch after Griff. Everyone needs to change their socks. Mrs. Russell, be sure to put your boots back on. If we are forced to leave in a hurry, you're going to want those already on your feet." He winked before turning and making himself comfortable in the driver's seat.

Valerie walked the remaining length of the RV, down four steps, and sat on the full-size bed. Scissors flew across the room into her lap.

"Cut the tape off your feet. You might not have time later." Hyka jumped and landed on the bed next to Valerie. "Also, don't tighten your laces all the way. Just tight enough they won't go flying off if you have to run."

"Thank you. I don't know if I could've come all this way on my own."

Hyka nodded but gave no other acceptance of the appreciation.

The old tape had served its purpose, leaving Valerie's feet blister-free. She replaced it with new tape before putting her socks and shoes back on. The soreness in her feet reminded her she was never supposed to be in Colorado Springs. Kevin was the one who was to find Max and hide out. Gia was the planned provision made for her. Valerie rolled over to question Hyka, but she was already asleep, so she rolled back over. No time passed before she was sleeping as well.

Valerie woke a few hours later to laughter and the smell of grilling meat. There was openness in the air versus the smothering walls of Max's estate, a welcomed change. Being so far from the city lent itself to her feeling of security. She climbed the stairs to the central area of the RV. Hyka was sitting at the kitchen table reading a book. She gave a backhanded wave without even looking up. Jack, Griff, and Major stood around a grill outside drinking beer. They looked comfortable and in their element.

In the daylight, she could see the mountains. They were miles away, but even in the distance they were breathtaking: still snow-capped from the winter season. The immediate area was flat with a hint of the green growth of spring. Foothills rose to the north and south. She studied the other RVs and trailers around them, but none appeared occupied.

"Val, you want a burger?" Jack asked as she walked over to them. He opened the hood of the grill and smoke rose into the air, releasing the smell of charcoal and well-seasoned beef.

Valerie was looking forward to a hot meal after eating mystery meat through the night. She took the plate he offered and pulled a bottle of water from a nearby cooler and took a seat on a bench fashioned from a fallen tree. Under different circumstances, this would have been an excellent way to spend the week. Griff sat down next to her with his plate of food.

"I feel like I should know everything about you, seeing as you're engaged to my closest fake friend." Valerie came off harsher than she intended. Gia had betrayed her trust, regardless of her reasoning.

"Gia was insulted when Mike approached her about being your nanny. She's a smart, successful woman with multiple degrees. She did not want to babysit a toddler on her days off. But once she met you and Caleb, she agreed. You're a good person, Valerie. You have what it takes to stop this."

She knew what he meant. Without the gene, Griff and Gia were in danger of being killed off by the CDC if she did not stop them. She owed them for helping her.

"Thanks to you, everyone else seems to be holding up pretty good, so far," Griff continued. "Major suggested we head out before dusk to cover more ground. Just let us know if you're not ready. A hundred miles is a long hike, even for me, and I do this kind of thing all the time."

"I'm doing pretty well, considering," she said, smiling back at him. She needed to figure out how to become a useful member of the group rather than cargo.

Valerie finished her lunch and made her way back inside the RV. She figured providing transportation was the best place to start. Sitting in the driver's seat, she took the keys from the cup holder and turned the ignition, but nothing happened. She was not surprised, but still felt a tinge of disappointment. Inhale, exhale. Even though she was unsure of how she produced the energy before, knowing that she could made her more determined to get the vehicle running. She held her hands apart, palms facing each other with no reaction from the machine. Then she held them out. Still nothing.

"What are you doing?"

Hyka's voice startled her. The woman was stealthy.

"I'd like to get this thing to work if I can. Being somewhat helpful is the least I could do after all everyone has done to help me."

"You don't know this, but without you being what you are, Max would have traded us for his sons the first chance he got."

"But, I. . ." Valerie had not told anyone about her conversation with Max. Hyka nodded at Valerie. Without any expression, Valerie was oblivious as to if the woman was angry at not being told, or proud of herself for knowing information Valerie never offered.

"There are perks to being a woman. Like getting a man to tell you the cipher code to the control room and sneaking in while no one is manning the station. I don't blame you for not divulging. I would have done the same thing. Screw that guy. Had you not turned out to be a diaphragm, my dad would still be old, and we would all be in captivity without ever having a chance at stopping all of this."

Valerie laughed at Hyka's repeated stab at her new status. Maybe she was starting to crack Hyka's tough exterior, but she was still terrifying.

Hyka stared out the window for a while, deep in thought. Valerie remembered what she had said about her mother and how Hyka had opened up to her the night before. The conversation had been a sign of trust. Valerie stared out the window at the same nothing.

"I used to work in the emergency room at the main hospital when we still lived in the Springs near Mom and Dad. I was on shift during the big snow storm last year. Rain turned to snow which all turned to ice in a matter of hours. Scott was in Denver at engineer training, and my sister-in-law was watching Caleb for me. I was in line to receive the next critical patient. We got a call giving us a heads up about an accident involving a bus which had jumped the median into southbound traffic. The bus and three cars were involved. My mom had been behind the bus by maybe a mile. So, she stopped to help people get out of wrecked vehicles. She helped about twenty people to a safe distance over the course of five minutes. Just before the ambulances arrived, some guy weaving in and out of traffic, too fast for the conditions, had drifted into the median where my mom was heading back to her car. She coded before even getting to the hospital. I have never felt so helpless in my life." Valerie choked on her words but continued to stare at nothing.

The RV door opened, breaking her train of thought and bringing her back to where she was. She looked over just as Hyka slipped to the back of the RV. Major walked backward into the RV with his hands in the air. Valerie looked out the window again to see what was happening. Jack and Griff were standing by the grill with their hands up, and the barrel of a shotgun pointed at them, though she could not see who was holding the gun.

"Look, sir. We don't want any trouble. We will hand over whatever you are looking for. There is no need to be pointing guns at us." Major's voice was steady and conversational despite his situation. Another man holding a shotgun entered the RV with him. Major continued to back himself into the driver's seat where Valerie was as if to block her from sight. She made herself as small as possible next to the door, gripping the handle. She could run if need be, but only if Major lost control of the situation.

"We saw you were having trouble with your RV, son. Lights were flashing and such. You got keys to this thing?"

Valerie pulled the keys from the ignition and pressed them to Major's side. He reached down and took hold of them, then held them out in front of him with his thumb and index finger to the man.

"I think it might be the alternator. My brother, Jimmy, is the owner. He's letting me and my buddies hang out while he's in quarantine. Was going to show this young lady a good time. We got here just this morning and had been trying to get the engine to turn over." Major continued to offer the keys, but the man held firm to his shotgun. He stood at the top of the steps, blocking the door.

She could not see the man's face, but she could smell him. She knew the smell. He was an addict of some sort, and he had not showered in quite a long time.

"Maybe the problem isn't with the machine but with the operator. Why don't you come out from behind there, honey?" the man requested, his three teeth exposed by his sloppy smile.

Valerie sat up, but Major backed up further into the seat to where she could not move one way or the other. She lost her grip on the handle. Major had her pinned so she could no longer reach her escape. She looked out the windshield again to see Jack holding the shotgun, steadying the barrel at a thin woman in a black tank top and dirty, cut-off jean shorts.

Hyka, having somehow gotten out of the RV from the back, appeared in the door behind the foul-smelling man. The sharp edge of her knife against his throat startled him into pulling the trigger. Major was not fast enough and was peppered by the buckshot on his right cheek and ear, knocking him back and to the ground. In a fight-or-flight response, a burst of an electrical current shot from Valerie and went through everyone inside the RV. The force knocked Hyka backward down two steps and onto the ground outside. The RV's engine turned over. The radio and TVs turned on at maximum volume, though the ringing in her ears muffled the sound.

Valerie went into treatment mode and assessed Major's wounds while maintaining power to the RV. The electrical current had started the healing process. His injury had stopped bleeding almost immediately but was still raw. Jack ran into the RV. Valerie stared at him with wide eyes and conveyed she was okay. She sat back in the driver's seat to get out of the way, staring at the intruder lying face down on the RV floor.

"Just a flesh wound, pal. We've got to go," Major said to Jack with a calm urgency.

Jack nodded and helped his friend up. Griff helped Hyka off the ground outside, the woman behind them screaming all the while. Jack stood over the man, who still was not moving. He kicked the rifle to

Major before kneeling next to the man's head. He pressed two fingers to his neck. His gaze met Valerie's.

"He's dead," Jack told her.

She already knew.

Major pulled the man out through the RV door by his ankles. Griff met him at the bottom of the steps and grabbed the man under his arms to finish getting him outside. Valerie could see the woman outside the door. Her screams became more frantic. She was sick-looking, and grief distorted her face. Tears built up in Valerie's eyes, blurring her vision. Hyka climbed into the RV with a grin on her face. She kissed Valerie hard on the mouth, then moved throughout the RV securing cabinets and gear to prepare the RV for travel.

Once the RV was road ready, the men entered one by one. Jack skipped over two steps and held out his hand to Valerie. Once she stood up, Griff took the driver's seat and slammed the shifter into drive. Major closed the door, muffling the screams of the woman, and took up a position next to Griff.

Jack faced Valerie. With his hand on the back of her head, he pulled her into his arms. She did not fight, but she did allow those silent tears to fall. She curled her arms up against his chest and just let him hold her. He rested his cheek on her head.

"It was an accident. They would have turned in every one of us, killed us, or worse."

"I stopped his heart," she whispered. "I meant to kill him."

CHAPTER ELEVEN

The RV lurched forward. The rocking of the vehicle knocked Valerie into Jack. He caught himself and pulled her up to her feet, searching her eyes to make sure he had heard her correctly. He had.

"What do you mean?" Jack demanded, his grip tightened on her arms.

Valerie shrugged free of Jack's grip and balanced herself.

"I wanted the RV to run, and I wanted the man dead. I panicked and focused my energy on him. Well, some of the energy grounded through Hyka. I saw the tiny spark in the man's chest, making his heart beat, and then I took the spark." She searched Jack's face for understanding. The gunshot had forced her abilities to manifest and, like the lights in the cabin of the RV, her awareness of the power had become apparent. Valerie could see and feel so much more than she was able to articulate. She could see the energy moving through each person, to her, and out to the RV. She could finally focus on the energy inside, manipulating it to her will.

"Dear God," Jack cursed.

"You're a weapon," Hyka stated from the dining table. Her head was propped up on her hands like she was watching television.

Jack and Valerie both looked at her for an explanation. Hyka smacked her lips at them and rolled her eyes.

"If they get you and pair you with another DiaZem, they will use you to kill everyone in the Midwest. Right now, I bet you could kill an entire city. They are so nervous about pissing you off and taking your kid because they don't know how much you know, which makes you dangerous." Hyka shrugged.

Valerie unbuckled the holster she carried on her leg, set the gun and carrier on the bench, and slid them both toward Hyka. The fear of using a weapon seemed to dull in comparison to what she could do without one. She wanted to disconnect from everyone's energy, but they had to keep moving. She stayed plugged into the RV's electrical system with little effort. Like breathing, she was aware, but doing so was involuntary.

"A weapon," Valerie said to herself as she sat. She remembered the slimy smile plastered on Lucas' face. She laughed at his title: Head of Research. Valerie needed to hone her abilities and fast. She had just killed a man and could have accidentally killed Griff, too, had he been in the RV. She looked up at Hyka.

"The only way I can explain this is we are a part of one battery. You collect energy by pulling the electricity from everything around you. When you do this, you render the object useless. If I reach out to someone for energy, I can convert the energy back into whatever I want. I complete the circuit. But I'm also an entire circuit by myself? I still don't completely understand."

"Good thing you aren't more emotional. Seems like you can only perform when you're about to lose your shit."

Valerie knew by now that Hyka was helping, in her own way, by appearing unimpressed as usual.

"I don't know how to control when I use my powers. But when I release a conductor's stored energy, I rejuvenate them, make them younger, heal them, too. Maybe the only time I let my guard down is when I panic. I don't make a habit of trusting people or reaching out for help," Valerie admitted, trying not to sound insensitive.

Jack sat in deep concentration. The longer he sat, the more upset he got. His worry showed on his face. Griff maneuvered the RV in the direction of the highway.

"Dr. Jarrett said I could power an entire region if I were in proximity to another DiaZem. I know right now I could power more than just this vehicle. Not much actual electricity is needed since vehicles run on gas. I can keep everyone from pulling the energy put out by the alternator."

The possibilities started running through Valerie's mind. She could find Scott and Caleb. Then, with the help of her friends, they would run. With their collection of skills, they could find a rural homestead and live in peace, away from the threat of the CDC. She would do anything necessary to preserve the lives of the people she loved, but she would have to start leading them in that direction now. Convincing them would take a lot of work.

The RV accelerated as they reached the on-ramp to the highway then slowed. Traffic was moving, but only just. Only one northbound lane was open. There would be little room left for escape if circumstances called for them to evade.

The overall mood in the RV was positive. Hyka flipped through channels on the TV looking for the latest in CDC propaganda. Jack sat staring out the window as Griff merged into traffic and joined the unaffected population on the road. Major left his post in the front to join them, leaving Griff to drive.

"You did it, young lady," Major said in his Southern accent. There was a twinkle in his eyes, like a child on Christmas morning.

Valerie, however, was not thrilled about their conflict ending with a fatality. In the moment of the shot, she rationalized the circumstance had come down to life or death. She gave Major a weak but appreciative smile. His wounds were still pink but had almost healed.

"You look a lot like your mama, you know," he said after studying her for a couple of seconds.

"Thank you." Valerie regretted not ever knowing these people before they became her friends. They all seemed to know her far better than she knew them. She would have had an easier time rallying them to her plan if she knew them already.

"Your pops is the most honest SOB I have ever met. Got him into trouble a lot, but you have to respect a man who will risk insubordination before jeopardizing the welfare of his soldiers. He was a smart man. Always stayed five steps ahead of the enemy. I see a lot of that in you. You're a quick one, Mrs. Russell."

"You all can start calling me Valerie or Val. I feel like we've been through enough to skip over the pleasantries."

A reasonable request. Major nodded.

"We promised your dad to keep you safe. As a simple man, I know enough to know that little good is going to come if we let them take you. Deep down, you know they could find another DiaZem to complete their plan. We can't stand idly by. You are the key to stopping them. You are what the good guys need to keep order in this world."

A weapon. Valerie was either going to be a weapon for right or wrong. Major's eyes searched hers for a positive acknowledgment. She had none to offer. Finding her son and husband were her top priority. She had a difficult time seeing past their safety to a bigger picture of overthrowing a rising world government. She wanted to preserve what life she had left and never leave her family again. She was not oblivious to the fact that she needed this group of people and was aware of what they risked by helping her. If she could offer them safety, maybe they would see her vision and abandon the idea of sending her on an impossible mission. Valerie struggled to find a way to satisfy Major's lingering suggestion.

She stared him down with raised eyebrows, refusing to agree to his idea. Major gave a long sigh and returned to Griff's side. Relief and anxiety rose in her as she knew this would not be the last time he brought up the proposition. He needed her buy-in as much as she needed his. They would continue to disagree until one of them gave in.

Valerie rested her head in her hands. She was stuck in a place where every decision came at a steep price. She felt helpless, like the night she lost her mother, except this time she was the driver who was going too fast. As a nurse, she was charged with saving the lives of others, but the weight of saving people she knew and loved was far heavier than she had ever experienced. If she could not find a way to control the situation, more people would die. Staring out the window as the parked cars passed by, she bit her knuckle, hoping the small bit of pain would calm the anxiety bubbling under the surface. Smoke rose from the mountains miles away. Millions of people populated the surrounding area. Yes. If her plan were successful, she would have her family; however, she was unsure if she could live with herself, knowing she was the key to saving so many more and chose to run. Her child would be safe, but what of every unaffected child? This was impossible, and she might lose everything for even trying. She swallowed the ball in her throat.

The sun sank behind the tallest mountain on the horizon, though it was still mid-afternoon. They had spent hours inching forward in the RV. The rest was welcome, and they covered more ground than if they had continued on foot. Their relaxation was short lived. Griff spotted the reason for the slow traffic. A checkpoint. Of course, there would be a checkpoint.

"No," she whispered as Griff accelerated. "Griffin, slow down."

"I can bust through. They don't have chains or gates. Just a soft checkpoint," he said, continuing to accelerate. He swerved onto the crowded shoulder in an attempt to gain momentum to run through.

"Major, we can't draw attention to ourselves." She tried to remain calm and authoritative.

"You think the soldiers at this checkpoint are just going to let us waltz right on through? What do you think will happen once we get there? I suppose we could hide in the cabinets and hope for the best." He was getting anxious, angrier, and desperate.

She could feel it in his heart rate.

"No," Valerie said louder and more direct. Everyone looked at her.

Hyka stood up and went to the bedroom of the RV. Car by car, they got closer to the checkpoint. She knew the CDC would take them either way. Valerie struggled to keep her fear under control. The doubt displayed all over her company's faces did not help.

"Please trust me. I can do this. I need to start figuring this out. No one else has to die. If we fight, that is exactly what will happen," she pleaded.

"No? Because you want to sabotage your own safety to prove a point? To try and figure it out now? Dammit." Major answered her request by returning to the passenger seat and giving the order to slow down.

"Please, just trust me," she said through clenched teeth as they pulled past a set of guards holding out sensors, scanning the RV.

Major turned to address the group. "Rendezvous point is the first exit off the east bypass." He spoke loud enough Hyka could hear him in the back but never took his eyes off Valerie. "If anything happens, we meet up there. No one gets left behind. All of us or none of us."

"This one is hot, Sarge," a voice yelled from outside the RV.

A loud but muffled alarm came from one of the guard's sensors. Griff slowed the RV to a halt. Seven CDC-clad soldiers stood behind barriers with unusual looking weapons at the ready. Two more soldiers made their way to the RV door. Griff looked at Major who gave the nod. He rolled the window down to take commands.

"Sir, we know you are harboring affected people in your vehicle. Please place the RV in park, hand over the keys, and everyone needs to exit the vehicle. Please follow directions or you will be forced to comply."

A rapping came from the other side of the RV. The two soldiers were getting impatient. Griff followed the orders and stood up to be the first out. He glanced over his shoulder at Valerie. She chewed the inside of her cheek. Major offered a protesting look as he walked out the door, hands in fists and head high. She followed behind him. Hyka reappeared from the back and fell in line behind Jack.

Valerie did a mental assessment of the checkpoint as her shoes hit the pavement. Her heart pounded, and she was still in touch with the energy around her. If she gave in to her fear, she would be consumed by the power that bombarded her. Her finger was on the pulse of every person in that checkpoint. Scared even to breathe too fast, Valerie realized then that she was indeed a weapon. There was no good side of taking the lives of so many people, regardless of the cause given to justify it. War was evil, and she wanted no part of either side. A prayer escaped her lips in a whisper. All her focus was on maintaining control.

The checkpoint spanned three lanes. Beyond the checkpoint, traffic moved quicker with two lanes open instead of just one. Guards led the 'Squatch team to a holding area next to a makeshift command tent. A grid was spray painted on the ground, five squares deep and nine squares long. They each were instructed to stand on a separate square. The square Jack stood on had a dried blood stain.

"Good evening, folks. My name is Staff Sergeant Stephenson. It has been brought to our attention that your vehicle is harboring individuals affected by the Event. No one here is in trouble or danger. However, if you refuse to comply, you will be forced to comply. No, you may not contact your lawyer. No, you do not have the right to refuse. And lastly, no, I do not care. Specialist O'Connell here will test you. If you test negative, then you are free to go. If you test positive, my troops will escort you to a facility in Denver for observation. The facility is a nice place where you will find the accommodations quite appealing."

Staff Sergeant Stephenson nodded toward a young man, Specialist O'Connell, to proceed. The young man's uniform was crisp and new. His arms shook as he pointed a wand-shaped contraption at Griff. Valerie studied the response of the wand. If she could manipulate the reaction of the device, they would all be released.

O'Connell moved down the line to Major; the wand went off for a second before she could block the reading. Valerie concentrated harder, mimicking the negative response given to Griff. The young man gave a startled look at Stephenson and waved the wand over Major again. This time Valerie caught the reaction before the alarm alerted them again. Major was negative. She let out a soft sigh and continued to focus on the wand.

The young man looked to the staff sergeant again. "I need another wand, sir."

"Goddammit, kid. I'm not a sir. Call me Staff Sergeant, or I'll beat you with your wand. What's wrong? Didn't you design this thing?"

O'Connell flinched at Stephenson's questioning. The boy did not have the same air about him as the other soldiers. He was too young, too scared, unbroken by military training. His invention must have given him a first-class ticket to join the CDC front lines.

Stephenson radioed to the command tent beside them to bring out a backup device. The young man started again. Griff was negative. Major and Hyka were both negative. The wand came closer to her. An alarm sounded from the device, triggering multiple alarms around the checkpoint. In seconds, they were surrounded by an additional fifty soldiers. All guns pointed at her. Blue sparks of electricity balled at the ends of their plastic-barreled weapons, using energy as their ammunition. They were charged and ready to fire.

She was running out of time, but lucky for her, the strange weapons were nothing more than stun guns. They were electric. She exhaled a laugh before changing the blue sparked charges to red. She had found their lethal mode. The strength of the electrical weapons coupled with a small magnetic piece within gave her the power to pick and hold their targets. One by one, the soldiers shifted and pointed their electrical weapons at each other against their will. It was just a show of power. Major took one step toward the staff sergeant, but in a split second, Stephenson produced a 9mm and steadied it on Valerie's forehead.

Valerie's heart was in her throat, and she fought to remain calm. Strangely enough, it was not the first time she had been in a situation with a gun in her face. Her experience did not offer much solace, but she had a small understanding of the man's psychology. He would not shoot her, with her being who she was. But unfortunately, her companions were more acceptable targets.

"If you know what I am, then you know what I am capable of," Valerie said in her best Hyka tone, flat with no expression.

Stephenson kept the gun steady on her, took a step, and whispered in her ear, "And I would love to see that in action, but maybe with fewer spectators." He took a step back. "O'Connell, run inside the head shed and grab about five guys without those plastic toys. Let the LT know what we've got here, too."

"Please don't shoot, her," Specialist O'Connell requested. "She's special. More important than anyone else in the world."

"Dammit, O'Connell. Does this look like a public execution to you? Grab some zip ties while you're up there. And stop questioning orders. Didn't you get some briefing before they just sent you out here? Undisciplined turd."

The young man backed away, unable to take his eyes off Valerie. Getting impatient, Stephenson pointed the gun in the air and fired a round. The young man flinched again and tripped over his own feet. Valerie used the distraction to try to grab the weapon from Stephenson, but he was faster and stronger. He anticipated her move, grabbed her throat right under her jaw, and held the gun to her head.

"You're really pretty, you know that? Of course, you do. Is that how you got these low-lives to follow you? I bet you even spread your legs for this bitch who looks like she wants to kill me. They might be afraid of you, but I'm not. Don't expect me to worship you. You're nothing but a whore. They'll take you to the facility and use you up. You think I'm joking? Why do you think they are so desperate to find a female DiaZem?" Stephenson kept his remarks to a whisper.

She tried to block out the images he painted in her head. All she could think about was how Max had looked at her, how Dr. Jarrett had looked at her. She kept her jaw clenched and balanced on her toes to alleviate the pain from his grip. She could smell the carbon smoke emitting from the barrel of the gun, less than an inch from her head. If she killed him, then she might have to kill all the soldiers at the checkpoint. Still, she knew he would not shoot her. No one had to die. Valerie disengaged the electrical weapons and returned power to the soldiers who held them.

"Atta girl," Stephenson said as he released his grip. The gun still steadied at her face.

She lowered herself to flat feet and glared at him. Her neck still hurt, but she would not give him the satisfaction of knowing. She brushed her hair out of her face with her left hand in a show of defiance.

"Oh, you're married?" Stephenson questioned in amusement. "To him?" he said, pointing to Jack. "Does he know they are going to whore you out at the facility?"

Stephenson got the reaction he was looking for from Jack who charged at him. Valerie felt one of the electrical weapons charge. The energy built up before a red stream shot toward Jack. She considered taking the hit from him, but in the transfer, the shock could move to Stephenson who held his index finger on the trigger of the gun still pointed at her. The trauma would cause his finger to flex, firing a bullet. Helpless, Valerie screamed as the red stream hit him. The shock pulsed through his body twice before he could absorb the energy. The amount administered would have killed a regular person. Jack fell to the ground, writhing in pain until he stopped moving altogether.

CHAPTER TWELVE

"I don't play their high-techy games," Staff Sergeant Stephenson said, waving the barrel of the black 9mm in Valerie's face.

O'Connell came barreling out of the command tent. He gave a visible sigh of relief when he saw Valerie was still standing. He slowed his pace to a brisk walk.

"But I cannot get over the fact I found the precious DiaZem," Stephenson said, touching his free hand to her cheek. "I'm sure the CDC has a medal for something like this."

"You won't get a medal for this," Major said. Valerie kept her gaze on the gun, but in her peripheral, she saw Major had grabbed Specialist O'Connell by the hair and held a knife to his throat. The door of the command tent swung open, and three men jogged over to the group. No one seemed concerned about the men approaching, although it was apparent they held positions of authority.

Sweat poured from O'Connell's face and mixed with silent tears. Major's jaw was tight, and he didn't drop his gaze from Stephenson. The staff sergeant's smile faded and he pushed the barrel hard into the side of Valerie's head, standing so close to her that his chest touched her face. Her fear was stronger than ever, but she would not give in. She could not. No one else had to die. Heart pounding, she decided to act. Valerie reached out to one of the electric weapons and fired two paces in front of the three men, stopping them in their tracks.

"Stephenson! Drop your weapon! That's an order, Staff Sergeant, and I won't say it again!" the tallest of the three threatened.

Stephenson gave Valerie a look of absolute hatred. He lowered the handgun from her face.

"Ma'am, I am Captain Franklin, the officer in charge of this checkpoint. Dr. Jarrett has ordered your safe passage. He runs the CDC facility in Denver."

"I know who he is," she said, loathing the mention of his name. She did not need his permission. She hated even more that he knew where she was.

"Sir, she's a DiaZem," Stephenson yelled in protest. "The one we've been out here screening for the entire time. And we are just going to let them go? The one thing holding up Phase Two shimmies through our checkpoint and points our goddamn weapons at us, fires at us, and we don't retaliate?"

"Staff Sergeant, I suggest you stand down now, or you're going to regret what happens next," Major said without loosening the grip on O'Connell.

Rage filled the staff sergeant's eyes. He took two long strides toward Major. Major flung the crying young man to the ground and took a fighting stance with his blade in hand. Jack, still lying on the ground nearby, grabbed O'Connell by the ankle and held him down.

Another electrical weapon fired. Stephenson fell.

"Stop!" the captain shouted. Silence fell over the checkpoint except for screams from the man writhing on the ground. Valerie had not fired at him. She looked into the crowd of soldiers. The weapons were all disengaged but one held by a woman who stood raising hers over her head. Valerie noted the blue setting of a stun gun. Not enough electricity to affect the heart, but enough to attack the nerves. Fellow soldiers approached the woman, detained her stun gun, and zip-tied her wrists together.

The captain left the medics to tend to Staff Sergeant Stephenson and walked toward Valerie. Jack stood up between them, maintaining his firm grip on O'Connell

"We mean you no harm," Captain Franklin offered. "Our orders are to let you pass, however, without the use of your vehicle. We know who you are, Valerie Burton. We know what you are. This little crusade you are on is pointless. Dr. Jarrett has offered an escort to your residence in exchange for your friends. You'd be home by the morning, ma'am. Your husband will also be notified to meet you there. A win-win option for everyone. No more running. You'll be back with your family."

Jack looked back over his shoulder at Valerie. She hesitated, but she knew what would happen after she reunited with her family. Lucas would have her captured and brought to the facility anyway. They would use her family as leverage to make her do what they wanted. Phase Two was dependent on her cooperation. Major was getting red in the face, and the captain was getting impatient. She realized they still had not located her son. If they had, they would not have given her the option to walk away.

"We are taking O'Connell." Valerie walked to the far side of Jack, away from the captain, and pulled the young man from his grasp. "And her. Let her go."

Valerie waited while the soldiers cut the restraints of the woman's wrists and let her go. Stephenson was trash. Anyone who would stand up to a man despite the consequence was someone she wanted on her side.

They walked out of the checkpoint. Hyka grabbed O'Connell's other arm, and they picked up the pace. Major glared at Valerie and waited for the three women to pass before he followed with Griff beside him, keeping his eye on the captain and the recovering staff sergeant. Jack waited until Valerie was out of earshot to point a finger at the captain's chest. Judging by the two men's posture, their exchange was not a pleasant one. After he spoke his piece, Jack jogged to catch up with the team.

Valerie released her hold on the young man. He was thin, wiry, and a few inches taller than her. His red hair was too long for military standards, and his skin was bright red from the stress of his situation. He was scared. She felt sorry for him, but she needed answers. He did not belong with those soldiers. He did not belong with the CDC. He belonged with them. His wand knew more about her than she did.

The woman kept pace. Valerie could tell she was a conductor, though she appeared Valerie's actual age.

"Thank you," she said, pushing her glasses up her face. She kept her chin high as they walked, unapologetic.

"Thank you," Valerie answered. "You would have faced a court martial over that, no doubt."

"I'm not even in the military," the woman laughed. "I am a journalist. I was at the government building, trying to get my paperwork in order so I could be a war-time correspondent. Then the Event happened, and I had a choice of quarantine or the front lines. Naturally, I wanted to be where the action would happen. So, I lied about being affected. They threw me a uniform, handed me a giant taser, and sent me out here."

"Shooting that guy jeopardized everything for you."

"It didn't really. I've watched that guy harass women for two days. If I just saved one person from that disgusting piece of shit, then I think it's worth it. If I've learned anything in my line of work, when you witness evil in the world and do nothing to stop it, you're just as responsible for the outcome."

Valerie thought about the woman's justification for a long time. The consequences of failure were still too high a price. Losing Scott or Caleb was not a path she wanted to risk, but the moral obligation was too great to run from.

"What's your name?" Valerie knew she had just gained another ally.

Smiling, she answered, "Courtney Dominguez."

"Valerie Russell."

"It's nice to meet you, Valerie Russell, and thanks again. I'm glad to be on the side of the good guys."

O'Connell did not try to run. He did not trail behind or even leave Valerie's side. His tears subsided after a few minutes, though his cheeks remained red. Ahead, Major and Griff navigated the team for two hours to their rendezvous point. They covered more ground without the burden of their packs, but the lack of supplies would cause more trouble later on if they did not restock.

When the group reached the off-ramp for the city of Parker, they stopped to regroup. Griff went up the hill to a gas station off the exit for water and food. Jack and Major held a quiet but heated discussion. She had spent hours calculating the distance between her and her son. Twenty-eight miles would have been a short drive. She could pick any vehicle littering the shoulders, median, and ditches surrounding the highway. But the only moving cars on the toll road they traveled were the blue CDC trucks. They would be stopped and forced to repeat the incident from the checkpoint. She did not have much farther before reaching home, but knowing they just barely skirted detainment was hard to stomach. She did not have the time or energy to go through another CDC encounter.

Courtney found a seat on the curb and pulled out a pen and paper. Specialist O'Connell sat down, too. Hyka nodded at Valerie and then sat next to him, as a guard.

". . . Just a matter of time," she heard Major say before he realized Valerie had walked up to them. Valerie knew they were talking about her and what had happened and Major was not happy about the additional people.

"You did alright, kid," Jack said and pulled her in for a side hug.

"I should have scrambled their communications. Now Jarrett knows where we are."

Major, with his brows drawn together, stomped past them and toward the young man sitting with his daughter. O'Connell was an easy target for his anger, but the kid knew it, and he had not taken his eyes off Major since the checkpoint. O'Connell stood up fast and took a few steps back to add more distance. He was about to turn to run, but he tripped on the curb and fell on his hip. Major grabbed him by the collar and yanked him off the ground with ease.

"Start talking, boy," he said, pulling O'Connell's face within an inch of his own.

"I . . . I found the DiaZem."

"Major, put him down. He can't tell us anything if you rip his head off," Jack said, annoyed.

Major lowered the young man's feet to the ground but kept his grip on the front of his shirt.

"What do you want with the DiaZem?" This time Hyka asked the question as she stood up. "How did you develop a screening tool in a week without having met one?"

"There is one, at the CDC facility. The technology wasn't hard, like testing a circuit for power. But DiaZem in their defensive state will deflect certain energy. I can't believe my invention worked in the field. I can't believe I found another DiaZem."

Hyka jabbed him in the side hard enough for him to wince.

"What do they want with a DiaZem?" she asked again.

"Phase Two. They can't start Phase Two until she's safe at the facility."

"Why?" Valerie asked.

"I don't know. No one knows what Phase Two is other than Dr. Jarrett. But your safety is of the utmost importance. We vowed to give our lives to keep your life intact. I have a place in the New World now. Creating the wand was easy, but I can't believe I found you."

Major shook the young man until his smile faded.

"Who is Dr. Jarrett?" Major asked him, growing more impatient with Valerie's celebrity DiaZem treatment.

Specialist O'Connell laughed at his question. "Dr. Lucas Jarrett is Head of Research at the Denver Facility. He is the mouthpiece of the World Council in the Central region of the United States."

Major shoved O'Connell to the ground. He let out a surprised yelp as the ground knocked the wind out of him. Major had heard enough. He shot an angry look at Courtney.

"Curse it! Why am I always right?!"

Valerie looked at Major, scared to say anything lest she received the same treatment as O'Connell. She did not have the slightest clue what he was right about. The young man had not said anything they did not already know. She was relieved when Major walked away and hoped he had left to calm down. She knelt by O'Connell who gazed at her, star struck.

"You are more beautiful than I had ever imagined," he whispered.

Courtney chuckled and shook her head.

Embarrassed by how he treated her, Valerie tried to steer the conversation better. "Well, thanks. But I have questions. Who is the other DiaZem?" she asked.

"There are two. I met one, though. I am not quite sure who the other is. He must be pretty important because they keep him protected. The DiaZem I tested on will be sent to the San Francisco facility once you are safe. He's just some lucky schmuck who won the genetic lottery. A nobody."

"But if all they need is two DiaZem, why are they still after me?"

He wrinkled his brow and tilted his head at the question. "After you? We are trying to find you and save you. Why would you not want yourself and your son protected? There is nothing more important than preserving your life. What do you think you are running from?"

"Just answer the question, alright?" Hyka said and kicked the kid in the arm.

"Ow! You people are worse than those soldiers," he said, rubbing where Hyka kicked. "The combined energy has to do with sex. Um, gender, I mean. Not sex. Imagine a magnet. Every magnet has two poles: north and south, a positive and negative. Hidden in the human gender chromosome is a charge. XY is negative, and XX is positive. When they come into proximity, the magnetic charge of two male DiaZem deflect and cause a lot of problems, a huge mess. Hypothetically, the same goes for females, regardless of their compatibility otherwise. But when a positive charge meets a negative charge, their bond becomes inseparable, and their power can sustain a civilization past Phase Four."

"You think she's going to leave her husband for some DiaZem to fulfill your kooky power triangle? Val, this dude is hot for you. Maybe he is the other DiaZem. How does that make you feel?" Hyka laughed once, which was as much as her stoic posture would allow.

Courtney let out a giggle, too, and continued her writing. But the joke was not amusing to Valerie or O'Connell who huffed and stuttered, causing Hyka to laugh twice more. His face turned a shade redder.

Griff showed up before the boy could collect himself. Food was a welcome distraction. Valerie tossed a bottle of water toward O'Connell. Hyka intercepted the container. She threw another to Courtney, who dropped her pen in time to catch it.

"He doesn't need this. He's not coming with us." Hyka threw the bottle to her father who had made his way back when he noticed Griff's return.

"Where is he going to go?" Valerie threw her hands in the air, referencing their temporary campsite on the side of the road. She had had enough of being undermined and second-guessed. "He's been inside the facility and worked with a DiaZem. He can help us," she explained.

"We will keep them around a bit longer," Jack said, coming to her rescue. "Neither of them poses a real threat. Search them, though. Who knows what kind of techy equipment that one might have on him. And it's high time we start listening to Valerie. Once shit hits the fan, she might be the only one to bring us out."

Valerie was glad Jack stood up for her, but the endorsement made her uncomfortable. She did not want control, but just one person to be on her side. It felt like everyone had their own agenda for her except Courtney, but her acquaintance was too new to determine where she fit into all this.

"He's a liability, Jack. The girl is fine to stay, and I can see how he'd even be helpful, but I'm with Hyka. That kid will sell us out before he'd help us," Griff said. He looked tired. He was not able to recover as fast as the others. Valerie was so caught up in being close to home she had not noticed the toll the journey was taking on him. The RV had been a nice break for everyone with the gene, but Griff did not get any rest during their drive.

"Let's take a few more hours to rest, but he stays with us until I get home. I need him here," Valerie said, trying to be firm and compassionate.

"What the hell are you trying to prove?" Major demanded of her.

She knew this conversation would not be pretty, but she needed to stand up for herself.

"What?" She just wanted to hear him admit he did not want her taking charge.

"You're reckless. You are making decisions you have no experience making."

She could feel him holding back his rage.

"You, sir, are reckless. We know nothing of what they plan to do. If he is our chance to shine some light on what's going on in there, I'm at least going to let him have a drink of water." She knew the young man was not the real subject of this argument. She wanted to hear Major admit his power struggle.

"He is lucky to still be alive, and she deserves whatever punishment they have lined up for her. Every second they are here puts every one of us at risk. I would have slit his throat at the checkpoint if I had known he'd be your little tag-a-long. Both of them will tell you what you want to hear to get you into the CDC compound. Hell, I should end this right now." Major motioned to his knife. O'Connell flinched and flung his arms in front of his face to shield himself.

Courtney just sat and watched.

"Your answer is to kill everyone? How does murder make us any better than them?"

"You and I both know you could have shielded Jack from the taser. I hate to be the bearer of bad news, Your Majesty, but the world is at war. Something I have a lifetime of experience in and you have none. You might have one mission right now, Princess, but we are here for something much bigger than a toddler. Your spawn is a tiny piece of this puzzle, and the sooner you get your head out of your fourth point of contact, the less you'll keep putting a visible target on our backs." Major's face was red. Sweat poured from his brow. She knew he was about to break.

"You used me to kill once; it won't happen again. I could have stopped the taser, yes. But the shock would have transferred to the man with the gun. His finger never moved from the trigger. If he had gotten electrocuted, his finger would have flexed, putting a bullet in my head. So, I'm sorry I had to let Jack get hit, but I did not have a choice.

"You can guide this mission and call the shots on when and where we stop, but you forget, sir, when the smoke clears I will be the one to fix everything. The reckless one here is you. I will not be a weapon. Not for them, and not for you."

A gun went off, loud and right in her ear. Major's face relaxed as blood trickled from the hole in his forehead. Valerie's world went numb and seemed to slow. Jack tackled O'Connell and Hyka grabbed her father as his lifeless body fell to the ground. Her face twisted in anguish. She let out a scream, muffled by the ringing in Valerie's ears. Courtney yanked the gun from O'Connell's hand and threw it away from him.

Hyka pulled the knife loose from her father's belt and turned to O'Connell. Jack was beating him with his bare fists. She used one hand to pull Jack away, but Griff grabbed her around her arms before she reached O'Connell. She screamed and kicked the air, trying to free herself.

Jack faced Valerie. His lips formed her name, but she could not hear him.

"Valerie. Valerie. Can you save him? Valerie. Wake up." He slapped her full handed across the face.

"Valerie. Can you save him?"

She looked at him, trying to decipher the foreign language he was speaking.

"Valerie! Fix him!" He shook her and yelled in her face.

She looked at Jack in full consciousness and understood. She moved to Major's body and felt for a pulse on his neck. He was still breathing and still had a heartbeat, though both were weak. She pulled open a medical pouch on his belt. The exit wound she found while wrapping the gauze around his head left her with little hope. She could feel his energy fading.

"Griff, call 911." She did not care about the consequences of being found. She just needed a backup plan. She put her hands on his chest, one on his right pec and the other on his left side. Valerie exhaled a silent prayer as she pulled the combined energy of those around her and focused her power on Major's fleeting heartbeat. Inhale.

She exhaled, and the very breath created sparks that traveled from her mouth to Majors. He sucked in when they reached his lips, and the connection stayed. Valerie could feel her own energy drain. It was not enough. Desperate, she pulled any power she could find. Soon, even the air around her was positively charged as visible streams of electricity moved from Jack, Hyka, Griff, and even Courtney. Valerie reached out further for power. The sky answered with a bolt of lightning.

Major's body arched off the ground, and Valerie could feel the connections of neurons in his brain. Firing. Reconnecting. Rebuilding. But the power was running out. She pushed as hard as she could to keep it going, but without another power source, within minutes it was all over.

CHAPTER THIRTEEN

Despite her elaborate show of power, Major lay lifeless under Valerie's hands. She searched his eyes, hoping he would return. She needed him. She needed him to tell her what to do next. She needed him to be her father's voice of reason in his absence. His energy had not faded, but he was not there. Out of desperation, she began chest compressions.

"Griff, call 911. Please!" Tears rolled down her face.

Major's head jerked with every thrust. His eyes stared into nowhere.

Jack placed his hands over Valerie's, but she did not stop. She would keep Major's heart beating even if he could not. Only when Jack wrapped his muscular arms over hers did she let the defeat overtake her.

The confrontation, the blood, the lifeless man who lay in front of her. If she had listened to him, she could have avoided all of this. She saw her mother where Hyka's father was. She had picked the most impossible of occupations—trusted to save lives, yet incapable. She saved hundreds of people in her career, but when love was involved, she had failed again. She feared this to be the fate of everyone close to her.

Valerie forgot where she was, who she was, and why she was there.

Grief poured from her soul into a tiny ball which kept growing into a hollowness in her chest. She wished the emptiness would collapse on itself and swallow her. She was numb to everything around her but the breaking of her heart.

The passing of time was only given away by the growing darkness casting the team into shadows. Valerie's adrenaline wore off, and the pain of kneeling on the concrete was becoming more apparent. She shifted her body to lay flat on the ground. Jack was next to her, his shirt still wet with her tears. His eyes closed. His right hand rubbed his forehead hard and slow, caked with dried blood from O'Connell's face.

Valerie stared up at the dark sky that had flashed bright with lightning as she had never experienced before. The failure drained her emotionally and physically. Her eyes were swollen and raw from crying. She wanted to run away. Leave them all. She did not want the responsibility which came with her awakened gene. She did not want to be a DiaZem or bear the impossible expectations of others. She did not want to be the one to stand by and pick up the pieces of destruction left in her wake.

Hyka lay next to her father with her head on his chest. She, like the rest of the group, was silent. No sobs or mournful sighs. She just stared down at his shoes, not even shifting for comfort. Griff sat facing the bloody pile of Specialist O'Connell. Dirt, blood, and sweat were only washed clean by the tears he allowed to fall down his cheeks. He reminded Valerie of the degenerates along the road to Max's: stripped of their loved ones and desperate for answers. Courtney sat beside him, both staring a thousand miles away at the same nothing.

"I have to keep going, Jack. I just don't know how," Valerie whispered. A tear rolled from the corner of her eye and across her temple. Her heart broke for Hyka, and she felt selfish for even breathing the words.

"You and I can go on. We'll take the girl. Eight more hours. Griff can stay with Hyka and Major. Once we reach Caleb, we will come back for them and regroup." Jack sounded like he had been rolling the idea around for as long as she had.

O'Connell coughed, sending a ball of clotted blood straight into the air which landed next to his face. Hyka slid to a stance in a fluid motion that conveyed she had been waiting for this exact moment. Griff attempted to head her off, but she had anticipated his interception as well and maneuvered by him with ease. Hyka straddled her prey, and with a quick jerk of her arm, her father's blade pulled over the young man's throat. She stayed there, blood pouring over her knees until the flow stopped and Specialist O'Connell's body lay lifeless. Only then did she stand and walk toward Valerie, stopping short and pointing the bloody blade at her.

"You did this. To both of them. Is this your idea of leading? You haven't even picked what side you're on," Hyka yelled in anger, but she did not cry. "This is not just about you. Stop pulling everyone along if you're just going to ditch us the first chance you get. We're here because we believe you're the one to stop this, but you need to stop straddling the fence. Pick a damn side already. You're just going to get the rest of us killed."

Her words felt like poison, and Valerie dared not interrupt. She knew the grieving process all too well. Hyka was the one hurting and needed to place blame and direct her anger. Valerie had no business trying to defend herself. Hyka would not have listened either way.

"You didn't search him," Jack said without looking at her. "I told you to search him, Hyka. This was as much your fault as any of us."

"Hyka," Major whispered from where he was lying.

She lowered the knife she had pointed at Valerie and stepped back to her father.

"Everything's alright. I'm fine. Just a little weak," Major coughed. Griff brought him a bottle of water and helped Hyka prop him up to drink.

"She did it. I can't believe she did it," Griff said to himself, wiping a tear away with the back of his hand.

"Give me a little time, I'll be ready to go," Major said, sitting more upright. He took another drink, then looked up. "I saw you, Valerie, in my dream, and bits and pieces of events. I saw the other DiaZem. And I saw. . ." He looked at Griff and then at the ground. "We need to keep moving. We're running out of time."

Jack patted Valerie hard on her back as he walked over to O'Connell's body.

"I can't," she said, anticipating another request. "I don't think my ability works the same for regular people."

"Nope. Not this one. He deserves what he got." Jack looked back at her and smiled. He looked over at Courtney, who seemed very much out of place. "Got a hand?"

"How did you do that anyway?" Courtney asked, grabbing under one of O'Connell's shoulders. "Did you know the lightning would work?"

"No, I didn't, but once I started, the electricity stimulated the stem cells in his brain to repair itself from the inside out." Feeling better about the situation, Valerie grabbed a bottle of water and cleaned her arms of the blood. "The damage was corrected. Maybe it just took some time for his brain to reboot. I was scared he wouldn't wake up."

"Well, you did good, kid," Jack grunted as he and Courtney pulled the body to the middle of the road.

"If it is of no concern to anyone, I am pretty close to home. I have someone I need to check in on. It's been days. I imagine she's worried about me," Courtney said, looking between Jack and Valerie.

"No one will force you to stay. We're all here to protect that which is dear to us. Yours is not any less important." Valerie wished Courtney would stay, but would not try to convince her.

"Thank you again. I know one day, I'll be able to repay your kindness. Be safe."

Courtney walked away, and Jack turned back toward Major.

"Are you just going to leave him there?" Valerie pointed to O'Connell's body in the middle of the road.

"They will find him better here than tucked behind a bush. Someone needs to take him back to his family. Just won't be us." Jack continued to walk over to Major, who was getting to his feet.

"How are you doing, old man? We thought you were down for the count. Can't keep Austin Major down." He grasped Major's arm and pulled him in for a hug.

"Yeah, I think I'm ready. Two shots to the head in one day? Let's get out of here. Birds are starting to circle."

Valerie looked up; there were no birds in the night sky.

The last leg of their journey gave Valerie plenty of time to digest what Hyka had said. Even in her rage, she had been right. Valerie needed their guidance now more than ever. With the near loss of Major, the attempt to bring him back was a natural choice. The mission to save lives was embedded into every part of her being. Valerie could not risk losing anyone else. She would fight against the CDC, but still needed to figure out how, and fast.

"What did you see when you were out? What was your dream?" she asked Major after an hour of walking and out of earshot of the others. He was silent for a few seconds, then let out a long sigh and shook his head.

"They die. They all die. All the regular people, until the only people left are the DiaZem and the conductors. It's happening soon, and I don't know how to stop it. Hell, I don't even know what 'it' is." He balled a fist and shook his head. "I've known Griff for twenty years. We grew up in the army together. I've never had a more loyal friend. I wouldn't have met Hyka's mother if not for him, and he was there to pick me back up when she left." He looked up ahead of them at Griff. He wiped his eyes.

Valerie noticed the drastic contrast from the man he was earlier in the day. Whatever he saw in his dream, he believed it was real.

"He's tired. Griff," Major said. "We should stop, but we are running out of time. We'll be at your place before morning. We'll rest and stock up there. Gia would have taken Caleb somewhere safe and left behind a clue of some sort. Something in plain sight the CDC wouldn't pick up on. Something only you would understand."

"I hope so."

Their pace had slowed by the time they crested the last hill. Valerie could see the rooftops of her neighborhood. Even with miles left on their journey, she began to run. She passed Griff who had fallen back to let Jack take the lead. As she moved beyond the team, Jack picked up his pace and joined her.

"We'll go at this pace as long as you can."

Her lungs burned, and her legs were sore, but the end was in sight and she picked up her speed. Valerie's heart raced faster than her legs would move. The cold air in her face made her eyes water. She let the tears fall and pushed out any negative thought of failure. She had done something otherwise impossible. She had fought with everything she had to make it this far. The end was within reach. Home represented safety, unity—even the slight promise of reunion. In her space, she could center herself, rest, think. Find the clue and find her son.

Valerie slowed to a walk once she could see her house. The street was quiet, but this was nothing unusual. Her yard, however, was littered with the contents of the garage. Even her porch furniture rested in the bushes. The CDC was so desperate to find her son that they had left nothing unturned. They had also left the front door open.

"Let me go in first," Jack said as he moved past her with his handgun drawn and ready.

She followed him through the threshold, heart pounding in her chest. Jack moved, clearing the downstairs. She stood in her living room while he finished a sweep of the second floor. Pictures had been pulled off the wall and smashed on the ground. The couches were torn apart, and tables flipped. Her TV was gone. The CDC must have left an easy target for looters.

"House is clear," Jack announced as he made his way back down the stairs.

Valerie could not hold back the tears. She leaned her weight against the wall and slid down until she sat on the floor. She pulled her knees up and rested her head.

Jack, without a word, began working. He put the tables right side up and replaced the cushions on the couches the best he could in their state. He dusted glass off an armrest and placed a pillow he found on the floor in the corner of the sofa. Then he moved to her. Jack scooped Valerie up and laid her on the couch. He pulled up a blanket and shook hard to free the cloth of debris and covered her. Valerie curled up on the couch. She breathed the familiar air of her home deeply, closed her eyes to shut out the disheveled state of her sanctuary, and was soon asleep.

"Hello?" Valerie jumped at the man's voice, but Jack beat her to the front door.

"Who the hell are you?" Scott had a handgun pointed at Jack, who stood with his hands in the air.

"Scott!" Valerie ran to him and almost knocked him over. She hugged him hard and buried her face in his neck. She kissed him long and hard before he pulled her away.

"Hon, what are you doing here?"

Scott was not alone. Behind him outside were two men in CDC uniforms waiting by their blue truck. They carried the plastic weapons she had seen at the checkpoint.

"Where is Caleb?" he asked.

"I don't know where he is," she answered, and she slid out of his embrace. Though he was in regular clothes, she remembered seeing him in his own CDC uniform in the video Lucas had shown her. She stepped back away from him.

"What happened to you?" Scott started. "Why aren't you in quarantine? I thought you were at the CDC facility. They let me come home to get Caleb, and we were going to meet you there." Scott stepped toward her with his arms still open. He noticed Jack again, still standing with his hands in the air, and motioned to him. "Who is this?"

Before Jack could answer, a confrontation broke out by the blue truck, distracting them. Major overpowered one of the men and took his plastic weapon. Hyka had the other in a choke hold. She released him when he stopped struggling. She relieved the man of his gun and shot a stream of blue electricity at him.

"I think he pooped a little," Hyka said, pointing over her shoulder as she walked up the stairs to the front door.

Scott just stared at her as she let herself in the open door.

"Is this your dude?" Hyka asked Valerie with a nod toward Scott.

"Scott, this is Hyka, Jack, and Major." Valerie motioned behind Scott outside at Major, who was zip-tying the CDC men.

"Could use some assistance," Major yelled toward the house.

Hyka ignored her father and walked toward the kitchen. Jack went outside to help Major, leaving the couple in the foyer to talk.

"They are after me, the CDC. But I won't go. I needed to make sure Caleb was safe. Gia took him somewhere, and we have to find him before they do." Valerie had no idea where to start.

Scott looked over her shoulder at the destruction in the living room.

"Who did this?" He continued to the dining room and into the kitchen, cabinets were open, and their contents appeared flung across the room.

"The CDC and then probably looters after. We can't stay here. We need to find Caleb."

While she had already assessed the physical state of their home, Scott was still trying to process the scene.

"Where is he?" Scott asked again, his frustration and anger at the situation building.

"I don't know. Gia was supposed to leave a clue. Something I would find and the CDC wouldn't. But we are running out of time."

She stopped, realizing while Major had dreamt of the death of his friend, he had, by proxy, also witnessed the death of her husband. They were, indeed, running out of time.

Hyka stood watching them while eating from a bag of potato chips like popcorn at the movies. Her crunching was enough to shake the image from Valerie's mind.

"We need to search the house. I'll start upstairs in Caleb's room if you want to try down here."

Scott nodded at Valerie's suggestion. "What am I looking for?"

"I honestly have no idea."

Caleb's toys covered the floor of the loft playroom. The TV, DVD player, and all of Caleb's movies were gone. Looters had even taken his race car bed frame from the boy's bedroom. She picked up an action figure. Caleb's current favorite. She tucked the toy into her pocket. The violent state of the room broke her heart. This was once a safe place for her son to play and sleep. She would never feel safe here again. She could never feel safe anywhere. She was still lost in thought when she heard the tune "I Love Paris" coming from downstairs. She left the loft area and walked to the balcony overlooking the living room. Scott was standing with a musical birthday card in his hand.

"Happy 356th Birthday, Mommy," he read out loud. He threw the card down in a pile he had already gone through.

"That!" Valerie said and ran down the stairs to retrieve the card. The music did not play when she opened it again, but her excitement indicated she had found the clue. "Something I would know and no one else would."

"She found the thing," Hyka yelled down into the basement where Jack and Major had taken the CDC men.

Soon the entire company was in the living room waiting for Valerie to explain how the birthday card told her where to find Caleb.

"There is a brand-new resort west of the airport that just opened, twenty minutes from here. The whole place has themed rooms and restaurants. For Gia's birthday, I took her and Caleb to a restaurant called Little Paris. Caleb told her she was old and said some ridiculous number. But I think this is a room number. They must be staying at the resort in room 356." Valerie could not contain herself.

"Can we drive this time?" Griff asked from the couch. He had arrived when Valerie was upstairs.

"We have uniforms and a truck. We can travel as CDC without being questioned," Major offered.

"You guys change," Valerie suggested. "I'll grab supplies from the basement. We can't stay here. If they've been holed up at the resort this whole time without being caught, then we should be safe to hide out there for a while until we figure out what to do next. Hyka, can you help me carry stuff up from the basement?"

The women left the men to change into their borrowed uniforms. The basement was unfinished and empty except for a few boxes, and the two men who were zip-tied and still unconscious. Valerie opened a closet next to the stairs. Looters had already picked through the barren shelves.

"So much for that idea," Hyka said.

"The closet is a decoy. We keep dead batteries here to satisfy thieves, thinking they scored a huge stash. Wait here—I'll open the door." Valerie stooped down and followed the closet under the stairs until she came to a small door, just tall enough for her to crawl through. She punched a series of numbers to unlock the miniature door. A couple of seconds later, a section of otherwise empty wall space opened next to Hyka. Valerie grinned so big her cheeks hurt. Hyka walked into a hidden room lined with shelves full of emergency provisions.

"Impressive." She let out a small laugh.

"Six months of supplies for the three of us. We have cots, rainwater collection in the window well, food, ammo. The windows are bullet-proof and fortified but make for fast egress if necessary." Valerie handed Hyka a couple of five-gallon buckets of shelf-stable food, not knowing how long they would hide out at the resort. Once they sent up the last of the supplies to be loaded, Valerie stole some time alone with Scott as she freshened up.

"You are so beautiful," Scott said as she pulled her shirt up over her head and turned on the shower.

"A side effect of this whole mess, but something about me makes me different than the rest. They've been hunting Caleb to get to me."

"I can't wrap my head around any of this. Please, start from the beginning," he requested.

Valerie explained the week's events, including her conversation with Max and what Lucas had told her. She told him how she killed a man and brought Major back to life. When she had finished her story, she opened the shower door and reached for the plush towel she had set out. Scott stood from the side of the bath and crossed the space between them. Valerie dried herself. This was the last place he had kissed her goodbye. She regretted not staying in the moment with him before and would not allow the opportunity to escape her again. His eyes locked with hers and she welcomed his gentle touch, running his rough hands over her damp skin around to the small of her back.

With a sense of urgency, she pulled his body against her, kissing his mouth with all the heat and need that had been missing since their last time together. Deepening the kiss, he picked her up, and Valerie's long damp hair fell forward, brushing against Scott's cheeks. Exiting the bathroom, he took little time crossing the room to the mattress, which was shoved into the corner. As he leaned her back against the crisp sheets, he knocked aside the debris that stood in the way of their reunion.

Valerie felt in control and powerful. She felt whole again, connected to someone who honestly knew her. The feeling of being in his arms was what she had been missing, needing. She collapsed against his chest, his arms around her, caressing her hair as he pressed a kiss on her head. She hoped their passion hadn't drawn the attention of the guests downstairs, but none of that had mattered the moment that she was back in his arms.

In a fleeting thought of apprehension, Valerie considered the slight chance of the two of them returning home at the same time. If she had not run the remaining miles or if she had not been able to save Major's life, she would have missed this opportunity. The reunion seemed almost too good to be true, but there they were, together again. Things were starting to turn in her favor. She put her arms around her husband and held him as tight as her strength allowed.

"There were times I thought I couldn't keep going," she cried into his shoulder. "I thought they'd catch me and I'd never see you again. I knew I had to fight and push on. I need you, Scott. I can't do this without you."

"You'll never have to. I am not going anywhere. I shouldn't have left you to begin with. I beat myself up the whole time we were apart. We both should have stayed home. I'm sorry I dismissed your concerns. You were terrified, and all I could think about was how beautiful you are and how lucky I am to have you. I brushed you off and doing so almost cost me everything," he said, kissing her head, her neck.

She pulled him away from her and looked up into his eyes. "But you don't understand. Even when we get Caleb, you're still in danger. We have to run as far away as we can. Now I have you, I don't ever want to let you go. Everyone keeps wanting me to fight this huge war, but all I want is you and Caleb." Tears fell down her cheeks. "I feel like I can only have one or the other and I can't risk losing you. How can I be strong enough without you?"

"Valerie Marie Russell, you are my wife. I didn't marry you because you needed me. I married you because you make hard choices without blinking an eye. You raise our son to be kind and fair, and you are breathtakingly good-looking," he laughed. "You never needed me to be those things. I am lucky you chose me to share your tenacity. I'm sorry I don't spend much time telling you how amazing you are. You keep this house, our son, and our whole lives together. All while handling all the stuff you have going on with work. We will do whatever you choose. If you want to fight this guy head-on, I'm right beside you. If you want to find a cabin in the woods and spend the rest of our days living off the land, I'll grow a beard and become a mountain man."

Valerie smiled through her tears. After years together, she had never loved him more.

He pulled her tighter against him. "Let's go get our son."

CHAPTER FOURTEEN

Valerie held Scott's arm and rested her head on his shoulder in the back of the package truck. He stroked her hair with his free hand. She was almost complete. Having her husband by her side made the entire journey seem trivial. She was minutes from reuniting with her son and would have time to rest. With Scott, she could figure out how to take on the CDC and free the rest of her family.

With no windows in the back compartment, the only light came from strips at the seams of the door. Griff was snoring, and there was no doubt Hyka was napping as well. Jack and Major were in the cab wearing their new blue uniforms, navigating to the resort.

"I'm so sorry," Scott whispered in the dark and kissed her head. "I had no idea you were in danger. I'm sorry I wasn't there to help you. I'm sorry I couldn't stay home with Caleb. I had to wait an entire day to get the word you were alright. They had me take a train to get the affected in Kansas and said I could pick up Caleb and meet you when I got back. I can't believe I helped them."

"They were hoping you would lead them to Caleb. I am thankful for Gia. Did I tell you my dad hired her? Remember how I wanted the other nanny, but she declined at the last minute? I'm just glad everything worked out in the end." Valerie smiled and found her husband's hand. "How lucky are we? I love you more than anything."

"I love you so much." Scott kissed her hand.

She held him tighter as the truck turned into the resort parking lot. When the vehicle stopped, Major and Jack got out of the cab and walked around to open the back to release the rest of the team. Valerie had a renewed sense of strength. The fear which had gripped her during her trek washed away. When she stepped out of the vehicle, the afternoon sky was thick with clouds threatening rain. Her journey was over, and she welcomed the weather. The parking lot was quiet, and just a few cars were in the lot. No one came in or out, and there was no power to the massive building. The sliding doors stayed open and warm and humid air blew from the inside like the building was breathing. There were a few people in the lobby who disappeared when they noticed the men in blue uniforms.

"This way." Valerie led the team in a jog to the farthest corner of the hotel. She knew where she would find Caleb. The clue was so smart, and she had no doubt what Gia intended to convey with the French birthday card. Valerie ran down a hallway that opened into a giant atrium. A stream running through the hotel was stagnant and lightly smelled of algae. She followed the water around to a bridge. The artificial island hosted a cluster of restaurants like Little Paris where she had taken Gia for her birthday. The restaurant was empty, and with a quick once over she decided there were no more clues.

"The room is on the third floor. 356." She found the stairs, heart pounding, and ran up as fast as she could. 395 was the first room. She sprinted down the balcony of rooms overlooking the restaurants and the stream. She flew past each room until she came to the right one. Her heart sank to her stomach. The door was open. Without bothering to knock, she pushed the door to see Gia face down on the bed.

"Gia? Oh, Gia!"

At the sound of Valerie's voice, Gia lifted her head. She had fresh blood coming from a cut on her lip and a significant bump on the side of her forehead. Tears poured down her face. She shook her head to Valerie. Caleb was not there.

Valerie collapsed on the floor as Griff walked in and lifted the girl from the bed. He held her tight, brushed her hair aside to examine her head wound and kissed her mouth.

"They took him and just left. They must have planted a bug in the house. They knew where we were. I'm so sorry. I tried to stop them," Gia cried to Griff.

Griff rocked his fiancée and reassured her.

Valerie watched the two in disbelief. She had been so close to him. Caleb was in this room just minutes before she arrived. She was numb. Scott stood next to her in the doorway, his eyes heavy with defeat. He moved across the room to a sitting chair, picked up Caleb's security blanket he carried everywhere, and held the fabric to his chest. When he turned to her, the sadness in his eyes broke Valerie's heart.

Lights in the room sprang to life, music could be heard down toward the island, and the pumps moved the water in the stream. Valerie stood up, confused. A loud rumbling came from overhead.

"Planes," Major said, entering the room. He stopped and looked at the two on the bed.

The sprinkler heads popped down from the ceiling and sprayed water all over the room and everyone in it.

"No," Major whispered. He looked at Scott just as the electricity exploded into the room.

"Valerie, stop," Jack yelled over the volume of the surge.

"It's not me!" As the words left her mouth, Scott was hit by the electricity, then Griff, then Gia who was still in his embrace.

Valerie screamed as Scott fought the pain. She reached out to him, trying to pull the energy away, but the current carried on through her and continued the path to the couple on the bed. She tried to control the power, but could not. She wrapped her arms around Scott and held him as tight as she could. What felt like an eternity was over in fifteen seconds.

The current, sprinklers, and all power stopped at once. Still screaming, she lowered Scott's weight to the ground. Major fell to his knees at the sight of his dear friend embracing the young woman on the bed. They heard more screams coming from outside the open door behind him. Jack held Hyka out on the balcony as she stared at the destruction.

"Phase Two," Hyka said to no one in particular.

Major had seen this event in his dream. He had known they were going to lose Griff, Gia, and Scott. She should have been able to stop it. Her pain turned to anger. Valerie kissed her deceased husband on his forehead, letting tears fall onto his lifeless face before standing. She did not dare look at the bed, at her friends. She moved past Major, who was sitting on his knees. She walked out the door to the balcony.

"There are survivors. Like us. We need to bring everyone together, as many as we can find. Jarrett has taken everything from us. I'm going to make him pay." She clenched her teeth hard, fighting the tears, but could not stop them.

Just as her knees buckled, Jack scooped her up like a child and carried her to the next room. He kicked the door in with little effort. The room was covered in water but was vacant. He stood her on her feet, opened the closet, and handed her a dry robe.

"Change your clothes." He did not ask her, and she did not argue.

She went through the motions, turning on the light without touching it and closing the bathroom door. As she took her clothes off, she realized they had been burned and left little covered. Her shoes had even melted. She removed what was left of her garments and covered herself with the soft hotel robe. The thick cover reminded her of the one hanging outside of her shower at home. One Scott had bought for her. Her mind was a battlefield of wanting to tell him how sad she was and then remembering why she was so sad. A cycle on a loop making the pain worse with each iteration. Everything reminded her of his body in the next room. But his soul was gone. She pulled open the door to receive her next set of directions, too disoriented to think of what to do on her own.

Jack had flipped over the mattress of the bed, offering a dry place to lie down. He had also pulled out the sofa bed and had taken his boots off, lain down, and closed his eyes. She knew he was not sleeping. None of them would sleep.

Valerie opened the mini refrigerator and without glancing at the labels, grabbed three small plastic bottles. One by one, she drank. Grief dulled her senses, and she was unable to taste the alcohol. She tossed the empty bottles into the trash can and crawled onto the mattress. She lay down facing the wall and stared, waiting for the liquid to take effect. The hole in her heart felt more significant than its host. She was empty. A shell of her person. She did not want to talk or even breathe. Despair shook her soul and with her tears came a scream so loud she threw up. She pulled a wet pillow into her and squeezed the bundle close to her body. She buried her face until it hurt, trying to stifle the emotional pain. Every time she would open her eyes something would trigger a memory. A small desk lamp reminded her of Caleb's bedroom and how Scott would turn the little light on and hold Caleb during thunderstorms when he was scared. Scott was everywhere. Everything brought his memory back to her mind, ripping her apart over and over again. For hours she lay like this, rocking back and forth, cycling through various intensities of sobs until fatigue finally won and she fell into a dreamless sleep.

In the middle of the night, the phone rang loudly, and a small red light blinded her in the pitch black. Her head pounded. She was dehydrated and confused, groping in the dark for the receiver.

"Hello?" she answered, groggy and unsure of where she was.

"Ms. Burton, I'm calling to convey my deepest condolences for your loss," a man's voice said on the other end.

The death of her husband the day before seemed like a horrible dream, but the slimy voice with his audible smile brought back the reality of the situation.

"Thank you, Dr. Jarrett," Valerie answered.

No one had come or gone from their party, yet Lucas knew where she was and the fate of her spouse. She had to be careful of what she said and did. He was watching her somehow, but she needed to gain the upper hand despite being underneath his watchful eye.

"It is my pleasure to inform you: young Caleb is safe and having a great time with Grandpa Burton. Would you like to talk to him?"

The mere suggestion choked her.

"Say hi to Mommy, Caleb."

"Hi, Mommy!" Caleb's sweet voice was oblivious to the situation and loss of his father.

"Hi, Sweetie-Petey." Valerie could not help but cry from heartbreak and relief.

Lucas had won this battle. He had made it to Caleb before her. He could now dangle the child on a string to get Valerie to cooperate. Lucas needed her for his plan and knew she would do anything to make sure her son was safe.

"I love you so very much, Baby. You be a good boy for Grandpa and Uncle Kev."

"Okay. I love you too, Mommy."

"Now, Ms. Burton, I would send a vehicle to you, but I no longer have drivers, and my conductors cannot operate a vehicle on their own. This would require me to make a personal appearance. Since you have yet to cooperate, we are behind schedule, and I must tend to matters here in the facility. So, neighbor, why don't you take a trip down the street and see your family? They miss you."

Valerie could hear the amusement in his voice while she fought to keep her frustration and tears silent. She had to pull herself together and buy some time to develop a plan.

"Have the decency to let me bury my husband. You can expect us this evening." She did not wait for a response before ending the call. Hearing her son's voice left no question in her mind of where she was going next. She had to look forward, or risk losing herself in the trauma of the previous day. She just wanted the entire world to stop and mourn, but her son could not wait. Scott's end was not the end of the fight. His death was just the beginning. Valerie lay back down on the bed and closed her eyes. She cried until she fell back to sleep.

HYKA PUSHED THE DOOR OPEN, slamming the heavy wood against the wall. Jack jumped to his feet from the sofa bed, but Valerie did not move. Lucas was no longer hunting her. He could not take anything else from her.

"You up?" Hyka asked Jack who was caught off guard

He could not articulate his anger at being woken up. Instead, he huffed trying to find the words.

"Everyone is waiting at the French place downstairs."

Valerie got up from the bed and walked past Hyka out the door to the balcony. There were about fifty college-aged kids assembled at the restaurant with a few smaller children. One girl held a tiny baby.

"We gathered everyone in the hotel. The power surge took their energy, so they all regressed in age like we did. There are about seven other casualties, not including ours. We collected them in one area to say some nice words." Hyka tried to be as sensitive to the facts as her vocabulary would allow.

"Where is Scott?"

"They are still in the room. We laid him on the other bed. We knew you wouldn't want us to move him without you knowing."

Valerie nodded and was satisfied with the answer. She remembered how Hyka had once scared her, but now she found her to be something steady in her life that she could count on.

"Dad wants to give Scott and Griff military honors. Not one hundred percent protocol, but the gesture would mean a lot to him. Also, there is a backhoe out in the far south parking lot. If you could help us out, that would save us hours of digging."

Hyka was the best person to handle these details, and Valerie was thankful someone had taken the lead. She gave an approving nod to Hyka to proceed with all plans for the deceased.

Despite sleeping, she still did not feel like herself. She had horrible vertigo and was weak. She looked again at the group gathered at the restaurant, wondering how she was going to rally these people to action so soon after the tragic events of the night before. Many of them were hurting from loss. Valerie turned to address her friends who were exchanging whispers of their own. She lost her balance and fell backward, hitting her back on the balcony before falling to the floor. Jack caught her head and guided her to the ground as her eyes rolled back.

Valerie woke up in the room Jack had taken her to the night before. She had been stripped of her robe, but dry blankets were pulled up to her chin, and she had an IV hung next to the bed.

"You feeling alright? You got dehydrated and passed out. I am disappointed those three little shooters would knock a DiaZem on her ass," Hyka joked, trying to keep the mood light.

"I don't think it was the alcohol. I threw up before I even got a buzz. Stress. My body is telling me to stop, but I can't. I don't have the luxury even to mourn the loss of my husband," Valerie said, rolling over to hide her tears. Just when she needed to lead them to vengeance and victory, she could not even keep her eyes open. She was broken.

"You need to rest. There is no rush," Jack spoke up from the other side of the room.

"If you help me outside, I can help with digging. Not physically, but I could keep the backhoe going. I need some air. This place is so humid." Valerie needed to occupy her mind. Sitting unstimulated in a room, letting her thoughts wander back to Scott and the fact that he was gone was torture. She also needed to talk to Jack outside, and away from any surveillance the CDC might have access to. There might not be anywhere safe, but being around heavy machinery could offer a better environment for secrecy.

"No," Jack said with paternal authority. "You've been out for two hours, and frankly you look horrible. There are a few volunteers from the group to help outside. No one needs to see you like this. Just rest."

Anger welled up in Valerie's throat. She understood what he meant, but denying her human emotion in front of the masses was infuriating. She felt her current state to be justified.

"I am going outside. Someone will drive the digger machine, and we all need to talk. Get my clothes from the truck and bring me something to eat. I am starving." Valerie felt a tinge of guilt for being so demanding, but she did not want to divulge too many of her suspicions. She had told Lucas they would be there by the evening, but at the rate things were going, they would not be there on time.

Outside, the air was refreshing compared to the dank, humid atmosphere of the resort. The sky was the same overcast as the day before, but evidence of a recent rain still covered the ground. Valerie walked to the area where the backhoe was and where they would say goodbye to their loved ones. Five young men were already working in the area, three digging and two breaking down furniture to fashion wooden crosses to mark each plot. They rotated these jobs before noticing her approach.

The backhoe's engine turned over with ease but startled the workers out of their focused tasks. Jack gave a thumbs-up to one of the workers who took up a position in the driver's seat of the vehicle and wasted no time getting started.

"Dr. Jarrett called last night. He has Caleb and is expecting us to arrive this evening. He knew where I was and what had happened to Scott. I imagine he tapped into the hotel surveillance. We should assume he can see and hear everything, regardless of where we are." Valerie stopped and took a seat on a parking curb close enough to the running machine that her three companions had to strain to hear her. "The only way to face this is head-on. We have to go in, but I have no idea how to fight once we get there."

Major exhaled hard and rubbed his brow. "I'm not going with you. Someone needs to stay back and gather reinforcements. If you can't fix things from inside someone should figure out a different angle. Valerie, I do not doubt your ability to see this through, but you might find yourself in need of pocket aces."

Jack nodded in agreement which helped Valerie. She did not have the energy to argue. She understood Major was looking out for her.

"I'm going in," Hyka said, in case anyone wondered where she stood on the matter.

Valerie smiled and nodded.

"I'm coming," Jack said next. "I'll meet up with your old man and brother and try to pull others to our cause. Once they know the fate of everyone they left behind, hosting a revolt from the inside should be easier. Then all you have to do, Val, is play the game."

"How long do you think all this will take?" Valerie asked, motioning to the men making progress on the makeshift cemetery.

"As long as you're well enough, a couple of hours. Once we get two or three done on this side, we can move down the way and dig more. Give people room to pay their respects while we're still working. We'll do Scott, Griff, and Gia's last before we leave, but that still will put us into the evening. We should wait until morning to move," Jack suggested, unable to mask his concern for her physical state.

Valerie shrugged. "Jarrett knows where to find me if I'm late. What else could they do?"

The sky above them cracked with lightning, releasing a downpour of rain.

CHAPTER FIFTEEN

They provided Valerie a chair next to the grave intended for her husband. She sat in silence in a black dress that Hyka had procured from one of the resort's stores. She had also brought Valerie a pair of sunglasses, though the clouds overhead were still thick bringing daylight to an early end. The wind blew a cold breeze through her cotton dress. She shivered and folded her arms. Words from the other services that began before Scott's carried on the wind, but she was too exhausted to do more than stare into the hole.

News of her status spread amongst the hotel's survivors. Some stared at her, others were afraid. No one had explained to them their genetic change and what that meant. They were trying to keep themselves together like she was. She still did not know what to say to them when the opportunity came. Valerie had little solace for herself, much less any to delve out to strangers. They had not even developed a plan moving forward from the funerals.

One by one, the deceased were carried to the burial area. Others walked behind them holding candles and crying. A young couple followed a tiny silhouette hidden under a sheet. They held on to each other; heads hung while they walked. Valerie choked, imagining Caleb under the small covering. She closed her eyes to push the thought from her mind. Inhale, exhale. When she opened them again, three more bodies were carried to the area; American flags covered two of them. Once they reached their prospective plots, Major made his way to a central location. As the other services ended, those who had finished their respects gathered around. The same five-man detail began to fill the graves as the mourners dispersed to the final ceremony.

"I thought retirement meant I didn't have to do these anymore." The corner of Major's mouth frowned, and his chin quivered ever so slightly. He, too, took a deep breath and continued, "Edward Francis Griffin was my best friend. We started our careers in the same infantry unit a couple of decades ago at Fort Bragg, North Carolina. He's seen me at my best and my worst and stuck around. He helped me raise my daughter and was more like a brother to me than a friend. This stubborn guy walked one hundred miles without complaint. He came all this way to be with the woman he loved. Gia Murphy moved to Denver at Mike's request to keep you and Caleb safe. Griff had a plan to move, too, after he proposed to her." Major dug into his pocket and produced a ring. "He was bringing this to Gia. Yes, he wanted to be sure we were safe, but love kept him going. And no one deserved love more than these two."

Valerie got another chill, but not from the wind. From guilt. She felt selfish and ashamed. She had made the journey about her reunion with her family and had never considered that her companions had missions which were just as important. Major continued to talk about his friend and how Gia's bright and contagious smile could light up a room. Valerie could not hold herself together. She shook with silent sobs remembering her friend who had fought for her son until the end. Who was far more loyal than she would have ever hoped. Valerie could never repay her, or even thank her.

Jack took Major's place in the center and retrieved a piece of paper from his pocket. His hands shook as he read from it, "Scott Michael Russell served in the U.S. Army from 2001 until about two years ago as an indirect fire infantryman. He completed four tours of duty, including Iraq and Afghanistan. He is survived by his wife, Mrs. Valerie Russell, and their son. I met Scott on an occasion like this. He was a nice guy who loved his family. Those closest to him will miss him dearly." Jack looked at Valerie.

She nodded with her approval. Jack then nodded to Hyka who was accompanied by two others. Valerie stood and watched the ceremony, trying to forget why she was there. Hyka and Jack took their place at the foot of the fallen soldiers, and the strangers stood at the head. In unison, all four picked up their designated flag and began folding them. Hyka presented the folded flag that had covered Griffin to her father. Jack approached Valerie with the folded flag of her husband. She had attended military funerals in the past but never imagined she would be on the receiving end of the ceremony. She thanked Jack.

He leaned in, kissed her cheek and said, "We'll get him. What he did will not go unanswered." He hugged her and returned to the front of the crowd.

"Let us bow our heads," Jack announced. He was quiet for a few moments before beginning his prayer. "Over the course of a week, we have come to question everything we know as humans. So, if there is a God orchestrating all this, I pray you take our brothers home to heaven. I also pray their family and friends find peace with their loss. Amen."

Storm sirens broke the moment of silence, though the skies were as still as they could be. The men who were filling the graves with dirt stopped and put down their shovels to take cover inside the resort. Hyka wrapped her arm under Valerie's to help her walk back inside.

They found the power restored to the hotel. A fountain sprayed water in a small pond in the lobby, soft music played overhead, and all TV monitors displayed the same message: "Please stand by for an important message from your district DiaZem."

"Seriously?" Hyka said.

As they made their way to the French restaurant, people watched and whispered as Valerie passed. They knew she was a DiaZem, but soon they would all find out who was in charge at the facility. Valerie had her suspicions but prayed she was wrong.

After fifteen minutes, the sirens outside fell silent, and the hotel's occupants waited in the restaurant area for the pending announcement. Valerie dreaded hearing anything from the CDC, but she was anxious to see who the other DiaZem was. The lights dimmed, and the screen began to countdown:

3 . . . 2 . . . 1. . .

"Greetings. My name is Dr. Lucas Jarrett, and I am the former director of the Centers for Disease Control and Prevention and former administrator for the Agency for Toxic Substances and Disease Registry. I say former because these organizations no longer exist. I have been reassigned as the Head of Research in the Rocky Mountain Region. I am also the region's DiaZem. I am addressing all of you this evening to do some much-needed explaining.

"Five days ago, a natural event occurred, waking a gene in one-quarter of the world's population. This gene was otherwise dormant in humans over the past few thousand years." As he spoke, graphics filled the screen illustrating his explanation. "Characteristics of this gene revolve around conducting, storing, and releasing electricity. Every human being carries a small amount of electricity in their body to maintain their heartbeat, enable their metabolism, and send information from the nerves to the brain. Your abilities are not so limited. Although your new gift might seem quite the hindrance, causing you to live without power, society is all about to change for the better.

"As you are collecting energy, a DiaZem such as myself can draw stored energy from you and use your power to do a multitude of things. I am responsible for your ability to watch this message. I have returned power to the city of Denver and surrounding areas—although, due to downed planes taking out key infrastructure, conventional means of power are currently impossible in some places. I apologize for having withheld this energy, but as one DiaZem, I am limited in my capabilities. However, there are other DiaZem who cannot control their abilities at all and are a danger to you. I understand last night many people lost their lives in such an incident. Men, women, and children who were not protected by the gene were taken from you, and I want to offer my deepest condolences."

Lucas bowed his head in a convincing gesture of empathy, but his show of remorse did not fool Valerie. She knew he was behind the attack. She scoffed and stood up to leave, but one look at Jack's face told her something was wrong. He stood behind her with his hand over his mouth, stroking his blonde beard.

"We have built a community for the survivors of this tragedy. We converted the Denver International Airport into a refuge city capable of supporting 2 million people. We have clean running water, medical capabilities, food and, of course, electricity."

"There are a handful of these mega-cities in the world. Two DiaZem govern each city: a male and a female." Lucas' slimy smile returned. "Ms. Valerie Burton has refused my many invitations to join me here at our facility for proper training on her abilities. This has been at the cost of so many lives, including her husband's. She may try to blame us here at the facility; either way, she is dangerous and needs to be taken into custody and brought to me as soon as possible."

Lucas continued to talk, but his voice was drowned out by the group at the restaurant. Major moved to Valerie and picked her up without the courtesy of a warning. He took her up the stairs and to her room with a slur of curses under his breath. Lucas continued his announcements on the television mounted on the wall across from her bed.

"I knew that SOB was going to pin those deaths on you from the second his greasy face showed up on the screen. He sent a lynch mob for you." Jack paced back and forth as Major sat Valerie in the chair. Jack stopped and looked at her. "Val, are you alright? You look green."

She was in shock. Valerie could not think or speak. Her hands were shaking, and she felt sick.

"Can," she said. "Trashcan."

Major grabbed the closest wastebasket to him and threw the bin in front of her just in time. The contents of her stomach emptied into the container. Hyka combed the hair out of Valerie's face and held a handful behind her head.

"Dad, can you get a cold washcloth? Jack, grab a bottle of water from the mini-fridge. They're free. I asked," Hyka joked. "Let me know when you're good to move; I'll help you to the bed. Maybe you can use some of your voodoo magic and fix your sick."

Major cleared his throat and shook his head, indicating Hyka's last comment might have been inappropriate. Valerie swished around the water Jack had given her, spit into the can, and gave Hyka the thumbs-up to move.

"Search and rescue parties cannot proceed until Ms. Burton is brought back to the facility. Until she arrives, provisions are limited to the immediate area around the airport. When she is delivered, power will be restored to the entire region, a five-hundred-mile radius. Let me stress again, she is not to be harmed, and her crimes will be handled by the standing government here at the facility.

"We must come together in this time of great loss. We must rebuild what was destroyed and pick up the pieces. We must protect all we have left: each other. Looking or going back is not an option anymore. We must move forward and evolve to our new way of life. Please join me in rebuilding this great region. Our gates are open to all."

The screen went blank, and the lights dimmed to nothing. Valerie powered a small light in the bathroom.

"Why? What more does he want from me? What does he get if everyone blames me?" Valerie yelled in frustration, embarrassed at her physical state.

"You can't raise a rebellion without followers. He'll do what he can to ruin your credibility so no one will fight for you," Hyka said while setting up an IV in the dark.

"I don't think those are helping much. You're wasting supplies on me. I'm fine. This is just stress." Valerie tried to rationalize her condition more for herself than the others. Though they did not say it, she could tell they were growing more concerned about her health.

"Valerie, since this started no one has even twisted their ankle or coughed once. Aside from Major's multiple gunshot wounds, we walked a hundred miles without training or preparation. I don't think this is a stress reaction. I think something is wrong. We need to get you help, but unless you can power a vehicle long enough to get to the airport, we are going to have to carry you for ten miles." Jack had stopped pacing and sat in the chair across from the bed. He jumped back to his feet when someone knocked on the door.

Major opened the door to a young, dark woman and her tiny baby.

"May I speak to the deity?" she asked, meek and reverent.

"Mrs. Russell is tired and is not seeing anyone," he answered in a stern, authoritative voice.

"Let them in, Major. Fear breeds hate. Let them ask their questions or point their fingers. Whatever they need to do to heal." Valerie was growing weak, but she wanted the people to know the truth rather than see her hiding away like a criminal.

The woman entered the room holding her sleeping baby. She walked to the bedside, kneeled, and bowed her head. "Holy Being, I hope you understand my language. I have come from Ghana with my child to America for a better life. I walked here from the airport and stayed hidden to keep my daughter safe for fear they would take her from me like they did to other mothers. I know your heart is good and you did not hurt anyone. Please accept my deepest sorrow for your loss."

"Your English is excellent. What is your name and your daughter's? She is beautiful." Valerie smiled and welcomed her kindness.

"I am Alma, and this is my daughter, Fatima. And my language is Twi. You speak, and I understand. I speak, and you understand. We are connected." Alma held a hand to Valerie's heart. She had a sweet, genuine smile. She bowed again, stood, and left the room.

"Okay, no more visitors. Rest," Major said pointing a finger at Valerie, commanding her.

Valerie nodded in agreement, rolled over, and fell asleep for a short while. When she woke, Jack was still sleeping in the chair. Major and Hyka were gone. Valerie pulled back the blanket as slow and quiet as she could, keeping an eye on Jack, making sure not to wake him. She walked out of the room onto the balcony. The night was still and dark. The only light was given off by the half-moon which broke through the cloudy night sky and shone through the skylight over the central atrium. Across the building on the opposite balcony was a young man leaning against the rail with something in his hand. He was looking at her, expressionless. She smiled and walked down the hall to find more privacy.

In a stairwell, Valerie powered the red emergency lights to guide her way. Unsure of where she wanted to go, she decided the roof was as safe a place as any to clear her mind and mull over her next steps. She reached the top of the stairs and struggled with the heavy door. After much exertion, she opened the roof access wide enough to squeeze through. The night air was fresh and welcoming. She walked to the east side of the roof, where she could see the airport bright on the otherwise black horizon. Seeing the circus topped structure every day for the past year, she never thought the buildings were more than they appeared. She was thankful Caleb was with her father and not alone, but she was so anxious to see him.

Despite the breeze, she found herself sweating again, and her hands shook. The journey up the stairs had caught up with her. She sat down to catch her breath. The door to the stairwell opened. A young man walked toward her, and she greeted him with a smile.

"You look unwell," said the young man she had seen on the balcony. His smile faded and his tone was less than concerned.

"I am fine. This week has been stressful for all of us," Valerie answered as she pushed herself up to allow for a more formal posture.

"Does anyone know you are out here? May I help you return to your room?" he asked.

She did, in fact, need help, but the order of his questions threw up a red flag. No one knew she was there. He had been watching her room from the balcony and followed her out to the roof. She kicked herself for being so careless. The CDC was no longer her only threat. Lucas had turned the people against her.

Valerie tried to stand on her own strength but faltered. The young man bent down and appeared to be trying to help. She wanted to push him away, but he grabbed her wrist and yanked her toward him, burying a blade between her ribs on her left side. He removed the knife and pulled his arm back to strike again. Valerie knew he meant to kill her. She pulled his energy. All of it. Even the tiny bit keeping his heart beating. His grip released and the arm holding the blade fell away from her. She too collapsed on the asphalt roof.

Valerie lacked the strength to move herself back down the stairs to find help. She tried to scream but realized her left lung had deflated from the injury and she could not take a deep enough breath. She tore her shirt open to fit her right hand over the wound and applied pressure. To delay the inevitable shock, she tried to slow her breathing and control her heart rate. She needed to signal to Jack where she was, somehow. Her eyes searched her surroundings for anything that could aid her in getting back to her room. On the corner, by the door she had used to access the roof, was a large speaker. Valerie tapped into the wiring of the intercom system and traced the power back to her room where Jack was still sleeping. She prayed a whisper would wake him. There were no other options.

"Jack. Help me," she said as loud as she could, which was still a low and raspy murmur. "The roof. Take the stairwell to the roof. Help me, please." Valerie's vision was fading, and she knew her chest was filling with blood.

She was gasping for air when the door flew open. Her three friends jumped into action. She pulled their energy in an attempt to heal her wounds as she had done with Major, but nothing worked. Hyka taped a plastic bag over her injury.

"I'm going to stab you with this needle to release the air trapped in your chest cavity. Your lung should then be able to expand." Hyka pulled out a large needle and felt for space on Valerie's chest below her collarbone and right above her heart. Hyka pushed into the space between bones to ensure she had the right spot. Valerie did not have the energy to fight or protest as Hyka stabbed her deep in between her ribs. She retracted the needle, leaving a plastic catheter in place. The catheter hissed, releasing the trapped air which had collapsed Valerie's lung. She took a desperate breath and both of her lungs filled with air.

"Valerie, look at me. Are you able to focus your energy?" Hyka spoke three inches from Valerie's face to help her concentration.

"I need water. I want to sleep." Valerie's consciousness was fading. She caught glimpses of the stairwell, the balcony, and her room. She heard the phone ring. She could not make out the words but knew Major was giving a few choice and angry words to whoever was on the other end.

When she could open her eyes again, she heard another man's

voice. Not Jack or Major, but he was speaking to them. Her vision was blurry, but she knew the voice, warm, comforting, and familiar.

"Scott?" She knew it was not her husband. She had left him in the cold ground, uncovered. Valerie tried to sit up. Someone needed to fill her husband's grave. Lucas had interrupted the ceremony, and she had left him there.

"Lay back, Valerie," the voice demanded. He sounded angry, almost frustrated. "Tie her down."

Major erupted at the command, and there was loud arguing between the warm, familiar voice and Major.

"The minute you have M.D. behind your name is the moment you can question my judgment, sir."

Valerie stirred again, coming closer and closer to consciousness. She winced at a sharp pinch on her right arm and soon felt the IV fluid in her veins. Moments later, she was asleep again.

Her next flash of awareness came in some vehicle. The ride was smoother than a car, and from the sensation in her stomach, she guessed they were moving fast. She tried to roll to her side to vomit, but they had tied her to whatever contraption she was on.

"Hyk—"

A plastic bag appeared at the side of her mouth and Hyka did her best to hold steady to not make a mess.

"Water," Valerie requested when she finished heaving.

"No water. We have to get you into surgery." The warm, familiar voice was back but still sounded angry. She tried to focus on the tone and pin down how she knew him. There was little light in the vehicle to see his face, but she wanted to reach for him.

"Scott?" she questioned again, unable to pin down her affection to the voice.

"Valerie, I'm Dr. August Wilkes. We met a week ago when the incident happened, and I let you go. I shouldn't have. You've caused so much destruction."

Valerie cried from frustration, too tired to correct him or fight to maintain her honor.

They rode in silence for the rest of the short trip. When the vehicle stopped, doors slid open to allow her to be unloaded and wheeled into a nearby elevator. She had been on a train. The movement made her sick again, this time with no one to help her. She turned the best she could to reach her head over the edge.

“Stop moving so much. The catheter will come out of your chest again,” August instructed her.

“Hyka? Jack?” Valerie was terrified. They had left her alone with a man she wanted to trust, but could not, in a place she had fought so hard to avoid. She was out of control.

“Your friends were taken to In-Processing. If they play nice, they’ll be back to see you after surgery.” August seemed annoyed at her questions. He treated her with such disdain and did not once look at her when he spoke.

He walked with her as she was wheeled on a gurney down a hallway to another elevator, taking them down even further. She tried to memorize the way, but her head was spinning. She did not dare close her eyes again for fear she would be sick. So, she watched him. She could feel the warmth radiating from his body, hear his heartbeat, and sense the way his body moved. All primal sensations.

“Are you a DiaZem?” she asked. She could feel the flutter of his heartbeat and the clench in his jaw.

He had rescued her because he had the ability to power the train, and was an emergency doctor. The situation called for his expertise, not Lucas’.

“You can heal me.”

He looked ahead, lowering his brow at her statement.

“I’ll do what I can to patch you up, then I’m off to San Francisco. You and Luke are free to rule here. He has a background in internal medicine and can manage your recovery.” August’s tone was mocking. He almost spit when he made mention of them together.

The thought of August leaving her hurt. She wanted him to stay and help her, and to stop treating her with such disgust. Valerie knew her feelings were nothing more than the polar attraction of their nature. Knowing she would foster the same feelings for Lucas made her skin crawl. She cried.

They exited the elevator and went down a stark white hallway. Every turn looked like the room her father and brother were in during the video conference with Lucas. They stopped outside a set of swinging double doors.

"I'm going to scrub in. I'll see you inside." August looked into her eyes.

He stood there for a few moments, and she felt she would die if he stopped looking at her even for the few seconds required to see her in the next room. His expression hardened, and he looked away. He exhaled and pushed through a door just to the left of the double doors she was being pushed through.

Surgical lights blinded her, and she became more anxious as they untied her restraints. People in surgical gowns with masks over their mouths removed a blanket used in transport and directed her to hug her arms over her chest while they moved her onto the operating table. It was then she realized she was naked. No one else seemed to notice as they all continued with their assigned tasks. Her arms were pulled straight out from her sides and strapped down to the bed. A young Asian woman sat next to her head and placed an oxygen mask over Valerie's mouth and nose.

"Take deep breaths and count backward from ten," the woman said.

Valerie took the breaths and could feel the narcotics taking effect. She could also feel when August entered the room.

"STOP!"

His command was the last thing she heard before drifting off to sleep.

She woke up, free from restraints and in a hospital bed. A once connected IV pump stood on one side of the bed, and her vitals were displayed on a monitor on the opposite side, all reading standard for a healthy person. Valerie looked around for anyone to explain what had happened or where she was. A beep came from an overhead speaker.

"Stay calm, Ms. Burton. Dr. Wilkes will be in to see you in a moment," a woman's voice said from the speaker.

As promised, there was a soft tapping before the door opened. To her relief, August walked in.

"We did not do the surgery." August was still fighting not to make eye contact with her. "Luckily, once you could rest, your wounds repaired themselves. But, umm." He rubbed his brow with two of his fingers, the other two clenched a small piece of paper. He reached for her hand and pushed the writing into her palm, his warm hands lingering.

"I hope you feel better soon." August looked her in the eyes, and she could feel his heart breaking with hers.

She shook her head in a feeble protest, but he had already stood and turned to the door. The sound of the door closing broke her. She began to cry, and her loneliness became palpable. She covered her head with the blanket, leaving enough light to read what was on the paper.

"You're pregnant."

CHAPTER SIXTEEN

The raw, empty hole of her husband's passing ripped itself open and threatened to swallow her again. She felt stupid for not having put the pieces together herself. All the signs were there. She had brushed off her morning sickness and fainting as anxiety over her newly-awakened gene. Scott would never know their child was growing inside of her. Their son was only two years old. What memory he could hold of his father, she would have to fortify with stories of how much he loved them. Scott had lived through two wars, but her love for him was what led to his early demise. Lucas Jarrett wanted nothing more than to rid the world of his competition, but Valerie would hold on to her husband's memory until her dying breath. For the man she loved, continuing their bond was the least she could do.

She resented her title, her genetics, and her involuntary attraction to the doctor. She hated herself for what had happened. She hated being drawn to another man while mourning the loss of her lover. In her delirium, she had even thought August was Scott in the ambulance. The way his voice filled her heart with warmth, the familiarity of his touch. How just his presence had revitalized her. She wished her husband had returned somehow from the clutches of death to be with her. Fight with her.

But Valerie was now a widow. A single mother of not one, but soon-to-be two children. She could not protect the one she had, and she struggled to see a happy future for the one she carried. Being so hopeless, if just for a second, she hoped the child would not grow. Her selfishness turned into shame, and she wished to fall asleep and never wake up. Scott had been her strength, and he was gone. Her will was gone.

She held her breath to stop the sobs from being audible. She could feel the pressure build in her head. Then someone knocked at the door. Her heart fluttered. Maybe August had come back. The thought brought back her shame and anger until the door opened, and Hyka peeked in before opening the door the rest of the way. She wore all white. Her pants, long-sleeved shirt, and tennis shoes were bright white, a sharp contrast to her tan skin and black hair. Valerie had never seen her wear so many clothes. Behind Hyka, at thigh height, a boy peeked into the room, just as Hyka did before her entry.

Valerie released the breath she held and the tears she had fought to conceal. She tried to smile as she reached her arms out to her son, but her face just twisted with a mix of emotion. The boy pushed past Hyka. Valerie's father and brother filed into the room after him.

She wrapped her arms around her son. She knew she would never let him go. Caleb would never leave her side again. She would protect him and keep him safe as long as she had air in her lungs and her heart continued to beat. Valerie rocked him. He let her, nestling his face into her neck as she kissed his head.

Mike Burton crossed the room and sat at the end of her bed.

"I didn't do what he said I did. He lied." Valerie's voice broke, and tears streamed down her face into Caleb's hair.

The boy did not seem to notice nor care. Mike nodded to his daughter in understanding, but Kevin stayed tight-lipped next to Hyka. Valerie could not look at them without breaking down again.

"Where is he?" Valerie asked moving herself to the edge of the bed still holding the boy. "This is going to end now."

Hyka clicked her tongue and jerked her head to a glass ball on the ceiling. A camera.

"I don't care. I am not going to let him take anything else from me." The rage balling up inside of her was a sharp contrast to the tenderness of her son's embrace. She wanted to scream, break everything within reach. But instead, she cried and kissed Caleb's head.

"Are you sad?" he questioned. Caleb lifted his head to face hers. He used his finger to trace down the tear streaks on her face. "Don't have a sad face. Have a happy face."

Caleb smiled as big as he could, and Valerie tried to mimic his expression.

"It's okay, Sweetie-Petey. I just—I missed you so very, very much. Did you have fun with Grandpa?"

"Uh-huh, and Uncle Kev! We played Pac-Man."

Valerie smiled, cupped the boy's face, and pulled him in for a kiss. She hugged him again and through tears mouthed the words "thank you" to Mike and Kevin. Hyka cleared her throat to get the room's attention.

"Duke needs us to take you to In-Processing so they can issue you a badge." Hyka held up a card attached to a lanyard around her neck. "This is how we get around this place, and how they track where we are." Hyka released the card, the badge snapped back into its reel.

Even her son had one. She held the card up to examine it. It was white with a blue border and had his cute little face in the middle. At the bottom: Caleb Burton, Level 10 Access, Minor.

"Duke, what? And why, for the love of everything, do they refuse to use my name? I haven't been Valerie Burton for over a decade. What do these do? What are the colors? Levels?" Valerie held up the card to her father.

"We're all here now. Max, Duke. Everyone but Major. The badges come in levels. Level ten means he needs an escort everywhere since he's just a little tyke. I have a level seven. I think because we're still considered an inside threat. Everyone else in the facility, depending on their profession, ranges from three to five. Level six, I think, is for teenagers who are considered adults but not quite at their peak age. Levels eight and nine are younger kids but older than Pac-Man here. The blue around our badges is the second-highest class so to speak.

Lucas and his henchmen have a green border. I imagine yours will look like theirs," Mike explained.

She knew there was much more, but the little information he offered made her nauseous.

"I have to do all of this now? I just. . ." She glanced at the camera and decided her family would have to wait to hear the news she had just received. "I'm just tired. A man attacked me. Lucas told people I caused the bad thing to happen." She chose her words, not wanting to subject Caleb to too much, too soon. She still had no idea how she would explain where his father was.

Hyka pressed a finger to her ear and rolled her eyes, sighing, "They are bringing a wheelchair for you."

Another knock came at the door. A young man, dressed in all white, pushed a wheelchair into the room. He apologized for interrupting and explained that he would assist Valerie to In-Processing.

"I'll take her." Kevin snatched the chair away from the young man who was far too intimidated by Valerie's brother to argue. "We can manage, thank you."

Valerie helped her son off the bed before swinging her legs over the edge. The small movement brought on another wave of nausea. She reached for a designated blue bag on the side table just in case. Mike and Kevin held her hands and supported her as she transitioned from the bed to the chair, which rolled back away from her. Hyka caught the chair and repositioned the seat under Valerie before she crashed to the ground.

"Seriously?" Hyka looked at the men.

Valerie grabbed Caleb under his arms and set him on her lap.

"Faster! Faster!" he squealed before they were even into the hallway.

Valerie tried to memorize the hallways they went down, but again they were all the same. Not until they reached the elevators did she notice anything distinct from her arrival.

"There are no windows. Where are we? How long have I been here?" Valerie asked while they waited for the elevator to arrive. She was not lying when she said she was tired. If anything, she had downplayed her exhaustion. She could guess the time was either early afternoon or late evening by how much Caleb let her snuggle him, close to his nap time or bedtime.

"We are underground, about six floors. In-Processing is on the first sub-level of the airport. The second level is the subway, which stretches all the way to downtown Denver. This place would be like if Beijing were underground. Every family has the equivalent of a hotel suite to live in. They built a city with the capacity for millions right under our noses," Kevin explained. This was the most he had spoken. Even though he came off as impressed by their arrangements, there was still an underlying bitterness in his words.

"We've been here thirteen hours," Hyka answered the one question Kevin omitted. "It's 11 a.m. We'll go eat after you get your badge."

The elevator opened and let a few people off. They stared at Valerie as they passed.

"Hurry up," Hyka told someone who was lingering too long and stood in the way of the chair.

Kevin caught the door and forced the elevator to stay open. He stepped in first and continued holding. Once everyone was in, he moved his arm and touched his badge to a black box. A small red light turned green, and he pushed the button for Sublevel 1 until the number lit up. The movement of the elevator caught Valerie's stomach off guard, but she was able to maintain its contents.

Soon enough the doors slid open again; they had arrived at the In-Processing floor. Dozens of blue-clad, weapon-bearing young men and women guarded entrances, exits, check stations, and even the bathrooms. What unnerved Valerie most was how suffocated she felt. She knew the people filing through were conductors, but something about the room counteracted their ability to pull energy. Mike, who walked ahead of her, shuddered.

"You know the feeling when your ears pop because of the elevation? Some sort of advanced technology lines the walls to temporarily mute the gene, but not completely. While we don't draw energy, they can still test us," Hyka explained.

Hyka was right. The atmosphere on Sublevel 1 was stifling, but there was also something else. Valerie could feel him watching her, like a small breeze offering relief in a hot furnace. Her ability was, indeed, muted but she could still feel her attraction to him. She searched the faces of the people in white, but he was not there. Hyka continued to push the wheelchair behind Mike as he led them to the first station.

"Ms. Burton, if you could look right here into this lens, we will take your photo for your access badge."

"Be sure it reads 'Valerie Russell.' My name is Russell, not Burton."

"Uh-huh," the young man answered.

She set Caleb on the ground to free her face from obstruction, but she did not let go of his hand, and she did not smile. The photographer took the picture regardless. She scooped Caleb back into her lap and hugged him. As they passed to another station, she noticed the In-Processing staff wore earpieces. She looked behind her at Hyka.

"You have an earpiece, too?"

"Yeah, I'm your personal assistant. Want some coffee?" Hyka asked.

"No, thank you. I'm fine," Valerie laughed.

They reached the second station: *Occupational Assignment.*

"She's the boss," Hyka told the person at the desk. They looked at Valerie with indifference and motioned to the next station. *Medical* was written on the subsequent banner. She could still feel him watching her, but the feeling did not grow as she moved forward. It was not him at the medical station, but an olive-skinned young woman who glared at her when she approached. She wore a white lab coat over her white outfit. Valerie remembered her pregnancy. Her heart pounded when she watched the woman pull out the same wand O'Connell had used on her at the checkpoint.

"Ma'am, you'll need to put the boy down so we can scan you."

Terrified they would find her out, Valerie did not protest but set Caleb down.

"Stand with Grandpa, Little Man." She kissed his forehead and released his hand. She whispered a prayer for the separation to be short.

The woman pointed the wand at her and pushed the button. The center of the rod exploded from the inside, splitting in half. Valerie jumped, but the woman's hateful expression did not change.

"I would appreciate if you didn't attack me, ma'am," she said through her teeth.

"Excuse me? I didn't do anything. I'm just sitting here!"

The woman rolled her eyes and walked through a door behind the desk. Valerie could not hear what was said, but the woman was furious. Kevin leaned down to Valerie's ear.

"They broadcasted the video here last night. Dr. Jarrett told them you murdered their families outside of the facility." Her brother didn't say any more.

She wished he had used a different word, but murder was appropriate for her to feel the weight of the situation. In their eyes, she was a murderer. Valerie's stomach knotted. She then noticed the whispers around her and the angry energy from those nearby.

The woman behind the door stopped ranting, and something changed. She felt the tiny breeze get stronger. He was getting closer. He was coming to whisk her out of the horrible stifling room of hate. Her heart fluttered with hope and regret. She pulled Caleb back to her lap and watched the door. Valerie wanted the feelings to go away, but the closer he came, the more she wanted him there. She needed him there.

The angry woman came back to the desk and motioned for them to proceed to the next station. A fitting area. Hyka pushed the chair to the following table. Valerie reached for the forms to fill out as a small sign instructed.

"Ms. Burton, here are your clothes. The changing room is right through there." Another woman directed her to a booth against the wall. The woman was doing a better job than the woman at the medical station at concealing her animosity.

"Need me to dress you, Barbie?" Hyka asked her.

"No, I should be fine. Caleb, come with Mommy, please." She held his hand and sauntered to the booth. After a couple of steps, she got her bearings and felt confident she was not going to pass out. The pile of clothing was stark white, down to the undergarments that she imagined were far more embellished than what they generally issued. She held up white, lace thong underwear with her thumb and index finger. They had included a matching bra. Caleb played with his reflection in the mirror as Valerie slid out of the hospital gown she woke up in. In a moment of complete nakedness, she knew he was there, just on the other side of the thin changing room door. Her face flushed and her heart raced. She felt like a girl in the locker room. Vulnerable and bashful. She slid the panties on. They fit just right on her lean figure. The bra was made for her. And then he spoke.

"I hope everything fits alright."

His voice wrapped her in heat and took her breath away. She rushed to pull on her white fitted t-shirt and white uniform cargo pants. She debated opening the door and then putting her shoes on, but knew she would forget about her shoes after she saw him.

She bent down and grabbed Caleb's hand. "You ready, honey? Come on; you can sit on Mama's lap again in the chair." She picked him up to help calm her nerves and held him close as she opened the door.

"Lord, you are the most beautiful woman I have ever seen." Lucas Jarrett stood there with his slimy, curled smile and thin trimmed dark beard. He was tall next to the armed guards around him. His tailored suit a contrast to the uniformed occupants of the facility.

Valerie tried to stop his heart like she had the homeless man and her attacker. She cursed the technology that muted her ability. Despite her hatred and anger, she was drawn to him. He was the one watching her. Lucas was the cool breeze. His voice had washed over her and made her want him. She was disgusted with herself.

"This room is supposed to suppress the gene, but I'll be honest, I am having a terrible time keeping my hands off you," Lucas reached to brush a lock of hair from her face.

Valerie slapped him away. She could fight her primal urges with the hatred brewing inside. Her body screamed for him, but she was having a more difficult time keeping herself from physically ripping him apart with her bare hands.

“Luke, she’s had a long day. Now is not a good time,” Mike said as if she were a child and could not speak for herself.

Valerie wanted to spit. Her father and the man who murdered his son-in-law were on a casual first name basis.

“Oh? I thought she would be excited about wedding planning. We are short on time, dear.”

Valerie had endured about as much as she could handle. She lowered Caleb to the ground as calm as she could and pushed him in the direction of her brother. Her vision went red. She went after Lucas Jarrett with all her strength and intended to kill him. The moment her hands reached him, weapons fired on her.

CHAPTER SEVENTEEN

Valerie pulled the heavy blanket to her chin, savoring the comfort. Caleb rustled next to her, and she pulled him into her arms, nestling him against her. She smelled his hair and looked around the dark room. She had no idea where she was but accepted the illusion of safety. Silent tears soaked into her pillow. She did not want to wipe them away for fear she would wipe away the grief she felt for her husband and any semblance of who she used to be.

"Are you alright?" Kevin asked from the chair across the dark room. "I was keeping an eye on Caleb. You've been asleep for a while. Poor buddy was pretty upset and wouldn't leave you. There might be some cereal in the bed somewhere, too."

Valerie kissed her son's head. She was so stupid to put Caleb and everyone else in danger. She held no other regrets about attacking Lucas.

"I'm sorry, Kevin, for everything. He must have been so scared."

"Well, you missed all the real action. Dr. Jarrett got his ass beat by some dude. Whatever technology controlled the room was disabled. The whole place went black. Then all we could see were bolts of lightning shooting through the room. I'm guessing the other guy was another DiaZem. They fought for a while until the barrier was restored and Jarrett's goons shot the guy." Kevin stopped.

Valerie sat straight up in bed with her hand over her mouth. "Is he okay? Where is he?" Her heart pounded for fear of breaking all over again.

He squinted at her and answered, "I'm not sure what they did with him. Do you know him?"

"August," she answered, embarrassed at her reaction. "Doctor August Wilkes. We were together when everything started. Not together, like in the biblical sense. He was the doctor on shift at the ER. We didn't know what was going on then. Have you heard from Madi at all?" She tried to change the subject.

"Yes and no," Kevin sighed. "She's alive. When we first arrived, they were still trying to maintain the lie that we'd all be released. I called to check on her. She said she couldn't handle being apart and couldn't wait for me. She checked out. Said she was going back to New York and she had made a mistake even coming to Colorado."

"I'm sorry, Kevin. I could punch her in the face if you want. How is Dad holding up?"

"So, this is going to sound strange, but he grew his leg back."

"What?"

"The process started when he regressed in age. Once he got here, he told Lucas where you were under certain conditions. Lucas finished the progression. He's as good as new. He seems pretty at home here. He and Lucas have meetings once a day, about you I'm guessing." Kevin slumped back in his chair. "He doesn't tell me much, just reassures me this is the best thing for us right now."

Valerie could feel her face getting hot. She trusted her father, but having him conspire with Lucas was infuriating. Her older brother wore his emotions right on his sleeve. Valerie would need to do a better job at masking her suspicions.

"Bathroom?"

Kevin pointed across the room at a closed door.

She moved as quietly as she could, shut the door behind her, and flipped on the light. There was a marked contrast from the simple room she had seen before. Though it maintained the stark white of the rest of the facility, floors and countertops were marble. The towels hanging on the wall were thick and soft. There was even a large TV mounted behind the sink displaying the time, date, and the weather outside of the facility. There were other announcements as well: menus for the day and mealtimes, a schedule for live updates, and times when phones would be available for use. Just before she turned back to the sink, a picture of her came across the screen.

Please welcome Valerie Burton to the Denver Facility. You will treat her with reverence and respect as your DiaZem. She will assume her seat on the World Council alongside her DiaZem partner, Lucas Jarrett. We ask you to maintain order and peace during her time of transition. All your concerns will be addressed in the coming weeks. Thank you.

"Russell," she said out loud to herself. "Valerie Russell." She pulled her badge off and threw the card and lanyard across the counter.

Her white shirt had a black burn hole on the right side of her back, revealing smooth, unblemished skin. She had healed while she slept. She also realized that the energy emitted from the men fighting might have lent itself to her aid.

Valerie considered the deep-jetted tub situated in the middle of the room. The idea of soaking seemed bizarre and inappropriate, but if she could not relax now, she feared she might never have the opportunity again. Caleb was sleeping with Kevin there watching him. She turned on the faucet and held her hand under the water until she was satisfied with the temperature. She pulled what remained of her shirt over her head and stood again in front of the mirror. Her hands slid over her abdomen, giving no hint of the tiny life within. In the moment she had attacked Lucas, Valerie had not given a thought to its safety or if the shock could harm her child. She had no idea how far along she even was, and if her genetics were strong enough to protect the babe.

"I need you, Scott," she whispered and wrapped her arms around herself. The tears came again, and she removed her remaining clothing and slid into the hot bath. She took a breath and submerged herself. The weightlessness loosened any tension left in her body. The heat of the water helped her focus. She needed to come up with a plan, and fast. To ensure her family's safety in the immediate future, she had to appear agreeable to Lucas' plans for her. She did not know how long or how far she would be forced to comply. She feared she would never get the opportunity to fight if she did not start immediately. A smile spread across her face under the water imagining August blacking Lucas' eye.

Valerie came up for air with an idea. If Lucas could watch her, then she could trace the video feed and do the same, like how she used the speaker to call for help at the resort. If there were cameras everywhere, tracking August would take little effort. She looked at the mounted TV. The screen went dark as she traced the electrical wires to the camera in her bedroom and displayed the feed in front of her. She was comforted by the ability to see her son sleeping, like using a baby monitor. In the same turn, she was sickened, knowing Lucas Jarrett had video access to her room. He and Max were both disgusting. She shuddered and followed the electrical system further, displaying other various locations.

Valerie found the control room of the facility and displayed the view on the screen in front of her. Three blue-uniformed people manned a control panel in front of surveillance screens. A much older man looked like he was in charge. He would point, and the surveillance screens would change at his command. And then there he was, on one of the many screens, in a white room. August was sleeping in the glow of his TV display. Just seeing him made her want to find him, be near him. She traced the video feed deep underground and down miles of tunnels opening into thousands of housing units. She could feel him. She could find him. And she did.

She watched him for a few moments, forgetting why she had tried to find him in the first place. She just knew she needed him to help her. He could not leave her there. Lucas would never let her be free. She would hold the title of DiaZem partner, and Lucas would control her.

Valerie took a quick breath and August's eyes opened as though he had heard her. He looked back at her. Startled, she broke the connection. He must have felt her watching, the same way she had sensed Lucas. She did not think he could see her, but in any case, she pulled the plug from the drain and got out of the tub. Just as she snatched a towel and covered herself, a knock at the door made her jump.

"Here is a set of clean clothes." Kevin opened the door and shoved the clothes through the small opening.

"Thanks," she said, blushing. Thankful at least her brother would respect her privacy, she was angry for never remembering to lock the bathroom door. She took the clothes and closed the door. Valerie was careful to dry off so as not to risk her white outfit being transparent. To her relief, the undergarments were far more appropriate than what Lucas had given her.

She tied her hair back in a band and looked over at the TV to make sure the standard display had returned. 3 a.m.

"Kevin, where's Dad?" she whispered, closing the door behind her.

"He's right outside. Hey, come here," he said, motioning with his arms open to hug her. Valerie let her brother hug her, but the embrace felt forced and awkward. "Val, I am sorry about Scott. I wanted you to know that. We need to be smart about—OUCH!" Valerie pinched his side, and once she had his attention, she moved her eyes in the direction of the camera in the corner, hoping he could see in the darkness. He glanced up, noticed the black ball in the ceiling, and nodded.

"I'm going to go talk to Dad. Care to watch Caleb for a bit? I won't be gone long; I don't want to wake him," Valerie said, studying his face. Her brother had never fussed over her before. Then again, she had never lost her husband before, and Madi was not there to make every situation about her. "Are you okay?"

Kevin shrugged and hugged her one more time. "Be careful."

Valerie opened the door to the hallway where Mike Burton lay asleep. He was in an oversized armchair on one side of the suite's living room area, and Jack McGuire was on the other. She kicked Jack's shoes together, and he jumped at her. Valerie let out a tiny scream and laughed.

"Jesus Christ on the cross, Val. I could have killed you." Jack hugged her instead, and she laughed again.

Jack had been so mean to her when they first met, but now he felt more like a brother to her than Kevin ever had.

He pulled her away, holding her at arm's length to look her over. "Are you alright? They said you healed yourself like you healed Major on the road."

"Yeah, I'm fine." Valerie turned to her dad as he stood from where he had been sleeping in the chair. "Are we stuck here? Can we leave the building at all?"

"Lucas likes being macabre, so your suite is on the thirteenth floor of the airport hotel."

Valerie noted his further familiarity with her enemy but kept the concern to herself.

"We're in the U-shaped building at the end of the terminals." Mike turned and motioned to the wall of windows to his left. "We are on the west side toward the mountains. All the lights are coming from the airport to the north across a small walkway. Lucas' suite is in the east tower, the same floor but separated by the architecture. You are free to walk around as you please within the hotel. Our rooms are on the lower guest floors, but under the circumstances, no one wanted to be far away from you. Luke is power-hungry and impulsive. He's a dangerous person."

"Eric Earl is here. So is Max," Jack added. "Also turns out the guy who treated you at the hotel is a DiaZem. Duke is his personal assistant like Hyka is to you. I was with Duke getting updates when you woke up in the infirmary."

"Well then, we've got a man on the inside," Valerie said, unimpressed by her old acquaintance's new title. She'd never trusted Duke. He had to have earned his position by betraying her trust like Max had done.

"Well, he's leaving soon, so we don't have an inside man for long," Jack finished.

"I think I need to walk around. This is home now, right?" She laughed but inside she wanted to run, find August, and escape. She was running out of time before he would be out of reach to offer any help to her at all.

Jack pushed the button to the elevators next to them and held the door open for her. She walked in. Jack stepped into the elevator to join her, but Mike grabbed his arm.

"Luke is a jealous man. We don't want to test his limits," he said to them both. Mike reached in and pushed the number six. "This will take you to the main lobby. Hyka will meet you down there. Use your badge to go through the doors. You need your badge to access everything. The outer doors and the elevator to the sub-levels are restricted. I'm not sure if he's granted you full access yet. There is a courtyard on the second level between here and the security checkpoint of the airport. You have free reign in there. No one comes or goes, but if you need to venture out, the terminals would be the best place to wander around."

Valerie smiled at her father and thanked him as the doors closed. She fell against the elevator wall. There was no winning. She knew what her dad said was right, but his knowledge of Lucas bothered her. She did not bring up his miraculous healing because she was not ready to know the part he had played in her arrival. Since she was always under surveillance, she just played dumb and did not push the issue. The less they knew about her concerns, the better chance she had of somehow escaping. Even if she did find August, she was not even sure how he could help her. Lucas seemed to know and control everything.

The elevator doors slid open to the hotel lobby. Neutral-colored lounge chairs were set up in groups along the windows to the left and right of her. In the middle of the room was a bar across from a reception desk. The generous space was quiet and otherwise empty. If this were a permanent living arrangement, she had no doubt she would, at some point, bump into Lucas in this space. She hoped to never be in the same room with him again. He could stay in his tower, and she in hers.

Valerie walked to the south side of the room where she could see the parking lot full of empty vehicles. Past the parking lots, the electricity stopped, but something on the western horizon caught her eye. She had to strain to see because the support wires of the hotel structure obstructed her view. There were lights in the distance. The resort had full power. Her former sanctuary was connected by a subway. There was a possibility Lucas was powering the resort, but she did not understand why he would need to anymore.

She moved away from the window and crossed to the opposite set of windows. The lobby was a comfortable sleepy space with dim lighting and a faint smell of fragrant hand lotion, not overpowering, but noticeable. What used to be a space of movement and change was now a luxurious prison with complimentary shampoo and conditioner.

Below her, she could see across the empty courtyard her father had mentioned and the airport terminals. All the lights were on as if a red-eye flight was expected. She looked down at the courtyard. To the left and right of the vast concrete walkway were hundreds of metal spikes on the ground. They seemed to move and flow with the wind, like a metal wheat field. They were each about two feet high and not even a foot apart, set up in a grid formation. She considered jumping from the window onto the spikes but knew she was not strong enough to break the glass. Lucas would not let her die. The DiaZem gene would not let her die. With every passing second, Valerie found it more difficult to see how her situation could improve. There was no winning.

Behind her, one of the outer doors granting access to the lobby had opened.

"You look like you could use a drink." Hyka walked across the lobby and behind the bar. "I borrowed a shirt, hope you don't mind."

Hyka was wearing one of Valerie's fitted t-shirts but had cut the sleeves into a tank top. Her chest was bare of the ink once marking her skin. Hyka slapped her badge against three different black boxes. Each blinked green and triggered different hydraulic shelves to emerge from their secure resting places below the counter. Lights underneath illuminated the liquor bottles which rose with the shelves. Hyka grabbed an ink pen and with a twist and stab, created a messy bun on her head with her string-wrapped strands still hanging free. She pinned a name tag to her shirt labeling herself Sammy Jo. Valerie smiled, and Hyka continued her smooth movements. She poked the computer screen and navigated to the music setting. 1980s pop music played overhead. She grabbed three bottles from the shelf with one hand and flipped them over into a shaker, scooped a glass tumbler full of ice, set the bottles down, picked up the shaker, slammed the two cups together and shook them. She looked up at Valerie.

"Ass-hat gave me a tour and told me I should make you feel at home. But the last time I checked you didn't have a full-service bar in your home. And yes, I did check." Hyka pulled the two glasses apart enough to drain the cocktail into a lowball tumbler holding the ice. She picked a napkin from a stack and placed it in front of Valerie with the lowball on top.

Valerie touched the glass. She had a strong urge to slam the alcohol back in one gulp, remembering the shooters she had at the hotel before she was aware she was with child.

"I was going to kill him, you know," Valerie spoke, studying the drink.

"Yeah, I had my money on the guards. Jarrett is such a coward. The ER doc got a good piece of him, though. I wish his eye would have stayed swollen shut a bit longer. He kept inviting me to his room while he was showing me around. Creep show."

Valerie felt a tinge of jealousy, followed by nausea. She hated him, but she could do little to prevent the involuntary attraction. If he stayed away from her, she could maintain her disdain. When he was close, she battled with herself. He killed her husband. He even tried to erase all connection to him. Valerie Burton, Caleb Burton. Their last name was Russell. She would keep his name until she died.

"I talked to Duke. Both guys have the hots for you. August is in a rush to leave because he thinks you killed everyone and knows when he gets away from you, the attraction will die."

"But you told him I didn't, right? Duke will tell August that Lucas killed those people. If he knows the truth, he won't go. He can't go. He is the only shot I have at being able to do anything."

"You know, I was joking before about the love triangle. One hundred percent real. Duke said the guy is a mess. He can't stand Lucas, but this is his territory. Also, every country around the world is involved. They have a World Council, and their main goal is to kill off everyone without the electric gene. They want a smaller world population so they can control everyone the same way. No one leader, just

DiaZem pairs running the show. Each pair runs a mega-city. August's partner in San Francisco is an eighty-year-old math teacher. She's all about killing everyone for equality."

Hyka kept talking, but Valerie was distracted by the mention of August's partner.

"I have a question," Valerie interrupted. "If two male DiaZem can't be in the same room together, how was August able to touch Lucas? Let alone punch him in the face?"

"So, like ole blood-stain O'Connell said, DiaZem are like magnets. The same charges expel each other." Hyka pulled four small round magnets off a refrigerator under the counter. She set two aside. "Okay, so two of the same charge cannot come near each other. In a DiaZem's case, everything explodes. Lights, circuit breakers, those stupid plastic guns they carry around. But if you add an opposite charge, like a lady," Hyka winked at Valerie and continued, "the two charges are joined by the opposite charge in the middle, making the entire circuit even stronger." Hyka pushed a third magnet between the two, and all three snapped together.

"So, thanks to you, someone punched that joker in the face."

They laughed together.

"Hyka, I don't know what to do," Valerie started, conscious of her words and who might hear them. "Can a magnet be un-magnetized? Is there a way to undo the effects of the gene? If they can find cures for other genetic diseases, there should be a logical way to become a normal person again."

Hyka looked at her but did not answer.

"I just want to be a nobody. I want Caleb to have a normal life."

"I don't think you want to be a normal person. You know what they do to normal people around here, right? But there shouldn't be any harm in finding out. There is a lab near the control room that researches Lucas' capabilities as a DiaZem and the effects on conductors. Lucas owns the lab, but other people work under him. Regular people even."

"Well, there's a start. I think we both know what needs to happen then," Valerie said. Then she felt the breeze. She wanted to look for the camera he was using, but she could not tell which one of the men was watching her.

"I'll work my magic and see what else I can find out. Duke and the doctor leave tomorrow afternoon. Duke thinks he's going to run and not go to San Francisco. He's not on board with killing a bunch of people. He's a doctor, after all. Do no harm and all that."

Valerie shot a look to Hyka, hoping she would stop talking.

She got the hint and changed the subject. "It's not going to drink itself, you know."

"Water, maybe?" Valerie smiled and pushed the cocktail away.

"I knew you were pregnant as soon as we got to your house."

Lucas knew. He was coming. She could feel his energy: excited, plotting.

"Dammit, Hyka. You don't know what you have done."

CHAPTER EIGHTEEN

"I have to get back to Caleb." Valerie pushed out of her tall chair and walked to the elevator. Lucas was far enough away she could get back to her room and give everyone a fair warning, maybe even tell them of her pregnancy before he did.

"He knows now, doesn't he?" Hyka asked, frustrated.

"He was going to find out either way."

"Who's the dad?"

Valerie stopped in front of the elevator and looked at Hyka, ready to slap her. "What the hell is that supposed to mean?"

"I don't know your life." Hyka threw her hands up in the air.

"It's my husband's child."

They stood in silence waiting for the elevator.

"This is taking too long. I was the last to use this elevator. It should have been here." Valerie paced.

When the door opened, a man in a black suit and necktie stepped out, blocking their entry.

"Dr. Jarrett would like to speak with you, ma'am. He felt you should be given a fair warning in order to collect yourself. I apologize for the late hour, but he asked the control room to notify him once you finished resting." The uniformed man maintained a smug grin and spoke only to Valerie. He kept his hand near a 9mm pistol secured in a tan leg holster.

Valerie was not impressed, nor was she threatened.

"Rest?! Is that what we call recovering from being shocked unconscious? Lucas is a coward."

"Ma'am, you will be careful how you speak of your DiaZem."

"My DiaZem? I am a DiaZem! You should be careful how you speak to me. I have been through a lot this week thanks to your DiaZem, and I am not looking to put up with much more."

He stepped out of the elevator, allowing the door to close behind him. The closer she felt Lucas was, the more anxious she became. She needed to be with her son. She needed to protect him. This man in the suit was standing in her way; something she vowed she would never let happen again.

"If you do not move now, you are going to need your own time to rest," Valerie said through clenched teeth. She did not want to kill him, but she did not know how to use her ability to hurt people without killing them.

Valerie blinked back tears of rage, but they escaped despite her best efforts. In the split second she took to close her eyes and release her frustration, she was staring down the end of his 9mm.

"Threats are not taken lightly here, Ms. Burton," the man said, remaining calm and collected. He held a finger to his ear and spoke again, not to her. "Yes, we are fine here, just coming to a mutual understanding. Yes, sir." He looked at her again, "Ms. Burton—"

"It's Russell, for the last time. Valerie Russell," she interrupted, teeth still clenched, fighting the quiver in her voice.

"Yeah, well, have a seat, and Dr. Jarrett will meet you momentarily." He dismissed her and holstered his weapon while keeping his eyes on Hyka, who could have killed him with the look on her face.

Lucas was not far away by the time she sat down, and all she could do was wait. She wanted to scream and fight the man with the gun, but doing so would put Hyka in immediate danger. She did not know Lucas well enough to know how he would react. She did not put it past him to hurt her family as retribution. She swore at herself for leaving

Caleb, for needing to go for a walk. She also cursed Hyka for guessing she was pregnant.

The attraction to Lucas grew stronger with every second. She chewed a cocktail straw and mulled over the magnet example Hyka had given. Two magnets of opposite polar attractions will always be attracted to each other. She racked her brain thinking of every science class she ever took. She knew there had to be a way to demagnetize a DiaZem if the properties were the same.

Her heart skipped a beat at the sound of the elevator opening. Deep down she still hoped August would get out, but knew it was Lucas. She fought her instinct to go to him and remained seated, not even looking in his direction.

"Ah, my beautiful bride," he said.

"You're such a pig," Valerie said before she could stop herself. She tried to refocus her rage at him, but she was weak.

Hyka spit out Valerie's drink she had helped herself to in disbelief.

"Now, I'm not that bad. I am positive there are worse people you could be paired with. I mean the pond is pretty narrow, my dear. The sooner you come around, the better. We don't want to give the World Council the impression we aren't in the game. The last DiaZem group to start a rebellion did not have a happy ending. The Council frowns upon such things." He stood behind her. She was so in tune with him, she knew how he was standing, how he motioned with his hands when he spoke, all without looking at him. Her heart raced, and her mouth was dry. Her instinct was to reach out to him, to be comforted and loved by him. The sensation ripped her soul apart at the seams. The emotional wounds from losing her husband were still fresh enough to help keep her wits about her. He placed his hand on her shoulder. Her head tilted just slightly, welcoming the warmth of his hand. She hated him yet wanted his affection. She did not know how long she could fight, but she would. Inhale, exhale.

"Where is August?" she asked, to spite him.

Lucas grabbed her by the hair and yanked her out of the chair to face him. The anger in his eyes faded and he pulled her closer, keeping his firm grip. She turned away from him, fighting her strong urges.

"You are far sexier angry than I could have ever hoped for. Maybe I should spread out the execution of your family to keep you in a constant state of rage. You're more fun when you play hard to get." The last words he whispered in her ear.

Hyka jumped up and was met by the 9mm held by Lucas' assistant.

"You are quite feisty, too. Having both of you will be a treat. A birthday present, maybe?" Lucas winked at Hyka. "Rob, what's going on?"

Lucas released Valerie and flung her toward Hyka.

His assistant held a finger to his earpiece for a moment before answering his boss. "I think the departure of Dr. Wilkes needs to be expedited."

Valerie looked at Hyka, who was listening to her earpiece. Hoping he would leave to deal with August, the women moved to the elevator.

"Oh, whoa, whoa, whoa!" Lucas shouted as he caught up with them. He grabbed Valerie's wrist and forced her hand into his. "This is a great opportunity to show you around, and you can even wave goodbye to your boyfriend."

Valerie could not handle any more. She chopped him in the throat with her free hand. When he released her, Hyka pushed her forward, and the women sprinted across the lobby. Two bullets whizzed by and hit the glass doors in front of them. A third caught Hyka in the leg. Valerie stopped running and glared at Rob, Lucas' assistant. She found the small spark inside of his rib cage flickering with his pulse. Then it was gone. His face went white, and he collapsed to the ground.

"Listen here, bitch," Lucas began.

Valerie tried the same, but Lucas absorbed every effort she made to pull his energy. He continued his advance, unfazed by her efforts.

"You are only here because I need you. Otherwise, you could die out there like the rest. You know why royalty can only marry royalty? Because of genetics. Because otherwise, the DiaZem gene would die out."

Valerie stood her ground next to Hyka and continued her defiant glare. When he was within arm's length, he backhanded her in the mouth. She did not budge. The pain fueled her resistance. She could never have affection for a man who hurt her. The taste of blood in her mouth kept her mind aware of the damage he had already done to her.

Hyka had made quick use of her white belt, wrapping the improvised tourniquet around her leg to stop the bleeding. Valerie knelt down and put her hand on the wound, ignoring Lucas standing over her. Once he saw what she was doing, he remembered his assistant, lifeless on the floor. Lucas waved a hand in his direction, and the man gasped for air.

"Now that you are done comparing packages, shall we?" He yanked Valerie off the ground by her shirt. "Rob, get up. You're fine."

Hyka's leg, though still healing, was now well enough she could walk. The four moved to the elevator in silence. Rob, a bit out of sorts, scanned his badge and pushed the button for Sublevel 2, where the trains ran.

"You know up until a week ago, I had no idea the facility existed beneath the airport. The gene I discovered in the 1970s grants the host a higher level of intellect. Conductors are predisposed to being smart, motivated thinkers. So, in one week we were able to move in, develop and supply the technology to assist in the collection of conductors and make life here in the facility more comfortable. Since our founding fathers had no idea what this gene could do, we had to act fast. We have endless resources here. Money is not a factor in the New World. Power is currency now. Pure, unadulterated energy." Lucas wrapped his arm around her waist and pulled her close to him. "And women love power. Do you know how many women wish they were you?"

Lucas tipped her chin up with his index finger and kissed her mouth. Valerie was filled with familiar warmth. Like she belonged to him. Before she could think to fight, she kissed him back. She pulled away when she realized what she had done. She looked down in shame, knowing Hyka would have something to say later. Lucas smiled down at her.

"You see? Not so bad. You're already starting to break. I'll give you another few hours before you're eating out of my hand. And we'll raise our children here in our kingdom and be one big happy family, eh Rob?" Lucas laughed.

“Please stop touching me,” she said under her breath.

“I’m sorry, baby, what did you say?” he asked, still mocking her inability to fight his affections.

“Stop touching me,” she said louder.

The elevator chimed. He slid his hand over her butt and squeezed before reaching for her hand and leading her out.

“Mmmm, you taste so good,” he said, licking his lips.

Valerie was mortified. The resolve she had found moments ago was beginning to fade; he was killing her spirit. There was no way she could fight him. She considered poisoning him, but no matter what harm she brought to him, he would regenerate the damaged cells. They walked along a corridor to the train platform.

“Where are we going?” Valerie asked.

“First things first. We must address your boy-toy who is causing quite the ruckus in the living quarters. Wait until you see. We can house millions of conductors underground. They have everything they need, food and water, and they provide the power for everything. There is no effort on their part, or ours. Their proximity to a DiaZem makes them individual generators. They absorb energy, and we serve as a conduit cycling it back into the facility. Otherwise, they would—in theory—age and die due to not being able to release the energy themselves. You, hot mama, and I are the fountain of youth for these poor souls.” Lucas walked her over to a balcony overlooking the living area. He gripped the back of her neck and forced her to look over the edge; it was like leaning over the side of a skyscraper, only underground. Valerie looked across at the other towers of individual housing units. She gripped the rail as hard as she could, so as not to fall the mile down to the bottom.

“Is this what you want to do to me?” Lucas questioned. “You want to throw me over and kill me? I can’t read your mind, but I can sense your energy. You need to remember something: I am stronger than you. If at any point you might catch me off guard, which I promise will not happen, these people are loyal to me. I saved them from you. You killed their families and friends. Remember your place, or I will do terrible things to the people you love." He pushed her further over the edge. "Or maybe you want to jump?"

Her arms were extended. He was powerful enough to break her grip from the rail, but he did not. "But you must think about more than just yourself now, mustn't you?" he said, winking at her and placing his hand on her abdomen. He guided her away from the rail.

Valerie pushed him away. She hated how Lucas' touch made her heart and stomach flutter. She hated how natural it felt to hold his hand and walk. Her body called out to him, and she fought with every fiber of her being to resist. She looked for anything to distract herself while they waited for the train. She counted the endless housing units, memorized the bizarre murals which seemed to be on every wall.

She could hear the train approaching in the distance. She could push him or jump in front of the train herself. The inner struggle was driving her mad. He was an insufferable narcissist, and she played the role of the battered girl. The longer she was with him, the more profound her suffering became. She felt like her spirit was fading into nothing, like the endless pit of apartments she had just stared down, but even it had a bottom. A cold, hard, definitive ending. She could not protect Caleb if she were gone.

The train arrived with five passengers. One, in particular, Lucas was excited to see. She wore a skimpy maid's costume, impractical for anything but what it was intended for.

"Teresa, right?" Lucas said, with the look of primal hunger he had flashed at Hyka earlier. "I am attending to business, but feel free to wait for me. Make yourself at home."

He laughed to himself until he met Hyka's glare. "Oh, you're welcome to join us. Or I'm sure Rob could use some entertainment. Eh?"

Rob still seemed put off by dying in the hotel. Hyka spit on Lucas' shoes.

"Dammit, you are disgusting," Lucas yelled and pulled a handkerchief from his pocket to wipe his leather shoes. "Get the hell on the train."

The doors closed behind them, and though the voice warned them to hold on, the velocity threw Valerie's weight into Lucas. He wrapped an arm around her waist and held the metal railing offered for support. She stopped fighting. Valerie remained in his embrace as her resolve grew weaker. She racked her brain for distractions. She focused on the puzzle of figuring out how to demagnetize Lucas Jarrett from her. Every second she was near him was torture.

Rob tapped Lucas on the shoulder. Nodding, he allowed Valerie to sit on one end of the train car with Hyka. Lucas and Rob moved a distance away to talk in whispers.

"August is flipping out. He's demanding to leave," Hyka said to her under the sound of the train.

"He must think I did kill all those people. I don't expect you to understand why I care, but please don't judge me. I love my husband more than anything, but these feelings I have for August are as intense as they are for this asshole. I can't help it. But I need August here. I need him to help me. I'm sure if he sees Lucas and me together, he's going to hate me more. But I can't fight Lucas on my own."

"You're not on your own. But all these favors I'm doing for you are going to start adding up, Your Majesty."

Valerie was not in the mood for Hyka's jokes, but she had a point. The more she involved Hyka and anyone else, she was putting their lives at risk.

The train stopped after a few minutes, the doors opened, and the overhead voice announced they were at the Main Control Center. Like most of Denver International Airport, the platforms were decorated with strange and abstract sculptures. The four of them stepped off the train and walked through a structure of thick copper wire. The massive statue was of two giant men engaged in a sword fight. Each leg was a pillar supporting their bodies. Thick copper wire wrapped around itself to form the figures. The art scaled three floors above her head, reminding her of Lucas' self-indulgence. She walked behind him now, as he puffed up his chest in his tailored jacket and exaggerated the angle of his jaw. He waited by a heavy door for Rob to use his badge and hold the door for him. Lucas walked through. Valerie did not follow. She wanted to stay behind and get as much distance as she could. Rob motioned for her to go in, but she did not budge. The connection between them grew weaker, and she felt the weight of him leave her. Then, just as gradual as the feeling had faded, it came back to her.

"I can feel when you're not here, you know. Let's go," he said, like an annoyed parent to a stubborn child. Valerie followed with Hyka in step behind her.

"I just want to tell you how bad I want to punch him in the face right now," Hyka whispered to Valerie.

"I know. I do too." She smiled.

Valerie walked past a set of windows. Behind the glass were people in white coats studying screens, looking into microscopes, and documenting on clipboards. Lucas stopped at the door labeled "Conference Room" across from the lab.

"Rob, could you please show Ms. Burton's assistant how to set up a conference with the Council? No fighting." Lucas pointed his finger at the two assistants and continued down the hall. Valerie stayed.

"Is this your lab?" she asked, hoping to stroke his ego enough to gain access.

Lucas turned around and walked back to her. "It is. I have brought together some of the world's finest doctors, scientists, and engineers to develop innovations to move the New World forward in my lab. Much easier now the language barrier no longer exists."

"No language barrier? So, everyone speaks English now?"

"Contrarily, we speak in the language we understand and hear in the language we understand. Do you remember the Bible story about the tower of Babel? My guess is the fall of the tower represents the moment the gene went dormant. With the awakening came a slew of mutual understandings. All of which are represented here in my lab. There are a handful of normal people, too. My most distinguished colleague turned out to not have the gene. He was the one who developed the technology to protect our nonconductor allies within the facility from your little attack that wiped them out of the city. He earned his right to live, and so owes his life to me."

"I didn't. . ."

"I'm sorry?" Lucas interrupted her with a daring look. When she did not make a further attempt to correct him, Lucas waved at the older gentleman Valerie had seen in the control room. He did not smile or wave back but tilted his head to Valerie. She nodded in return.

"May I?" Valerie asked, placing her badge on the black reader. The light turned green, and the door's latch disengaged. She did have unrestricted access after all.

"Yes, fine, but I have work to do. I'll be back for you in five minutes." Lucas held the door open for her.

Valerie stepped into the lab. Every person looked at her in silence. They were not angry with her like the rest. There was a palpable sadness in their energy.

"Mrs. Russell, I am Doctor Leonard Warner of the CDC. I'd be happy to answer any questions you may have," the gentleman offered, extending his hand.

Valerie took his hand to shake it, but he lifted hers to his mouth. Bowing, he placed a kiss on her knuckle. She thanked him and pulled her hand away.

"I guess I just want to see what you are working on."

"I am sure, with time, you will find the right questions to ask. This is nothing more than your run of the mill research lab. We are studying DNA with the gene in its active state to understand its capabilities better. I have two male DiaZem samples; would you mind if we drew a small amount of blood from you?" the doctor asked with a sincere smile.

"What would you do with it?"

Dr. Leonard leaned in close to Valerie's ear. "We would look for your weaknesses as well as your strengths. To protect you, we must also know what could harm you."

As he stepped away, Valerie knew there was something else at work here. She nodded in agreement. Dr. Leonard motioned her to a chair and was handed the tools needed to extract her blood.

"You're smart, like your mother, Janice. I have not seen her since she was about half your age," the doctor said as he made quick work of filling the vial with blood.

"Look at you, so compliant now," Lucas spoke, making her jump.

She had been distracted by the mention of her mother and did not see or feel him walk into the lab.

"Leo's studies are essential to the evolution of the New World. You'd be happy to know you are contributing to the right cause, my dear. Now, shall we?" Lucas ripped the bandage off her arm as quick as the doctor had placed it. Her wound had already healed.

"Five thousand mega-cities all over the world were built to house the quarter of the population that carry the gene. DiaZem are like the royalty of the conductors. The entire English royal family are DiaZem. Not realizing it, of course, they were able to maintain the bloodline through generations. The Queen of England has reigned for so long for a reason. Now, she will continue to rule with her youth restored. Her descendants host other mega-cities otherwise vacant of DiaZem. The United States has four mega-cities: Fort Knox, Dallas, Denver, and San Francisco. You were the last DiaZem needed for our country to come online with Phase Two. Dr. Wilkes will meet up with his partner in San Francisco, and you and I will marry and rule here." He escorted her down the hall while he spoke. He did not look at her, but for the first time, he seemed to treat her as an equal.

"You said they do something to those who don't follow through with Phase Two? Do they kill DiaZem?" she asked.

"Already trying to plot my death? Please stop fighting. You can't. I don't care if you don't want to be with me. I can force you to be with me, and there is little you can do to fight it." Lucas stopped in the hallway and slammed her up against the wall, pinning her there with his body. "So, you'll forget about Dr. Wilkes. He doesn't want you. He has his partner. And once he gets to his city, he'll forget all about you. He will see you in the Council and have no emotions toward you. You are mine, Valerie, forever."

She tried to turn away, but Lucas forced his mouth on hers, hard and painful. He slid his hand behind her and pulled her into him. Caught in between wanting him and wanting to die, she screamed when he released her mouth. This time his fist connected with her cheek. He held her upright, and she braced for another strike. None came. The taste of tears and blood fill her mouth again.

He placed his hand on the tender spot of his blow. "I can't have my missus sporting a shiner on her pretty face. What would the Council think? We don't want them knowing you don't want to join us. And yes, they kill DiaZem, the ones who do not cooperate with the New World. I know you would have let people, like your husband, live willy-nilly around the earth. Threatening our genetic superiority. How does someone like you end up with a regular anyway?" Lucas moved his hand between her legs.

She did not want him to stop, but she felt sick and humiliated.

"Did you not feel it deep inside? You are so much more than a man's bed warmer. You are a leader of nations. The mother of future leaders. His blood diluted your heritage. Caleb's lucky he takes after you."

At the mention of her son, all her emotions turned to anger. Her inner yearning extinguished. She looked at him in the eye and grabbed his wrist, pulling his hand away from her. Then she pushed him hard to free her body of him and the wall.

"There's my girl," he said, smiling in approval.

The door behind him buzzed open. A blue-clad guard stopped in his path, nervous to see Lucas waiting outside. He moved aside and held the door open for the two of them to enter. Lucas motioned in a gentleman-like fashion for her to proceed ahead of him. She rolled her eyes and walked inside.

CHAPTER NINETEEN

Valerie remembered the control room from her surveillance search for August. She scanned the cameras for Caleb. He was still fast asleep, and Kevin sat in the chair with his eyes closed. She let out a sigh of relief. On another screen, Jack and her father boarded a train. No one in the control room seemed to worry about the men wandering around the facility in the wee hours of the morning. She focused her attention on August. Glancing at Lucas, who was having a conversation with one of the guards, she retraced the camera feed, through the tunnels of the living area and up to his suite. Like before, her presence was felt. She tapped into the controls of the TV monitor in his room and wrote him a message.

I need you to know I didn't kill those people. Lucas is blaming me for the attack to turn the people against me. What the Council plans to do is wrong, and I cannot let them move forward. I can't fight Lucas on my own. Please don't leave me here with him. I don't stand a chance without you. If you won't stay, take us with you. Please.

August sat up on the edge of his bed, hung his head in his hands and rubbed his temples.

"It's not that easy. Every second I am here I want to kill him for even being near you. If his attraction is anything like mine, he'll kill me if I try to take you. Even if we find a way to beat him, the Council will be after us. There is no winning in this," he answered out loud.

She heard him and hid a falling tear from the others in the room.

I'm willing to take the chance.

August looked up at the camera and nodded. With his confirmation, she brought her focus back to the control room and wiped the tear away. Her heart fluttered with excitement and anxiety. Lucas stopped talking and looked at her. She wanted to smile at him but did not want to evoke any more attention. If he liked her angry, she would give him angry.

"Everyone, can I have your attention," Lucas demanded of the room. "This angelic being before you is my betrothed. You all know Ms. Burton from monitoring her for the past week or so. But here she is in the flesh. She is part of me and will be treated as such." Lucas winked from across the room and walked over to her.

The room remained silent, but those in attendance made notice of her before returning to their tasks.

"They should have the conference room ready to go. Once the Council caught wind of your arrival, they insisted August and I move forward with Phase Two. And since you have already done part of the work for me, our region will be easy."

On the screen, Eric Earl entered August's room, and the two men exited the suite. Lucas motioned her to the door. Without expression, she preceded him through the threshold and back down the hall. She could see Hyka moving in her direction with the slightest limp and Rob behind her trying to keep up.

"What is it?" Valerie said, once in earshot of her friend.

"Nothing. If I had stayed in that room any longer, I would have killed his assistant. But that's apparently against the rules," Hyka said, turning to face Rob, who ran into her.

"Stop acting like children," Lucas accused. "Is the conference online?"

"Yes, sir. New Zealand is having difficulty finding their male DiaZem, but otherwise, they are awaiting you and August." Rob straightened himself and took a step behind Lucas.

Hyka reached the conference room first and held the door for Valerie. She cut Lucas off to follow her in. Rob caught the door from slamming on his boss. The room was like a home theater, but instead of comfortable armchairs, a desk with two office chairs sat in front of the large projection screen. Names etched into placards labeled their seats. Lucas pulled out Valerie's chair before taking his own on her right.

The screen reflected hundreds of other DiaZem couples. Valerie could not count them all. Another large screen was reserved for the DiaZem team addressing the group. The label on the giant screen announced Beijing.

"Thank you for joining us at such an early hour, Ms. Burton." The Asian woman greeted Valerie by her maiden name, as it appeared printed in front of her. "The Council has taken into consideration your lack of training to date and are in agreement to overlook the course of events leading to your arrival at the facility.

"A partial initiation of Phase Two could have proven to be detrimental to your region. If a rebellion occurs before your circuit is complete, the inferior population could overthrow your facility. Your conductors would be scattered to the winds. To avoid this, you must take the oath of coronation, proceed to marry your DiaZem partner, and initiate the cleansing of your nation sooner rather than later.

"Dr. Wilkes will leave for his station, and both cities will initiate a complete Phase Two. This will reach the remaining half of the United States and should suffice since the eastern coast is already online with our plan, and their Phase Two accomplished."

"Can I be let in on the secret now?" August said, waving at the mounted screens.

Valerie was startled to see his face so large in front of her. She blushed and looked away. Lucas glared at her, sensing her excitement at the sight of him. His hands gripped the armrests. She was thankful for once to be on camera. He would not hit her on camera.

"What is Phase Two? I swear I'll comply, I want to know what I'm walking into."

This time Jacqueline Thomas, alone in her screen with San Francisco displayed under her name, spoke up. "To maintain the purity of our DNA and keep the gene from returning to a dormant state, the Council has agreed that the elimination of the inferior is the best way to maintain compliance, unity, and control of our governed regions. DiaZem who refuse this plan of action are, of course, removed from power and eliminated as well. I am sure you can see the danger in allowing them to live."

August looked away from the screen to his assistant who would not make eye contact with him. Duke whispered to August, "I think they are waiting for your answer."

"Yes. I'm on board. Jackie, you and I are going to rule with iron fists and cold hearts. What do you say?"

The Council took August's joke at face value. Jacqueline's expression lightened and she even almost smiled. The rest of the Council nodded in acceptance, except for Lucas, who interrupted the first light moment of the meeting.

"I expect, in the next twenty-four hours, the United States should be compliant with Phase Two. I motion to adjourn this meeting."

To Valerie's relief, the motion was reciprocated, and the conference was over.

"Good job, wife." Lucas stopped, studied her, and shook his head in disapproval. "You need something more fitting of royalty. I'll send my tailor out to find you something suitable for the coronation and our wedding. I'll pick out something for our wedding night. No more white for you, Missus Jarrett. Oh, when I'm done with you, there will be no way you could wear white." He laughed to himself and waved a hand at Rob to begin the arrangements for her clothing.

Rob nodded and answered a knock at the door. Valerie's father and Jack walked in.

"Ah! Pops! Just in time," Lucas said. The men gave each other a back-beating hug.

Her heart pounded. Seeing the men acting so acquainted more than irritated her.

"I'm sorry. What is this?" she asked, pointing a finger at the two men.

"There is so much I haven't gotten the chance to explain," Mike started. "Luke and I have known each other for a long time. I met your mother when we were kids. What we didn't tell you is we met in a genetic testing program run by Dr. Jarrett. Your mother had the DiaZem gene. I had the conductor gene. We ran away and got married, but knew either you or Kevin or both of you would carry on her DiaZem heritage." Mike waited for Valerie's reaction.

Lucas leaned against the wall, failing to conceal the amusement on his face.

Mike continued, "I wanted you to escape, but there is no outrunning this. I made sure Caleb was safe. I didn't think you had the DiaZem gene and just assumed Kevin did. So many things didn't go the way we planned. I didn't get the chance to explain. Luke took Kevin and me, knowing we were leverage over you. We were never in danger. Max was in on the entire thing, and for his help, he was granted life in the facility."

Hyka moved quick, sliding across the table separating her and the two men. Jack was able to dodge the right hook she threw at him. He grabbed her by the waist to subdue her, but he had left one arm free of his grasp. Hyka elbowed him hard in the ear. In retaliation, he lifted her off her feet and dropped her body onto the floor.

"Dammit Hyka! I didn't know, either! Jesus." Jack pushed her away from him and retreated, cupping his ear and looking at his hand for blood.

"Tell her the rest, Mikey," Lucas instigated.

"No one else knew," Mike continued. "Val, I love you. I never wanted any of this. I hoped time was on our side and we'd all be dead and gone before the gene awakened."

"Stop beating around the bush," Lucas yelled this time. "Tell her why she is really here."

Mike took a hard breath. "Given Dr. Jarrett's status and his discovery, he was promised his choice of partner. He chose your mother. When she passed, he chose you, if you were the one with the DiaZem gene. I thought it was Kevin with the gene, and that you were safe." Mike studied her face for any sign of acceptance or understanding.

She offered none.

"Oh, but Mike, she has secrets of her own! Come on, sweetie, tell him our big news," Lucas taunted.

"I am going back to my room now," Valerie whispered as loud as she could without her voice cracking from the tears she held back.

As she walked to the door, her father offered a hug.

"You don't get to touch me. Don't follow me. Don't talk to me. Don't talk to my son. Leave. I never want to see you again."

She walked out of the room with Hyka. No one else followed. Lucas even remained silent as she left.

On the train, in the elevator, and through the lobby, Valerie did not speak. When she reached her suite on the thirteenth floor, the sun shined red along the eastern horizon.

"Coffee?" Valerie asked Hyka.

"I'll get it. Decaf? You should get some sleep," Hyka suggested.

"No. I have some shopping to do for my wedding tonight." Valerie's tone was flat and defeated. She felt dead inside. She sat at the bar-height counter in the kitchen area of the suite. Her bedroom door opened, and Kevin stepped out. His hair was flat on one side and stuck straight up on the other.

"I'd take some coffee," he said, taking a seat next to his sister. He reached over and rubbed her back. "Caleb is still out. I barricaded him on the bed with pillows so he wouldn't roll off. You doing okay?"

Valerie hung and shook her head no.

"Your dad sold her out. He knew this whole time what was up," Hyka said, examining the coffee pot to ensure it was clean. "The shitty thing is, it was supposed to be your mom."

"Mom was a DiaZem," Valerie explained. "They met in a program run by Lucas when they were kids. Dad let me walk all the way home, knowing I wouldn't get to Caleb in time. He knew I would be forced to marry Lucas. Kevin, he didn't even try to protect us." Valerie wiped her face with the back of her hand.

A box of tissue flew across the kitchen, hit the counter, and slid to where Valerie was sitting.

"Thank you," she sniffed.

"It was supposed to be me," Kevin retorted.

"What?"

"All these years, I have trained, knowing I would have to use my status to stop the World Council from committing genocide. You don't have the skills or maturity to do what needs to be done. You never have. You just cry and complain instead of trying to figure it out for yourself."

Hyka's arm wrapped around his neck, obstructing Kevin's airway. The other arm twisted one of his behind his back into submission. He stood from the chair, and the two moved toward the door. Knowing what she intended, he grabbed the doorknob. Hyka released her choke hold and shoved him out the door, slamming it behind him and engaging the swing bar lock.

Valerie sat, mouth gaping in disbelief at what her brother had said. "Is everyone against me? Everyone hates me. They either think I killed their entire family or they are jealous? Of this? No one should live like this!"

"Man, your family sucks," Hyka said, returning to the kitchen and pouring Valerie's mug.

With her head in her hands, Valerie propped her elbows on the table. She was not tired, just needed to think.

"Everything is happening so fast. I'm just getting lost in it all. What in the world is a coronation? Like the cartoon princess thing? That's a real thing? And a wedding. Just saying the word out loud makes me want to throw up."

Hyka just stood next to her listening and holding Valerie's coffee until she noticed her. Valerie held her hand out for the cup. She inhaled and wanted to think about anything else than the agenda for her day.

"Why did you hit Jack and not my dad?" Valerie asked, trying to objectify the situation. She figured nothing more could surprise or upset her at this point.

"I don't know. Maybe after walking almost a hundred miles, he'd have let us in on the whole scheme," Hyka shrugged, turning back to the finished pot.

"Something is going on there, between you and Jack," Valerie put together, smiling. "He's old enough to be your dad. He and your dad are actually really good friends," Valerie laughed. She felt proud for having tapped into her friend's softer side, but deep down she also found it comforting to have a semi-normal girl talk.

"Dr. Wilkes could be worse of an asshole than Jarrett, and twice as old." Hyka stood across the counter from her, looking her in the eye.

"August is my only hope not to have to marry that sick, murdering, narcissistic chauvinist," Valerie was yelling.

The corner of Hyka's mouth twisted up, and she turned back to the coffee, satisfied with Valerie's reaction.

"See? Can't help who you fall for. Why don't you kill Lucas like that weenis who shot me in the leg? Seems like an effective trick." Hyka poured her coffee and looked at Valerie over the top of her mug while she drank.

Valerie sat back down in her chair. "I tried. Didn't work. We are cycling the same energy of the facility. I'm not even sure what kind of physical harm would be needed to kill a DiaZem. Someone in the Council must know, but I doubt I can just ask."

"They don't know either. There is a rebellion happening in New Zealand. Despite what they said, the Council doesn't have the country under their control. Because they are so isolated, the Kiwis aren't a real threat to the Council. You are a much bigger liability. The United States has a bigger influence. Maybe reach out to New Zealand and see what they are up to."

"They aren't going to hand over their secrets. I'd have to earn their trust. How can I do that in twelve hours?"

"Mommy." Caleb appeared next to Valerie at the table. She pulled him into her lap and brushed his sleep-spiked hair down.

"Hey, sweetie. Did Mommy wake you up?" she asked, kissing his cheek while he nodded his answer. "I am sorry Mommy scared you, but I'm okay. See?"

Valerie smiled to show her son she was not hurt or otherwise uncomfortable. "Let's go back to bed, Little Mister."

Caleb protested and choked Valerie with a tight hug around her neck.

She rubbed his back and rocked him. "Well, do you want to go shopping with Mommy? Maybe I can find you some candy."

"Candy, yeah!" Caleb answered and hopped off his mother's lap.

Valerie found some clothes for the boy and got him ready. The TV monitor displayed 6:30 a.m. and the sun completely shone in the sky. They found themselves alone as they walked through the lobby and the courtyard. They saw no one until they got to the airport. An old man sat at the security gate. When he noticed the two women come around the motionless escalator, he sat up straight and requested their badges. Hyka and Caleb's badges were scanned and compared to their faces. When Valerie handed over her badge, the old man stood from his chair and bowed to her.

"I owe my life to you, Ms. Burton."

The man's words confused her. She had never met him before.

"Why? What do you mean?" she asked, knowing she might receive an answer influenced by Lucas' lies.

"When the regular people were called to be with the Lord, you saved me. They fell around me, but I was the one left standing. Thank you for sparing my life. I am here to serve you." The man bowed again and scanned her badge.

Valerie studied the man. He was indeed a conductor, but there was something wrong. He had not regressed in age like the rest. When she focused her attention on his energy, she saw a small pocket under his skin with a mechanism sewn into him, connected to his heart.

"What's your name?" she asked him. She knew he did not have much time left unless he was able to release the energy he had absorbed since his dormant gene was awakened.

"Bernard Butler, my DiaZem," he answered.

"Mr. Butler, you have my permission to leave this post. I need you to go to Sublevel 2, catch the train to Living Area Nine. On the eighth level, look for a suite labeled Dr. August Wilkes. Tell him your pacemaker is broken and I request that he remove it as soon as possible. He will know what to do. Then you will stop aging, and can continue to live like the rest of us." Valerie was unsure the procedure would work, but it gave the kind man a chance.

"I will. Bless you!" The man hurried away.

The three walked down to the airport train to the terminals. On the platform, a statue of Jack Swigert stood ten feet tall.

"Astronaut," Caleb pronounced the word slowly and pointed to the figure. Valerie let his hand go, and he ran to the plaque at the foot of the statue.

"He died of cancer right before taking his seat in Congress. Isn't that some crap: survives space, dies of cancer," Hyka said, standing behind Caleb and reading the plaque.

"I wonder if he was a DiaZem," Valerie said out loud to herself.

"The gene we have does not allow for other genetic abnormalities like cancer. We're immune to disease as well. Have you ever had a VD?" Hyka asked without a wink of humor, but Valerie laughed.

"No! What? Seriously?" Valerie needed a laugh.

Hyka nodded with a solemn expression as the train arrived.

"Whoo, whoooooo," Caleb called at the train.

Shaking her head, she led her son aboard. They walked to the front end of the car. Caleb crawled up onto the seat to watch out the front window. Valerie sat to keep him from losing balance once the train began to move. Hyka stood and held a pole.

"I'm running this train. Lucas and I. Powering everything is involuntary, like breathing or blinking. I know when he is watching me. Well, I know when someone is watching. When I was at In-Processing, I thought it was August watching me on surveillance. But when we were at the bar, I knew it was Lucas. I can feel him now," Valerie explained, becoming more aware of how difficult her situation was.

"That's gross," was all Hyka would comment.

CHAPTER TWENTY

The train approached Terminal B, where Rob had told Hyka they could find women's clothing. As they crested the top of the stairs, a lingerie store awaited them.

"Tell me this is not what he meant by 'women's clothing,'" Valerie demanded. "I hate him. I hate him so much."

"They have makeup and stuff here, too." Hyka slapped her badge on the wall. As the gate rose, she ducked under and helped herself to a shopping bag.

Valerie let Caleb down. "Now listen. You can run and play, but you stay near Mommy, okay? Stay inside the store. When I say Marco, you say. . ."

"Polo," Caleb shouted, excited about the game his father had taught him.

As she looked over the sexy garments, her heart sank. She had no intention of showing anyone her underwear. She wanted to mourn the loss of her husband, the one man she was in love with from the beginning. She remembered shopping in similar stores when she was young and surprising him in the evenings when they were dating. Caleb had changed her body. So much so that no matter how much Scott had wanted her, she felt unattractive. She wished she had not stopped wearing these things for him.

"Marco?"

"Polo."

Having a difficult time concentrating, Valerie looked for things she would have picked before her transformation.

"Extra small," Hyka said over her shoulder. "You don't have mom hips anymore, remember?"

Valerie looked at the pair of medium panties in her hand. Embarrassed, she set them down and picked up the suggested size. She put those down as well and grabbed a handful of small panties and shoved them in her bag. Hyka returned and dumped an armful of cosmetics into Valerie's bag.

"I don't want any of these things," Valerie protested.

"Oh, those are mine, but I grabbed some stuff you can use for your crowning ceremony. Go through the motions, Val."

Hyka returned after each lap around the store with more things to put in the bag, until she just took the sack from Valerie.

"Marco. Marco? Marco!" Her heart pounded. She ran, hoping she could find him in the empty terminal.

"Polo," a man answered. The sound tied her stomach in a knot. She cursed herself for letting him sneak up on her. She reached the front of the store. Caleb sat on Lucas' shoulders with a smile on his face.

"Daddy. Daddy. Daddy," Caleb repeated while treating Lucas' head as a drum.

"No." She glared. "Put him down. Now."

Lucas just smiled and bounced the boy, making him squeal and giggle. Valerie pulled her son down and held him.

"What? He likes me. I don't mind if he calls me Daddy. They're our kids now."

"You listen to me. You can have my father, my brother, and whoever else you think you might need on your side. These are my children. They are Scott Russell's children. My name is Valerie Russell. My children's names are and will always be Russell. They will grow up knowing what you did to their father, and why. They will know what an abusive and sick person you are."

She spoke into her son's ear, "Caleb, baby, this is a bad man. He's stinky and mean, and he hurts Mommy. He's dangerous."

"Dangerous," Caleb answered, frowning toward Lucas.

"Getting them to hate me is only going to make things worse for you, my dear. The thing is, until about thirty minutes ago, I had no clue why Ole Bernie had not died with the rest of the old and plagued people who weren't under my protection. Until you looked at him. You looked at him and saw inside to what was ailing him. I guess I never take much time to look at people. But you found the problem. So then, I wondered what I would see if I looked at you, and boy, what an exciting discovery. Val, honey, do you want to know what I see when I look at you?"

Lucas raised his brows, waiting for her response. She did not care what he saw in her. She cared for the two children she carried: the one on her hip and the other in her womb.

"No? Not even a little curious? Because I heard Hyka tell you we don't get sick. We heal ourselves. But you, you were very ill until you got here. Your body was not regenerating as a DiaZem should. Like Bernie misdiagnosed with a heart condition, instead of maybe anxiety. Catching an unnecessary pacemaker was great thinking on your part. Your condition was critical. You were knocking on death's door until you got here. You were so very, very sick. So, what is ailing you? Your baby? Of course, pregnancy has certain symptoms, but should DiaZem be ailed if they are the most superior beings? The answer is no, Valerie. There's something else brewing in there. We're having a girl."

Valerie failed to see the relevance of her child's gender. She adjusted Caleb to her other hip, turned, and walked away from him. Hyka followed. Lucas did not pursue.

With her hands full, she let the tears blur her vision before blinking them free to fall down her cheeks. She could not raise her daughter to be strong and not be a victim while she let Lucas treat her so horribly. She could not teach her how to fight when she, herself, could not. Valerie considered putting the baby on a raft of reeds like Moses and floating her away from this place. But there were no rivers, reeds, or anywhere else she would be safe. She would have to fight, for herself and her children.

When they returned to the room, a dress dangled from a hook on the wall. It was labeled Coronation. Even though the white dress hung high, the tulle skirt of the dress still managed to touch the ground. With short, capped sleeves, the hand-sewn lace had jewels worked into a flower design down and around the torso. Next to the dress was a long, thick regal cape with a train ten feet long. Valerie walked past the ensemble to the bedroom and closed the door. She stood Caleb on the bed, and he began to jump.

"Come on, bed bug, let's snuggle. Mommy is tired." Valerie removed her shoes and socks, remaining otherwise clothed for the cameras. She crawled into bed and tackled the little boy. As she lay there with her son tucked into her arms, she noticed the closet door had been left open. There was a tiny tuxedo for Caleb and another long white dress with a slimmer silhouette than the coronation gown. Her wedding dress, which she had no intention of wearing.

Valerie sang her son to sleep. She lay there staring at the ceiling for a long while, racking her brain for a solution or plan of any kind. She lowered the mechanical blinds to block out the risen sun and dozed off. She was coaxed awake by the cool breeze of his presence. Forgetting for a moment where she was and who might be watching her, she let herself enjoy the refreshing feeling of his eye upon her. Then the TV screen mounted on the wall went black. She opened her eyes to the message he wrote:

We are running out of time. Come with me. We can leave here. We can live off the grid.

"You can't just smuggle me out. I won't leave my son or Hyka behind," she whispered under her blanket, unsure if he could hear her.

Nothing would make me happier than getting rid of Lucas, but what if we fight and fail? It's the most impractical choice at this point.

"Then leave," Valerie screamed at the wall. "I am not leaving my son again. I don't need you if that is my only option. Just because you're not a psycho murderer, doesn't mean I have to pick between the two of you! I don't love you. This is not love. This is an involuntary attraction. It's an insult to love."

The lights in her room burned bright and then dimmed once she realized he was gone.

"You good in here?" Hyka asked, cracking the door open. Caleb was awake as well.

"Yes, I'm fine," Valerie lied. The TV was still on, but the time, weather, and room service menu scrolled across instead of August's messages. 9 a.m.

"Cereal," the little boy requested.

"You're hungry, little guy? I forgot about your candy. Let's see how this room service works. You want to get the phone for Mommy?" The boy nodded, excited to have permission to talk on the phone. He crawled across the bed, picked up the cordless phone off the receiver, and held it to his head grinning from ear to ear.

After she assisted Caleb in ordering breakfast, the meals came within thirty minutes. The three ate together at the small dining table.

"So, are we going to talk about the giant white elephant in the room? We have about three hours," Hyka said.

"When the time comes for this baby to be born, would you take them away? Somewhere safe? If I go along with everything and can't find a way out, will you hide them?" Valerie pleaded. She struggled to find a solution, but nothing she could think of would change the day's events.

"That's a terrible idea. I don't even like kids," Hyka answered, snarling at Caleb, making him giggle with a mouth full of colorful breakfast cereal. She smiled back as milk dribbled down his chin. "So, you're doing this? The whole thing? Marrying this schmuck and becoming the Queen of Denver?"

"Do you have any other ideas?" Valerie asked with as much confidence as she could muster.

"I know you hate his face, but maybe your dad has some solid advice about all this?" Hyka did not look her in the eye as she made the suggestion.

Valerie scoffed. "He'd tell me to figure it out for myself like he always has. I have never mattered to him, not until he realized he'd told the wrong kid he was special."

Out the window, a plane taxied across the empty runway toward the airport. August's flight. Valerie drank from her coffee cup, wishing she could indulge in something stronger. "I do have to figure this out for myself."

When they finished eating, Valerie dismissed Hyka to get herself ready for the coronation ceremony. She ran a shallow bath and set Caleb down to play while she showered and watched him through the glass door. She sang a song. He sang back in a slur of baby gibberish of what he thought the words were. "Up-ah-bubba world so high."

Valerie did not know who she would be if she were not a mother. Even in the face of uncertainty, she cherished moments like this with her son.

When she was out of the shower and robed, she stood while he played in the bath. In his facial features, Valerie recognized her husband. Scott's memory would never be far from her. She would teach them about their father. They needed to know where they came from, not the lies and fantasies Lucas entertained.

When Hyka returned, she wore a tight black dress ending right at her knee. The sleeves were snug to her wrists, and the neckline cut deep between her breasts. Her heels were spikes, giving her height a three-inch addition. She pulled her hair up into a tight bun, including the string-wrapped strands which added the only color to her ensemble. There was an hour left before they had to depart for the ceremony.

Valerie had managed to pin her hair up but had no makeup on. Hyka pulled things from the shopping bag and sat Valerie down in front of a mirrored vanity. She did not protest and gave no guidance as to how she wanted her makeup done. The result was stunning, but all Valerie could see in the mirror was the beginning of her end.

Caleb's shirt, vest, and tie were white, and his pants, jacket, and shoes were black. Valerie wetted a comb and brushed his hair to one side, adding a tiny dollop of hair product to keep it in place.

"Well, there, handsome. Want to be my date?" Valerie teased her son. He smiled and nodded his head yes.

With thirty minutes until the ceremony, a knock came at the door. Valerie tapped into the camera in the elevator lobby. Once satisfied with the visitor, she nodded to Hyka to open the door. Jack walked in alone in an adult version of the same tuxedo Caleb was wearing.

"Whoa, man, we're like twins." Jack play-punched at Caleb, who retreated behind his mother.

Valerie closed herself and her son in the bedroom to give Jack and Hyka some privacy and to put on the dress and gaudy cape. She spent fifteen minutes securing the entire thing herself before she opened the door. The sun shining in through the window caught the jewels on her bodice, and the room erupted in rays of light. She radiated.

"Val," was all Jack could utter. He hugged her tight. "We can find another way. No good will come from this guy or this New World Council."

"It's fine. I'll figure this out. I have to," Valerie said, looking at her son. She placed a hand on her belly. Her mouth was dry, and she was terrified of the events soon to follow.

"The ceremony is in the central station of the facility," Jack began, giving her an overview of what to expect. "Think Kansas City Union Station, but underground and without windows. Top-tier residents only are permitted to attend. The rest will watch on any monitor they wish, because the entire procession will be broadcast throughout the world, to include the Council and to ensure your compliance."

Valerie nodded.

Jack continued, "The ceremony is simple: you'll repeat your creed after Lucas, swearing your unwavering allegiance to the Council." He paused.

Valerie nodded again. She was sure he was waiting to hear an alternate plan, but she had none. She sighed, "I could go for that cocktail right about now."

"Maybe not a good idea," Hyka answered. "It's time."

Jack took Hyka by the arm and escorted her out. Caleb trailed behind Valerie, holding the end of her train. She was pulling him along more than he was keeping her cape off the ground. Once to the elevator, she and Hyka gathered the material in their arms.

"Caleb? Where did you go?"

He poked his head out from behind a mound of tulle. "Peek-a-boo, Mommy!"

They reached the platform and boarded the train Jack had arranged to be waiting for her. They arrived moments later. The platform of the copper fighting giants was full of people; all formally dressed. They watched her, but no one cheered as the doors opened. Just solemn faces and glares greeted her. She picked up her son and held him close, letting her train drag on the ground behind her. Jack and Hyka led her through a wide corridor she had not noticed before. The ceiling arched high over her head until it gave way to a grand room filled with thousands of people seated in rows of chairs. The ground was adorned with brown and black marble arranged in a large grid, marking the aisle she would walk to the tall platform at the end.

As the group proceeded down the aisle, Caleb became more and more upset. He wiggled in his mother's arms and cried to be let down. Hyka stopped to assist her. Valerie handed him over. He held Hyka's and Jack's hand and continued down the aisle without a fuss.

Though everyone stood as she passed, the hostility toward her was palpable. They hated her. She wanted to scream the truth at them but knew they would not believe her. Lucas had already prepared them. She walked with her hands folded together. Her fingers were interlaced; otherwise, they would tremble. Her heart pounded in her ears, and she felt hot and lightheaded under the weight of her dress.

She focused her sight on the couple in front of her. They tried to tell Caleb not to jump between them. She did not bother to intervene. She did not care if he disrupted the whole thing. He gave her a distraction from the impending doom she felt.

As she neared the platform, Caleb caught sight of his grandpa and ran to stand with him. Anger swelled inside of her. She swallowed the bitterness. Best to conceal her temper lest she give the masses another reason to hate her.

After what felt like an eternity of walking she reached the platform. She wished she had walked even slower. She climbed seven marble steps and stopped with three left to go, where an X was taped.

Lucas smiled down at her from the top of the stairs. "So nice of you to come. You look lovely, my dear."

There was no way out. There was nowhere to go. She prayed someone or something would rescue her from taking the oath. She knew whatever she was about to swear to would be nothing but evil.

"Welcome, Ms. Valerie Burton," Lucas said, his voice projected throughout the room on speakers. He then reached his hand over her head to address the crowd. "Now let us begin."

The lights dimmed in the grand room, and a spotlight steadied over her and Lucas. A broad smile curled over his face. Her dull expression did not change. Inhale, exhale.

CHAPTER TWENTY-ONE

"Madam, is Your Majesty willing to take the Oath?" Lucas Jarrett asked, holding a large heavy book. He wore a simple but formal black suit and a black bow tie.

"I am willing," Valerie answered.

Lucas handed the book to her before proceeding with the oath. "Will you solemnly promise and swear to govern the peoples of your region with power, according to the New World Council and its rising laws and customs?"

"I solemnly promise to do so."

"Will you, to your ability, cause law and justice to be executed in all your judgments?"

"I will."

Valerie continued to swear her allegiance to the New World Council, to vote diplomatically and carry forth all tasks agreed upon by the Council; the penalty of noncompliance being suspension, expulsion, and reprimand up to and including the penalty of death. She agreed to the oath in front of the hateful crowd and tried her hardest to not focus on her image displayed on the large monitors hanging above Lucas.

Then Lucas paused and smiled, the next line dripped from his curled smile, "Do you swear to your bloodline that your children, should they be DiaZem, will be promised to and inducted into the Council at birth and sent to their own ruling city upon coming of age?"

The blood left Valerie's face. She had never considered the child she carried was a DiaZem. Lucas knew. Valerie had become ill because her daughter's genetics were killing her. The opposite charges given off by August and Lucas made her pregnancy viable. She could not escape Lucas Jarrett even if she had the opportunity. If she left, her body would reject the growing baby. She and her daughter had the same magnetic charge. Lucas knew this, too. Her own life depended on the man standing before her. He had far more power over her than she ever imagined.

With her mouth dry and tears welling, she said, "I swear it shall be."

"Will you, to the utmost of your power, maintain and protect the bloodline of those in your charge? Will you, to the utmost of your power, maintain the DiaZem bloodline for future ruling generations? Will you maintain and preserve inviolably the settlement of the genetically superior and the discipline and government thereof, as established by the law of the World Council?"

She went on, no longer hearing the words she swore to, "All this I promise to do."

Valerie kneeled on the step and Lucas relieved her of the book.

"The things which I have here before promised, I will perform and keep. So, help me."

Lucas extended his hand to her. Helping her up, he guided her to stand next to him on the platform.

"Ladies and gentlemen, it is my pleasure to present to you, your Queen DiaZem, Valerie Burton."

A soft, obligated applause met Lucas' announcement. The crowd dispersed. Lucas placed her hand on the inside of his elbow to escort her across the platform. She looked over her shoulder at Hyka, who nodded and took Caleb's hand from his grandfather's. She whispered something in the boy's ear, and his face lit up in agreement as they left the grand room. Jack followed.

"Why was my father present? I don't want him here." Valerie

asked, hoping he would not bring up her pregnancy again. She needed time to process the realization. Anger was a good distraction.

"Mike Burton is far more loyal to you than he is to me. He stole Janice from my program, even knowing they couldn't run forever. He tried to hide her, you, and your brother, not knowing the military was mine as well. He hates me as much as you do, if not more. And where you might think I am heartless, I can appreciate his stance. And above all else, I don't give a shit what you want. If I can find one more thing to break your spirit or make you cry, by all means, you can bet I will make it happen."

"When are you going to tell them you killed their families?" Valerie asked, raising her voice so anyone lingering in the grand hall could hear. She could play his game. She was determined to fight. Knowing the truth to his lie was the only angle she had over him.

A few spectators nearby turned at her pointed question. Lucas' grip on her hand tightened in anger. His brow creased and his face turned red. He led her to a door just off the central platform. In the dark, she could not tell what the room was.

Lucas slammed her body against a wall, and then slammed his weight into her. He yanked her cape apart with both hands, breaking the clasp, which held it together in the front. The bulky material fell from her shoulders to the ground.

She screamed out into the darkness of the tiny room, hoping an eavesdropper could hear her. Before she could scream again, he placed his forearm over her throat and leaned in, cutting off her voice and her air. She searched the room for energy and found a security camera. In her desperation, she broadcasted the feed to anyone who could help her. She wrote a message on the screen:

Someone, please help. He's going to kill me.

Tears streamed down her face, and her eyes grew heavy as she struggled for breath under his arm. He let up just before she blacked out. Valerie gasped for air. Lucas grabbed a handful of hair from the base of her neck and forced his mouth to hers. The primal attraction soon took over, and she gave in.

Where his hands touched her skin, her body reacted in ways she had never felt before. It was no longer a matter of willpower. The attraction between them pulled her closer like they shared the primal need to be as one. She was aware of every nerve in her body. Sparks began to light the room from anything that could hold a charge. She sighed under the weight of his mouth.

In a fleeting wave of inner strength, she tried to push him away. Lucas growled with frustration, pulled away from her, reeled back his fist, and hit her. Valerie could no longer focus on the fight. She lost the energy to call for help.

Lucas forced her back into another kiss. The lights on a dressing room vanity burst one by one. Her body begged for him as she cried, knowing he was trying to take what was not offered freely. Lucas released her mouth and pushed her, face down, onto a table. Valerie tried to stand, coming to her senses. She forced herself to fight against him, against her own raw desire for him. Lucas grabbed her hair again and slammed her head hard onto the table. While she was disoriented, he pinned both of her arms behind her back with one hand. She could not move.

"This is why I like younger women. They have so much fight in them. I am supposed to wait until we are married, but I've never been one to play by any rules when it comes to what I want. Maybe when your daughter is of age, I'll trade you in for her."

The words filled her with a rage she could not control. The red she saw at their first meeting was dim compared to how bright the lights grew in the room. Disoriented and blind, Lucas shielded his face and stepped away from her. She pushed herself off the table and stood to face him. With a scream of fury, Valerie unleashed every ounce of energy she held in her body. Every light bulb burst at the same time, shooting shards of glass across the room and past her like bullets at Lucas.

Valerie took the chance and ran, throwing the door open. She gathered her dress into her arms and sprinted through the great room. She ran past people, frozen at the sight of her. They moved from her path as she made her way through the arched corridor. No one offered her any help; their faces either blank or confused at the sight of her. She reached the platform where the copper wire structure of the sword-fighting men stood sentinel to the platform. She approached just as the train was coming to a stop. The doors slid open.

"August!" she screamed and ran faster toward him.

His jaw clenched as hard as his fists. She ran hard into his chest, and his demeanor softened, if just for a moment. He touched her arms. The shards of glass had sliced her exposed skin, but in her rage, she had not felt the pain. Though her wounds had already healed, blood still covered her. August looked her in the eyes. Without a word or need for explanation, he walked past her to meet Lucas, who was making his way to the platform.

The men exchanged blows as soon as they were within arm's reach. Their strikes echoed in the acoustics of the platform. August ducked past the punches thrown at him. Taking the opportunity of Lucas' exposed torso, he sent a knee into his side. Lucas connected an elbow to the side of August's head. They continued exchanging impacts. Both men were unyielding and recovered instantly from blow to blow. They moved fast and fluid, neither tiring.

Valerie's concern grew, and she approached the fighting men. She stood in her white gown, soiled with the blood of her struggle, helpless to aid August for fear of anything happening to her unborn child. It was evident that neither man would admit defeat. Her abilities were useless. Both men were far stronger than her. If she left, their energies could destroy the entire facility. Fear kept her eyes fixed on the endless battle. No matter how much she wanted it to stop, they kept up the brawl.

People filled the platform. The same people who had failed to offer her help stood to stare. Guards watched with their weapons on standby, awaiting the outcome of the confrontation. Lucas' assistant was at the forefront of the crowd. Rob stood with his arms crossed and maintained a look of indifference. Valerie continued to search the group for an ally. Just as she was convinced she had none, the door to the control room opened. Doctor Leonard Warner, as fast as his cane would assist him, walked across the platform to where she stood. Though their interaction in the lab had been short, she trusted he was coming to help her somehow. When he reached her, the scientist placed a hand on her shoulder and whispered in her ear. Confused, she gave him a look. He nodded, walked back to the secured door, and was gone. Valerie lifted her chin and walked toward the fighting men. She needed to separate them somehow; it was her only chance to overpower Lucas.

When she reached a massive pillared leg of the copper sculpture, August gained the upper hand in the fight. He had Lucas pinned down and held his neck in both hands. For a moment, Valerie thought it was over.

Rob yanked a weapon away from one of the guards and fired a red stream at August. Valerie screamed and fell to her knees. The current coursed over his body once before he was able to absorb the shock, giving Lucas a chance to break out of the choke hold. Once they had separated, Rob fired again, this time maintaining a steady red stream of electricity, knocking August back. He was within her reach. Inhale, exhale. Valerie grabbed the copper sculpture as tight as she could and reached for August, bracing herself for the pain to transfer to her. But when he grasped her forearm, there was no pain. The energy transferred to the tall copper sculpture of the two warriors battling. Valerie focused the electricity through the statue and onto Lucas. The thick copper cables melted. Valerie willed the current to form a coil of liquid copper around Lucas. Though it slowed him down, he continued to move toward them, making easy work of the soft metal.

"Kiss me," she yelled at August. She helped him to his feet. With sweat and blood smeared on his face, he leaned down and connected his mouth with hers. She kissed him as though she would never get the opportunity again. The power surged through her body, igniting everything in her being. Valerie pulled every bit of energy from every person and machine within reach of her ability. She transferred the power to the wire. The electrical current increased around Lucas. He struggled to move. His mouth opened to scream but nothing came out. The flow of energy grew brighter and brighter until Lucas' suit caught fire. He aged years in an instant. She could feel her attraction to him decrease as the flames burnt his skin. The current and heat had demagnetized him. Leo had given her the answer to the riddle plaguing her since she first met Lucas Jarrett. His skin glowed red, faded to gray, then black. When the two released their embrace, Valerie removed her hand from the coil. Lucas' body crumbled to the marble floor. He was nothing more than ashes.

Valerie collapsed.

"Are you okay?" August knelt down in concern.

"It's over," were the only words she had.

Across the platform, guards surrounded Rob. He turned his 9mm on them and tried to run from the scene. He fired three shots before the guards backed away from him, giving him a clear path of escape. August ran after him. Valerie followed. Once they entered the great room, Rob sent shots flying at August. Valerie dropped to the ground to avoid injury. August took three shots to his torso before Rob tripped over the stairs and put two more rounds in the ceiling. He was out of bullets.

August beat the man over and over, pounding his fists into his face.

"August, stop," she demanded. But he kept on.

Valerie grabbed August's wrist as he reeled back for another hit. "It's done." Inhale, exhale. She took the spark from Rob's body. This time, he would not get it back.

August stood and stared down at the lifeless man.

"He let Lucas hurt you," August said, looking up at her.

There was a pain in his eyes. Valerie realized he was still bleeding. She took his hand and concentrated on the three bullets. He touched her face and winced as they fell from his abdomen and onto the floor.

"You are going to kill us, too?" shouted someone from the crowd, which was moving into the grand room.

August searched the crowd for who had spoken the words, but Valerie spoke before August had the chance to take a breath.

"Lucas Jarrett killed your families," Valerie addressed the growing crowd. "I had no part in the attack. I was forced to watch the man I love die in my arms. My husband died because I loved him so much, and Lucas would not allow it. For that deep-rooted jealousy, he found the loss of your loved ones to be acceptable collateral damage. I swear to you, it was not my doing."

Valerie continued even as her face appeared on the giant monitors throughout the room, "Lucas Jarrett intended to fulfill the World Council's plan to maintain our genetic purity by eliminating anyone who is not like us. He threatened to hurt my son if I did not go along with the Council. I have been fighting against their plan to kill every regular human being on the planet. He lied to you and turned you against me to keep me from leading a rebellion against the World Council. Genocide is just a small glimpse of what they are capable of doing. As long as I can stand before you, I will not let that happen here.

"If you wish to leave the facility and return to your homes, no one will stop you. If you find there is nothing left for you out there, I will turn no one away from the sanctuary of the facility, regardless of their genetic standing. We can rebuild our society from what is left. I will stand against the World Council. We have a clear enemy, but it is not each other. It is not me."

When she finished, the screens went blank. The people remained silent. August placed a hand on her shoulder.

"Come on. You don't have to do this right now."

Valerie did not know what else she could say to get them to believe her. The monitors flashed on again displaying a surveillance feed of the control room. Lucas Jarrett stood shouting orders as he watched Valerie enter Gia's room at the resort. Valerie froze. She did not want to relive that moment, but she knew they needed to see the truth. Her eyes fixed on the screen, and she fought to keep herself together.

"Are the planes in place, Leonard?"

The scientist on the screen nodded to Lucas.

"Now, just wait. Wait until he is completely in the room."

Valerie watched again as Scott crossed the room to pick up Caleb's blanket. She looked away and buried her face in August's chest. Her screams echoed through the grand room. Through her screams, she could hear Lucas laughing.

Valerie heaved and gasped. August lowered her to the floor. She stayed there for a long time, sobbing. After she had exhausted all emotion, August lifted her from the ground and carried her to the train.

CHAPTER TWENTY-TWO

Valerie washed the blood from her arms and rid herself of the excessive makeup deemed necessary for the coronation ceremony. She had no tears left. No anger racked her nerves. Even her grief washed away, staining the white-tiled shower stall. For a long time, she let the water just run over her. The hate, the hurt, the damage had broken her. The time for grieving never came. Valerie's journey had yet to end. She did not have the luxury of being broken. She had to keep going to lead and give direction to the devastated city, and then the region.

Hyka—once a stranger, now her closest friend—had gifted her a red shirt to contrast the all-white dress code of the facility. She dressed and sat on the stark white bed. The mechanical blinds raised on her mental command, revealing the snowcapped mountains in the distance. They represented massive and ancient permanence. There was little she could do to move or change them. Just as she could not change the events of the past two weeks, she had to live with the gaping hole where her former life had been. Her husband Scott lie at the bottom of that hungry hole, along with many other things she loved but could no longer have.

Valerie opened the door to the rest of the empty suite and made coffee while she searched the surveillance feeds for her son. She found him a few floors down playing with Jack while Hyka made lunch. She smiled at the image. Jack, despite his initial reservations, had stood by her since the beginning. He and Hyka had believed in her when even she had doubted her strength. They pushed her to do the right thing, when all she wanted was to run away.

"You're looking quite domestic today." Valerie's voice carried through the feed and into Hyka's earpiece.

"It's literally killing me," Hyka said without skipping a beat. "Want me to bring him up?"

"I'll come down and surprise him in a little bit. And Hyka . . . thank you."

Hyka threw a thumb in the air and continued her task.

The entire time she spent in solitude, from the moment the door closed between them, Valerie's body had called out for August. She had not felt the breeze of his attention since he had delivered her to her room earlier in the day. She had spent much of her time alone rehearsing conversations with her partner DiaZem in case her attraction to him grew even stronger, and she lost her nerve. She understood they would lead together, but she maintained, in her heart, that they were not together.

Instead of seeking him out on surveillance, she followed the attraction. She walked where she felt drawn, hit the elevator button to where she thought he would be. On the eleventh floor of the hotel was the gym. She walked down the hall, thankful he was in a semi-public area and not alone in his room. She was still apprehensive about being near him at all. She had hated Lucas with every ounce of her being and yet he still had power over her. August would find her too easy a target to seduce if he felt so inclined.

She opened the door to the gym. Everything was still and quiet, the equipment in its proper place, unused. She could feel him, though he was not in the room. Behind a frosted glass wall in the gym, his silhouette moved swiftly before diving into the pool. Her heart fluttered, and her cheeks flushed. He knew she was there. For as intense as she felt when she was near him, there was no way he could not sense her pounding heart.

"I'm glad you're up," he said from the other side of the wall.

Finding the separation of the glass appropriate, she decided to stay in the gym to have their conversation. She could hear his body cut through the water. It made her thirsty.

"We need to discuss some things, before . . . I mean, it's best to talk about this now rather than having to . . . stop. . ."

"We can build glass dividers in every room if doing so would make you more comfortable," he said, pulling himself out of the pool. Through the glass, she could see his blurry shape emerge from the far end.

Her pulse quickened, and she looked away.

"Or we can use conference calls for all our communications." He rubbed his hands over his face and through his hair and sighed. "Val, this isn't easy for me either, but I want to respect you and everything you have going on. I could even go away for a while if you want."

"No," she shouted. "You can't leave me." She had rehearsed these lines many times in her room, yet was not prepared to say them out loud. "I could lose the baby. She's a DiaZem. Our energies repel each other. I would lose her, or she would kill me."

August was quiet for a while. "Remember when we first met? I had the door to the office closed for so long. The whole time, I was pacing inside. At first, because I couldn't make sense of the age regression, but then I began to fight the need to approach you. I hadn't seen you, but I could feel you."

"Why are you telling me this?" Valerie leaned her back against the glass and slid to the floor, pulling her knees close to her. She could listen to his voice forever, but remembering the time before was painful.

"Because I need you to know I'm not like him. I'm not going to hurt you. Even if this is all some involuntary instinct, I care about you. I died a little when you walked out of the emergency room. I never want to feel like that again. I will wait here as long as it takes for you to be okay. And maybe, when you're ready, we can go to dinner. Supervised, if that's what you want."

Valerie smiled to herself. She did want that, but she was not sure if she was quite okay enough.

"Are you joining the Council?" she asked him.

"I never intended to."

She nodded, going down her mental list of questions. "Do you have a family?"

"I do. I have two sons, about your age. One in Arizona and one in Chicago. They both have the conductor gene and live away from any facilities."

"Are you married?"

"No. I have some questions, too."

"Okay."

"Do you want my help here, or do you want to be the sole leader?"

"I have no idea what I am doing. I would appreciate your help."

"I think I can do that," he laughed. "Val?"

She loved hearing him say her name. "Yes?"

"Take it one day at a time. Don't expect to be alright. Healing takes time. I'll always be here, okay?"

"Okay." Valerie stood and left the gym. As she passed the door to the pool, she could not help but to get an unimpeded look at him.

He looked back at her, water still dripping down his bare chest and torso. He winked with a smile and dove back into the pool. She blushed and walked away.

Valerie knocked on the door where she had found Caleb earlier. The little boy, with some help, answered the door.

"My mommy," he squealed.

She swooped him up and spun him around. She glanced around. Caleb's toys were scattered across the room.

"Are these his? From our house?"

Jack cleared his throat. "We've been pretty busy while you were . . . resting."

"Dad went to your place to pick up some things you might need or want. Whatever was salvageable they packed up and brought here. Your entire house was loaded up and is now sitting in boxes in the next room," Hyka explained.

Valerie appreciated how forward Hyka was. Even her explanations ran the line of being too much for Valerie to handle, and Hyka only said what was necessary.

As if on cue, Major stepped out of the bathroom drying his hands. "Well, hey there, Electra."

Valerie smiled and greeted him with a hug.

He kissed her cheek and ruffled Caleb's hair. "This little man was worth all the trouble."

"Did you find more people?" Valerie asked.

"We can talk about those things later." Major skirted the question, but his expression was solemn. "I heard you pulled through and saved the day."

"Yeah, well, I had a lot of good help. Dr. Warner was the one who told me how to use the copper sculpture to reverse the effects of Lucas' DiaZem gene. With August and me connected, he told me to focus the facility's power on the sculpture as a metal conductor to melt the copper around him. It was the heat that destroyed him. He called it the Curie point. At first it wasn't working, so, I did the one thing I thought would intensify the bond." Valerie blushed. "Hyka, maybe tomorrow, will you see if Dr. Leonard Warner is available?"

"No, I can't."

"Val, we can talk about those things later," Major said with more emphasis, nodding to Caleb.

"What happened?"

Hyka sighed. "She's not going to stop until you just tell her."

"Show her the video then," Major answered his daughter. "Hopefully Caleb is too young to understand."

Valerie turned her attention to the television in the common area, unsure of what news the video would provide. She suspected the worst. Dr. Leonard appeared on the monitor after Hyka pushed a few buttons on the remote.

"Mrs. Russell, I want to offer you my sincerest and gravest apologies and condolences. I know the things I have done are far from forgivable. I am afraid, at the moment, I saw no other way but to be agreeable to my former colleague and contribute to his plan. That is until you came along. You have the fight of your mother. Something I could never forget. The same tenacity she had to run away from our program decades ago is what saved her from our experiments in the first place, and how you came to be. She fought against Dr. Jarrett then so that you could defeat him now. Something I was never strong enough to do.

"I am also sorry for replaying your deepest sorrow for the masses. They deserved to know the truth. And you deserved to know the truth about me. It is because of this truth I can no longer continue, knowing the damage I have caused. The damage I once thought necessary. To you and your children, there are no words to express my profound regret. Once you receive this message, I assure you I will no longer be with this world, and I hope that you, and whatever might be waiting for me, will have mercy on my soul."

The video ended. Valerie had no words or tears. She nodded and collected her son. Valerie spent the rest of the afternoon with Caleb in her suite in the west wing of the hotel. She picked through her salvaged belongings to make the living quarters a little more colorful and familiar. She fixed up a room for Caleb in her suite with a few of his toys and pictures of him and his father.

Hyka and Duke arranged a meeting with facility managers and her trusted circle of friends, which had become her family. August would also attend to discuss matters of the facility and the people in their charge. Soon enough, Hyka let herself into Valerie's suite to escort them to the meeting.

Valerie sat at the head of the long table across from August. Caleb, Hyka, and Jack sat to her left; Major sat to her right with two empty seats between him and August. Last to arrive, Mike and Kevin walked through the quiet conference room and took the empty seats. Valerie watched in silence. Kevin did not look at her but kept his head down. Her father nodded as he took a sip of water. Others she did not recognize sat in chairs lining the wall, away from the main table.

August cleared his voice, "Major, can you bring Valerie up to speed on the state of the city?"

"August has extended power to the region. Even rural areas have adequate electricity to continue life as usual, as much as they can. There are some downed lines due to the initial outages, plane crashes and the like, which are still a problem. The idea is the facility acts as a power plant. Giving the conductors the ability to use the power when they want to turn lights on and off in their home, et cetera. We can provide continuous power by proximity, as your power footprint reaches as far as Chicago, but that would power everything, all the time, which is not practical or comfortable for anyone. So, our first obstacle to rebuilding the city is to reconnect the damaged power lines.

"Second, we need to handle the aftermath of Phase Two. As the weather gets warmer, bodies will decompose. The task is not going to be pretty or comfortable. We're looking at two million fatalities. I have a few ideas on how to tackle this, but nothing as sensitive to the matter as it should be."

Valerie shook her head processing the information. Hyka kept her head down, taking notes.

Duke entered the conference room, breaking her concentration on the news.

"Sorry to interrupt. The Council is demanding a conference right now. They are waiting for you both."

"We don't have to do this now, Valerie," August said.

"We do. My son and I are safe. I need to keep it that way. Are we able to do a video conference in here?"

"We should take the call in another room and come back to this meeting later."

"Dammit, if one more person tells me what to do. . .! These people need to be here. This region is relying on us to keep them safe. Millions of other lives are at stake. They deserve to see the Council for what they are, and they need to know we won't stand for their disgusting practices. No one else should die. I cannot spend another second running from this."

"Well, then let's give them the news," August agreed.

The walls lit up with images of the Council members. Her caption had been edited to read: Valerie Russell, Queen DiaZem, Central United States.

"An improvement, I guess. Do I have to be a queen? Seems a bit extreme," she tried to joke her nerves away, but her hands shook with anxiety and adrenaline.

"Whatever your title, it is most definitely under question," the male DiaZem of Austria stated.

The screen changed to display a recording of Valerie's speech on the platform.

"He threatened to hurt my son if I did not go along with the Council. I have been fighting against their plan to kill every regular human being on the planet. He lied to you and turned you against me, to keep me from leading a rebellion against the World Council. Genocide is just a small glimpse of what they are capable of doing. As long as I can stand before you, I will not let that happen here."

Then the screen changed back to the Council. She noticed there were fewer members present. She looked for August's betrothed, but could not find her.

"Mrs. Russell, or whatever your name is today, is it your intent to start a war with the Council?" The Queen DiaZem of England posed the question.

"Your Majesty, it is not my intention to start a war, but we do not wish to be a part of the Council and are ready to deal with those consequences. Let me also add that you of all people should know the history of our countries. The United States is 'The Land of the Free.' I promise if you try to take it from these people, you will lose . . . again. There can be peace between our nations, but not if you continue to murder innocent people. This will end." Valerie's nervousness had transitioned to anger.

August and Duke whispered back and forth while she waited for a response from the Council. A few more council members' screens went blank before anyone spoke.

"Dr. August Wilkes, is this your stance as well?" the Venezuelan male DiaZem questioned.

"It is."

"Then I hereby, with the authority of the New World Order and its Council, exile you from the Order and Council. Your crimes of treason include the murder of your King DiaZem, and rebellion against the New Order, both of which hold the penalty of death. You will await official notice of penalty and reprimand."

With those words, the screens went black with a green blinking cursor. Valerie recognized the cursor from the written messages she and August sent in secret:

San Francisco stands with you, Valerie Russell. -Jacqueline Taylor

New Zealand stands with the United States. -Sophia Wilson

Let's give them hell. -John and Sylvia Hampton of Dallas

The screens filled with line after line of allegiance. They all watched in silence waiting for them to stop.

"Don't trust every olive branch stretched to you," her father warned, breaking the silence.

Valerie stood up and pointed a finger across the table. She opened her mouth to speak, but he cut her off.

"I have coached you your entire life to do and be everything you are right now. Valerie, you must understand, I did not want anyone to die. I did not want them to find Caleb, but I did want you to have the strength to stand up against the evil and corrupt in the world. I am so proud of you, Valerie."

"You're proud of yourself. You and Kevin will leave. Today. Because I don't trust every olive branch stretched out to me. If you are true to our cause, you will handle the deceased of the city with the utmost respect and sensitivity. I will provide all the tools you need to complete the task, but you will not return until every person is named. If you want to take credit for something, you can take credit for those lives."

She shook with anger. Mike and Kevin stood and left the room. Duke helped himself to Mike's former place at the table.

"Pizza! Mac and cheese. Chicken fries," Caleb said, poking Valerie's arm until she smiled down at him.

"The rest can wait until after dinner. There is an entire wedding feast prepared. Shall we?" August smiled at her from across the table. She nodded, and the meeting adjourned.

ABOUT THE AUTHOR

Dacia M Arnold is an author of adult dystopian and dark fiction. She enjoys writing main characters who are otherwise normal people with extraordinary abilities. Dacia is also a ten-year Army veteran who served two tours of combat as a medic. However, being a mother is the forefront of Dacia's life. With two small children, her life and work revolve around them. When she does steal a moment away for herself, Dacia is an avid karaoke singer, master crafter and a thrift-ster. She lives in Denver, Colorado with her husband, kids, and two beagles named Watson and Molly.

ACKNOWLEDGEMENTS

Dacia would like to thank the many, many people who made this possible:

Shaula B., Stephanie F., Ashley T., Kyria C., Monta (Mom), Kat and Nancy M., Tim P. of ChapterBuzz.com, Liberty H., and Tiana L.

Torrie, Jasmine and Kayla for wrangling my kids while I worked.

Corinne O., Jon M., Becky L., Liz D., Mike H., Mike S., Heather H., Brian Keene and Mary Sangiovanni for all your advice and for believing I was worth your wisdom.

To Holli Anderson, my Acquisitions Editor, and Immortal Works Press for taking a chance on me.

To My AMAZING Patrons: Jack W. F., Stephanie V., Laci S. and Jennifer T.

To my ever-patient husband who drives me crazy and keeps me sane. Thank you for sharing this life with me.

To everyone who has touched my life in any way. THANK YOU!

THIS HAS BEEN AN IMMORTAL PRODUCTION

CPSIA information can be obtained
at www.ICGtesting.com
Printed in the USA
FSHW011253150119
55044FS